"Good afternoon, Councillor."

Jerril Carson smiled at Carl with a precision that came from four decades of political smiling. The edges of his smile might have been measured in millimeters and never varied. "Good afternoon, Carl. Congratulations on passage of the Amendment."

"Thank you, sir. What can I do for you?"

"I really didn't think you would get it passed," said Carson conversationally. "With the Secretary General making his position against it so very clear—well, even with Monsieur Kalharri's aid, Tuesday's vote succeeded in surprising me." He looked thoughtful. "And the Secretary General as well, I believe. You controlled yourself quite well during testimony. I doubt if most of the Unification Council has the vaguest idea just how erratic and dangerous you are."

"Well, I hope not myself," said Carl politely. "It's always nice to be under . . ."

"Nothing," Carson whispered as the mask dropped from his face, and left something old and insane in his eyes, "has changed. Nothing."

The holofield went dead and faded.

EMERALD EYES

A TALE OF THE CONTINUING TIME

DANIEL KEYS MORAN

BANTAM BOOKS
TORONTO • NEW YORK • LONDON • SYDNEY • AUCKLAND

EMERALD EYES

A Bantam Spectra Book / July 1988

Grateful acknowledgment is made for permission to reprint lyrics
from "Lost Boys and Golden Girls" by Jim Steinman. Courtesy of
Jim Steinman.

ISBN 0-553-27347-7

Published simultaneously in the United States and Canada

Bantam Books are published by Bantam Books, a division of Bantam
Doubleday Dell Publishing Group, Inc. Its trademark, consisting of the
words "Bantam Books" and the portrayal of a rooster, is Registered in
U.S. Patent and Trademark Office and in other countries. Marca Re-
gistrada, Bantam Books, 666 Fifth Avenue, New York, New York 10103

PRINTED IN THE UNITED STATES OF AMERICA

O   0 9 8 7 6 5 4 3 2 1

DEDICATION

My life work, *The Tales of the Continuing Time,* is dedicated, first, to those men and women who taught the writer:

Poul Anderson, for David Falkayn and, most especially, Captain Sir Dominic Flandry;

Isaac Asimov, for Foundation and the Robots and his cool rationality;

Ronald J. Bass, for Gideon, who was Theo, who was Voleur, who was *The Perfect Thief;*

Marion Zimmer Bradley, for Lew Alton and Regis Hastur and Darkover;

Robert A. Heinlein, for my favorite book, *The Moon Is a Harsh Mistress;*

Stephen King, for my second favorite, *'Salem's Lot;*

John D. MacDonald, for Travis and Meyer and all the colors of the rainbow;

Gregory McDonald, for Fletch and Flynn and for teaching me to write dialogue;

Larry Niven, for Known Space and *Protector;*

Tom Robbins, for Amanda and Sissy Hankshaw and Nearly Normal Jimmy;

E. E. "Doc" Smith, for the Gray Lensman, and for teaching me not to think too small;

Mary Stewart, for giving me Merlin, and for giving *him* the music of the stars;

Theodore Sturgeon, for teaching me to write about love—by example;

Hunter S. Thompson, with Fear and Loathing and some respect;

J. R. R. Tolkien, for the astonishing *Lord of the Rings;*

And to those who gave hope to the child:

Asimov again, and Ted Sturgeon, Edgar Eager and Lloyd Alexander and E. Nesbit, Madeleine L'Engle and Susan Cooper and Sylvia Engdahl and Tolkien and, with love,

for C. S. Lewis. At the age of seven I wrote him a letter thanking him for *The Chronicles of Narnia.* I learned, years later, that he had died the year after I was born. Those who believe children cannot feel strong passion do not remember. C. S. Lewis never forgot.

> *There is good in the world.*
> —Daniel Keys Moran

DEDICATION FOR "EMERALD EYES":

Emerald Eyes is dedicated to my father, Richard Joseph Moran, who is one of the best storytellers who ever lived. He taught me to read, and bought me every typewriter I have ever owned, but I just got him a computer to do his writing and to keep track of his stocks, so I think we're even now.

He has pissed me off worse and more often than any other human being who has ever lived.

He is one of the very, very few people out there who cares about me even when I fuck up.

I love him a lot.

The gods can either take away evil from the world and will not, or, being willing to do so cannot; or they neither can nor will, or lastly, they are both able and willing. If they have the will to remove evil and cannot, then they are not omnipotent. If they can, but will not, then they are not benevolent. If they are neither able or willing, then they are neither omnipotent nor benevolent. Lastly, if they are both able and willing to annihilate evil, how does it exist?

—Epicurus,
300 B.C.

"IN THE
BEGINNING"

I am the Storyteller.

Hear now my voice. From out of the white noise of Creation, listen to my words . . .

They were our forerunners, and they made plans, yes, for they were human, even as you and I. I have told this story before, and I shall someday tell it again, in a different fashion; but for Now, know the story so . . .

They made plans, you see, and the universe, which cared no more for them than for you or I, struck them down; and its tool was nothing less than a pair of Gods of the Zaradin Church, one of them myself, fighting a battle in a war that was ended near sixty-five thousand years before they were ever born.

I will tell' you of those days.

Darryl Amnier was a man without a title.

A title makes one knowable.

"Tell me about them," he said softly.

"Oui." Amnier's assistant was French; a depressingly large number of government employees were these days. "The director's name is Montignet, Suzanne Montignet. She is French born, but arrived in the United States in 2015. It is thought that her parents were fleeing the European theater of the War. She was fourteen then. We do not have accurate records for her after leaving France; she arrived in America just a year before the Unification War reached that continent. Her parents were killed, apparently by Americans, after the War began. One would have expected this to turn a young girl against the country in which she found herself, but obviously not. When next we have accurate records of her, beginning in 2018, she was studying under a scholarship at the College of the Camden Protectorate, in New Jersey. She had by then, and retains today, a substantially American accent. Though she spells her name 'Suzanne' she had further taken to pronouncing her name 'Susan,' in the American style, a habit which she also retains. In 2024 she graduated with high honors; two years ago, her work in genetics—it says here, sir, dee en ay, and ar en ay, Monsieur Amnier, which are explained to mean—"

"I know what they mean."

". . . oui. This work led to her current position with the United Nations Advanced Biotechnology Research Laboratory in New Jersey, this 'Project Superman.' "

"Don't use that name. It's not correct."

The command did not seem to require an answer; after a pause Amnier's aide continued. "The Ministry of Population Control has granted her an unlimited parenting license. She seems apolitical, aside from her personal habits."

"By which you mean?"

"Monsieur, she lives in Occupied America, among a proud people who have been, hmm, conquered? Conquered. An apparent distaste for the United Nations might be expedient."

"Not when dealing with the United Nations purse strings."

"Oui. As you say."

"What of Malko Kalharri?"

"What of Kalharri?" Amnier's aide seemed to find the question amusing. "Sir, I think there is very little I can tell you which you do not already know about Colonel Kalharri."

With a shower of gamma rays I came into existence at the fast end of time.

A wind was raised with my appearance in the empty corridor. Had there been any to observe, they would have heard the sharp crack created as air was moved aside at greater than the speed of sound, and might have felt a brief warmth. Those with sharp eyes might have noticed a shadow in the fraction of an instant before I moved away from the spot of my appearance. They would not have seen any more of me. Even at my end of time they would have seen little to note; a human, dressed all in white, from the boots on my feet to the white cowl that covered my head. Even with the visual distortion that is unavoidable when time is sped so drastically, men of their century would have found the lack of focus upon the surface of a white shadow cloak a striking thing.

Of course they were not in fast time, nor could be.

I began trudging through the air, toward my destination. The corridor was almost entirely dark; flashes of ultraviolet light marked the passage of X rays, each flash illuminating the corridor like a small lightning. The normal visible spectrum was shifted too deeply into the radio to be of use to me.

I was in a hurry, pushing through the resisting atmosphere, and I am a man unaccustomed to hurrying; but I was being closely followed by an enemy who had promised to cut my heart out and eat it—and I rather believed Camber Tremodian would do just exactly that, given the chance.

I did not intend to give him the chance. At the fast end of time I hurried through the slow air.

**Monday, December 11, 2029; the United
Nations Advanced Biotechnology Research
Laboratories, in New Jersey.**

He arrived from Capital City just before eight o'clock;
security let Darryl Amnier into Suzanne Montignet's office more
than two hours early. They were uneasy, doing it.

But they did it nonetheless.

He sat behind her desk, in her chair, with the lights dimmed.
A small man, with paper-white hair and wrinkles around his
eyes and mouth that made him look far older than he was, he
found Montignet's chair slightly too high for his taste. He did
not readjust it. Her office had no window, which pleased him
to the degree that he ever allowed himself to be pleased. A
crank with a rifle was that much less likely to bring three
quarters of a million Credit Units' worth of research grinding
to a halt with a single shot.

The decor was standardized, little different from what
Amnier had seen in over twenty other research installations in
the last four months. Amnier was not certain whether that
surprised him or not. From a woman of such exceptional skills,
one might reasonably have expected anything.

The same comment, of course, might be made about Malko
Kalharri, the director of security for the installation.

An Information Network terminal, left turned on and
connected to the Mead Data Central medical database, sat
at attention immediately next to her desk. Amnier made
a note to find out what sort of bill the laboratories were
running up on the Network. An ornamental bookshelf against
one wall held reference works in too excellent condition.
There were no holographs, not even of Colonel Kalharri,
who was reputed to be her lover. Nor were there paintings.
The desk was locked. Amnier considered picking it, and
decided not to. There was unlikely to be anything inside
that he would either understand or find incriminating, and
whether he opened it or not, Montignet was certain to suspect
he had.

Which was the whole point.

The empty corridor in which I appeared connected the sterile genegineers' labs with the showers which led to the unsterile outer world, on the first floor of the New Jersey laboratories of the United Nations Bureau of Biotechnology Research. The entrance to the genegineer's labs was through a small room with sealed doorways at both ends. They were not airlocks, though the technology of the day was sufficient to allow the use of airlocks; indeed, at the interface between the showers and the rest of the installation airlocks were in use. But it was cheaper to keep the laboratories under a slight overpressure; when the door opened, the wind, and any contaminants, blew outward.

The door swung wide, and a pair of laboratory technicians in white gowns and gloves strode through. The resemblance between their garb and mine brought the ghost of a smile to my lips.

As they left, I, the god Named Storyteller, entered.

Suzanne Montignet stopped by Malko Kalharri's office on the way to her own. The lights in his office had not yet been turned on that morning. Entering the room from the brightly lit hallway, Suzanne found it difficult even to see Kalharri at first.

"Malko?"

"Yes?" The office lacked a desk; the man who was sprawled loosely on the couch, one oversized hand wrapped loosely around a steaming coffee cup, did not look away from the holo tank in the corner of his office. Kalharri did not resemble his name, which he had received by way of his grandfather; he was a big blond man with a tan. The channel light glowed at 35: S-STR, the political news station.

"What's happening?"

Malko Kalharri had been a soldier for too many years; he never moved quickly when the situation did not warrant it. After a moment he said simply, "The Unification Council is 'discussing'—this is the word they have used all morning for the screaming and threats—the feasibility of adding an amendment to their damned Statement of Principles, to allow the Secretary General to hold office for more than three four-year terms. Sarah Almundsen must be turning over in her grave; the first amendment ever proposed to that brilliant piece of writing being a tool to keep one of her more foolish successors in office a little while longer." He shook his head. "It's not going well at any rate; SecGen Ténérat didn't think this one through all the way, silly damn frog that he is." He paused a moment and without looking at her said, "No offense meant."

"None taken," said Suzanne Montignet drily.

"Not that the opposition has prepared for it either. The Unification Councillor for Sri Lanka opened the floor for discussion on the subject; so far this morning that's been the most coherent thing anybody's said."

"I see."

Kalharri turned his head then to look at her. He grinned broadly. "I've been watching this damned box all morning, you know. I tried turning up the brightness control earlier . . ."

"It didn't work."

"Afraid not." He turned back to the screen.

"Amnier's here."

Kalharri did not look back. He took a sip from his coffee before replying. "The guards told me. You're supposed to believe that he's gone through all of your documents in the last hour or so; torn your office apart, so to speak, however neatly. He's been there for an hour already; he knows you don't usually get in until 9 A.M., and he'll be expecting you to come charging up to your office as soon as you learn that he had himself let in to wait."

"Wheels within wheels. What do I do?"

"*Command,*" said Malko Kalharri, "bring coffee." The word *Acknowledged* blinked briefly in the lower right hand corner of the 3-D tank, and vanished. He lowered his voice slightly to normal conversational levels. "Amnier's appointment isn't until ten o'clock."

"So?"

Filled cups and condiments appeared on the floor next to the couch; memory plastic raised itself up from the floor to become a table at Kalharri's right hand. Kalharri took his cup and sent the table gliding across the floor toward Montignet. "I don't like surprises, my dear. They have a terrible tendency to be lethal."

"*So?*"

"Darryl's the same way, he doesn't like surprises. Right now he's expecting you to arrive any moment, angry. So, have a seat," he said cheerfully, "drink your coffee and watch the politicians, and make the bastard wait."

Excerpted from the Name Historian's *Looking Backwards From the Year 3000*; pub. 3018, Alternities Press, CU:110.00 Zaradin.

Wars which were, by the standards of provincial humanity, notably severe—the wars were referred to as World War I and World War II—brought home to the societies of the time the need for some social mechanism that would prevent similar man-made catastrophes from occurring again. With the development of thermonuclear explosives capable of ending all life within the biosphere of Earth, it became clear that some form of containment was required to prevent the species from destroying itself, and its planet into the bargain.

In 1969, a child named Sarah Almundsen was born in America.

Sarah Almundsen became Secretary General of the United Nations in the year 2014. With aid from members of the French and Chinese military, she assumed control of the orbital laser weaponry, formed the United Nations Peace Keeping Force, and declared the United Nations to be, under her "Charter of Principles," the sole legal government of Earth. China and France were the first two sovereign governments to agree to this; both were in grave geopolitical troubles at the time, caught between the vise of Japanese, Soviet, and American interests. Brazil followed, and before the end of the year 2014, two thirds of the planet acknowledged the United Nations as the Earth's legitimate government.

Three notable holdouts were, of course, the United States and the Soviet Union and Japan. Sarah Almundsen used tactical thermonuclear weapons and orbital lasers and sliced the USSR into ribbons. The Soviets, whose citizens were in open revolt after the second week of war with the United Nations, surrendered after Moscow was vaporized. Japan never surrendered; although members of the new government committed suicide after performing their duty, the United Nations did explode more than a dozen thermonuclear warheads over Jap-

anese territory until the Japanese were no longer capable of resistance.

North America, specifically the United States, was a more delicate matter; the United Nations offices were located there. Further, whole battalions of the U.S. Armed Forces deserted to the United Nations in the earliest days of the Unification War. Sarah Almundsen was an American, an honorable woman who was known to keep her word; sentiment to deal with her ran strong in many parts of the U.S.

The Sons of Liberty, a group of soldiers led by the President of the United States, composed of large portions of the Armed Forces, with nearly all of the Marine Corps, prevented that. The Unification War reached America in 2016 and stretched into 2017, and then into 2018. Throughout the first half of 2018, the Sons of Liberty fought a rearguard action as the better-equipped, better-fed, better-supported United Nations Peace Keeping Forces swept them north and east, across the Plains states and onto the Eastern seaboard. The Unification War, after causing more casualties than any other war in American history, officially ended in the summer of 2018 with the Treaty of New York, which detailed the particulars of the surrender of the mightiest nation the Earth had ever known, the United States of America.

The door slid aside at exactly ten A.M.

"What the fuck are you doing in my office?"

Suzanne Montignet was, Darryl Amnier thought in immediate surprise, an astonishing beauty. The holos in her files did her not the faintest trace of justice. Her blond hair was tucked up under a net that reminded him, strangely, of the hair net the Sisters had worn at St. Margaret Mary's, the Catholic school he'd been taught at as a child. She stared at him, waiting for an answer. He wondered at her anger; forty-five minutes ago it had undoubtedly been real. Now it was simply a mask stamped across features that were, perhaps, slightly too delicate. It seemed to Amnier that she was undernourished as well; she must have lost five kilograms since the most recent holographs of her had been taken.

Darryl Amnier rose belatedly from behind Montignet's desk, removed his hat, and sketched a bow. "I am Monsieur Amnier, here for my appointment." It was his best French.

Suzanne Montignet looked him over as though he were

something unpleasant she'd found in her salad, and shook her head in a tired motion. She dropped the pile of folders she'd entered with on her desktop. "Lights," she said in English. The fluorescent lamps came up bright, and Darryl Amnier realized that the odd gray of her eyes, which he'd assumed an error in her holo reproductions, was their true color. "I know who you are. Do you usually pop into people's offices two damned hours ahead of time?"

Amnier found himself caught in the challenge of her gaze. Without thought he found his posture straightening. With perfect honesty he replied, "Mademoiselle, only when I wish for the person with whom I am meeting to be ill at ease." He shook his head. "In this instance, I regret the use of the technique—and have for the last half hour."

Suzanne Montignet looked him over briefly, and smiled rather wearily. She held out her hand. "I have," she said softly, "been looking forward to meeting you, Mister Amnier." He took her hand, and was not surprised at the strength in her grip. "As has Colonel Kalharri."

Someday I shall tell you of the life of Jorge Rodriguez; it is the least one can do for a man one has killed.

It is the truth that I killed Jorge Rodriguez.

Like all truths it is susceptible to interpretation. I had taken all the precautions available to me that my visit to this time might not cause more damage than good; but it is never possible to know all of what may come from any course of action. This is as true of a God of the Zaradin Church as it is of any other sentient.

Jorge Rodriguez entered the small room with two doors only moments after his fellow technicians had left through the other. The doors were so designed that they could not both be open at the same time. I waited patiently as the man came through the door leading to the laboratories proper. There was time for me, despite the poor quality of ultraviolet light, to puzzle out his name badge, which was mounted on a piece of dark plastic with a strip of a clear film upon it. He entered as the door had just barely opened, and then stood in the doorway, preventing my passage, as the door slid shut again. It should not have been a problem; he would continue through the next door, and I would open the door to the laboratories after he was gone. It would appear to those inside as if the door had slid aside of its own accord; unusual, but given the relatively primitive stage of their technology, it would not be so strange as to cause excitement in and of itself.

A glitch, they would call it.

But Jorge Rodriguez did not leave immediately. As long minutes fled by on my personal time scale, Rodriguez slumped back against the door to the laboratories. With excruciating slowness he reached inside his coat and withdrew a small cylinder, which he placed within his mouth. As far away as the small room would allow me to get, I paced slowly back and forth to prevent my image from flickering into an instant of appearance. It must have raised ever so faint a breeze.

Rodriguez puffed on the cylinder, his back to the door through which I desperately needed to pass. It was likely tobacco or marijuana, two preeminent inhalants of the period. I could not recall how long a typical cylinder of either inhalant should have taken to be consumed, but it was soon apparent that whatever the period was would be far longer than I had available.

I came down into Time.

It was instantaneous for me; for Rodriguez I appeared as a frozen statue for most of a second. His eyes were opened wide in a surprise that would soon be terror, and he was drawing in air to shout. I reached past the rising wave of fear, into his forebrain, and sent him into sleep as gently as I was able. His body began to sag almost instantly; his breath exhaled in a loud sigh as he fell. I caught him before he had struck the ground, and carried him out through the door into the corridor. In Time I erased his memories of me, and in Time I returned to the small room where I had killed Jorge Rodriguez. I touched the pressure pad that opened the door into the laboratories, and as it opened I ascended into fast time once more.

The small badge that Jorge Rodriguez wore had turned from clear to black while he stood in that room with me. I had lived a thousand times as fast as he; the heat of my body had struck him as gamma rays for more than long enough.

"A remarkably impersonal room, this." Amnier stood in front of her bookcase, ran one finger down the spine of a text by de Nostri on fine neural structure. "No paintings, no holos . . ." Without subtlety, he watched her as he spoke. She held herself like a man, shoulders squared back.

Montignet moved by him, to seat herself behind her desk. She pressed her thumb against the lock and slid open the filing drawer. "I'm rarely here. I generally work downstairs at the lab. I have a desk there, and there are cots for when we draw night duty." From the filing drawer she withdrew two folders, and closed the drawer again. The drawer locked itself automatically. "The books are mostly gifts." Amnier turned back to her. "The de Nostri was from de Nostri; the man's an incredible egotist."

"Ah," said Amnier, and Suzanne had to repress a rather evil grin at how eagerly he leapt upon the opening, "an egotist, yes, but a *successful* egotist."

Suzanne Montignet did smile then, and watched as her smile struck Amnier. His face became very calm. So then, he was not, as Malko had thought, attracted *only* to boys. "I would not say that our work here has been a failure."

"But neither has it produced a clear success. De Nostri has—children, if that is the correct word—who are nearly two years of age."

"Children," said Suzanne Montignet with some anger, "is not the correct word. Mister, any fool can produce monsters. Mixing variant gene sets is not so very difficult. Slapping together genes from humans and leopards, among reputable scientists, that's known as playing mix and match. What we're doing is more difficult, and you know it. The foeti we have designed here, from the ground up, are *human*. They will be *human* children."

"But they do not live."

"Not . . ." *Not yet,* she had started to say; Suzanne Montignet clamped down upon her anger. It was almost as though Malko were there in the room with her, whispering in her ear. Amnier delighted in argument; directness was the way to handle him. "Did you," she asked slowly, "come here to shut us down?"

"I have come," said the small man, as honestly as he was able, "to decide."

They were still staring at each other when the alarms went off.

It was strange, looking down upon the bundle of amino acids which was my ancestor.

They had assembled him with lasers and viruses, in a

process that the histories said would be obsolete within a decade. It was a primitive process, far likelier to fail than otherwise; the histories were unclear as to how many times the technique had ever functioned properly in the decade in which it was employed.

There are moments when Destiny itself reaches out to trace a finger down my cheek, with the touch of a lover. I do not know if it is the same for Camber Tremodian; he is an immensely practical man in some ways. The tiny bit of matter before me was the great-grandfather of the first of my line; and it was right that it was with the Gift of the House of November that I reached out, and took the broken long chains of unliving matter, and brought them together in the pattern which would let Carl Castanaveras live.

Robin MacIntyre finished reading off status reports in a dull monotone. "We hustled the decon unit downstairs, and—"

"Radiation?"

"All over the place. Low levels most places, but—Jorge's badge was totally black." For the first time Suzanne understood the grief-stricken expression on Robin's face; Jorge, Robin's closest friend on the staff, was as good as dead. "They're taking Jorge to the hospital; I'm going to log out and go with him."

"No." It was Amnier, standing on the other side of the Information Network terminal. He could not see either Robin or the status reports that were filling up the other half of the screen. "You can't take him out of here."

Suzanne was not sure Robin had heard Amnier; she'd slapped down on the silence point as soon as he'd begun speaking. "Why the hell not?"

"If his badge is black," said Amnier patiently, "he's dead regardless. I saw enough of that during the war; so did Malko. Check with him if you must; medical technology hasn't advanced as much as all that in the last decade. Taking him to the hospital will be of use to nobody except this Robin person, and it will, by releasing knowledge of this radiation contamination into the general populace, place a very potent weapon into the hands of those who do wish to close you down."

Robin was gesturing on the terminal's screen. Suzanne lifted her thumb from the pressure point. "One moment, Robin." She pressed down again. "How so?"

"It will mean that you are either incompetent enough to have allowed radioactives to escape from confinement—"

"We don't even *use* radioactives."

"Irrelevant. Or it will mean that you have been targeted by ideologs." Amnier shook his head. "The Unification Council would find that an excellent excuse to shut you down. We have not the resources to guard an installation of questionable worth against a group of determined ideologs."

An override suddenly flashed on Suzanne's terminal. "Malko here. I'll meet you at the showers. Bring Amnier." The override ended, and Robin's form appeared again in the terminal.

"This is," said Suzanne, the instant the thought struck her, "a fascinating coincidence, that this should happen while you are visiting."

Darryl Amnier smiled at her, the first true smile she had seen from him. He spoke with chilling precision. "I have thought that myself."

Terence Kniessen, a tall fat man with a shock of red hair, met them at the showers. He was wearing his head bubble— a barely visible line of refraction ran five centimeters around the perimeter of his skull—but his gloves had been removed. Malko was already there, undressing preparatory to entering the chemical showers; Amnier flinched visibly at the sight of the long laser scars that crisscrossed Kalharri's body. Almost hidden among the marks of the lasers were the small round puckered scars where bullets had entered his flesh. Kalharri did not even glance at Amnier. He entered the first shower in the row as they began undressing.

Terence was sweating; he took Amnier's coat, babbling instructions at the man. ". . . and then gargle with the mouthwash, you'll have to swallow the second mouthful. I'll meet you on the other side and show you how to—"

Suzanne interrupted him. "Terence."

He stopped speaking instantly and glanced at her sideways—he was more of a prude than most of the rest of the staff. "Yes ma'am?"

"You took your gloves off."

Terence let out a low moan. "Oh, *damn*," he swore, and began stripping down even more quickly than the others.

The first thing that Amnier noticed, as they cycled through the double doors that led into the labs, was the faint smell of ozone. The bubble let filtered air through, and it was not supposed to filter anything so small as an ozone molecule; but before he could be certain about the smell, he was led through the inner door and found himself upon a catwalk that looked down upon chaos.

Kalharri was down there, with a pair of technicians wearing decon badges. Only one of the decon badges bore the radiating triangle insignia that meant its wearer had passed training to deal with radioactive materials. The tech who wore that badge was probably paid twice as much as the tech who did not; even today, eleven-and-a-half years after the end of the Unification War, there were not enough skilled radiation decon techs to go around.

The lab itself was huge; it was easily the largest room in what was not a small building. *This*, thought Amnier, *is where they work*. The things that had been missing everywhere else were in abundance here: comic strips had been inscribed in the glowpaint, and decorative calendars were hung in three different places. The dozen or so desks that were scattered across the place were personalized to various degrees; one that caught his eye held the holograph of a ballerina, turning eternally on point.

The laboratory was the first place Amnier had seen in the building where glowpaint gave an approximation of yellow sunlight.

A huge laser hung nose-down from the ceiling, pointing at a table that bore a ceramic depression nearly a meter in diameter. In the middle of the depression was a small transparent container that had been clamped into position; tubes so small that Amnier could barely see them from where he stood led to the container.

Amnier made his way down from the catwalk slowly. Montignet was already down at floor level. One of the technicians was showing her listings from the devices that were attached to the transparent container; Montignet rose up from the computer, shouted, "Ellie, get me nutrient flow *now,*" and went back instantly to the readouts.

Amnier reached the floor and found Malko Kalharri there, waiting for him. Kalharri was standing with his arms crossed, pale blue eyes calm and rather relaxed. "Hello, Darryl."

Amnier sat down abruptly on a step four from the bottom. It put his eyes almost on a level with Kalharri's. "Hello, Malko. How have you been?"

"Well. And yourself?"

Amnier shrugged. "Busy. I work. What is happening?"

"There was a source of radiation." Kalharri eyed Amnier speculatively. "It's gone now. Vanished. We haven't been able to track it down."

"Assuming," said Amnier, "that you yourself have not caused this excitement—and I do not put it past you, Malko —please accept my assurance that I am not responsible for whatever has happened here today." He looked directly at Malko. "Did you let them take this Jorge person to the hospital?"

"No. Of course not."

"It grieves you that you could not do so."

"It would have made Robin feel better."

"But he would still die."

Kalharri nodded. "Yes."

Amnier watched the technicians in silence for a moment as they rushed about at errands that he, and he suspected Kalharri also, found totally incomprehensible. "If a living foetus comes out of this, and what I am hearing leads me to believe it might, I shall find it all most suspect."

Amnier thought a smile might have touched Kalharri's lips for an instant. It was difficult to be certain. "You're flattering yourself, Darryl."

"Perhaps. It is a danger in my profession." Amnier paused. "Our profession, I might say. You have not forgotten how the thought processes operate, at any rate. I have not needed to say a startling number of things."

"I have been thinking," said Kalharri, "about what you said to me the last time we talked."

Darryl Amnier stared at him in utter, complete amazement. "Malko, that was seventeen years ago."

"I think you may have been right. The United States was crumbling, in some ways." Kalharri spoke slowly, with what was as close to reluctance as Amnier had ever seen from him. "I mean politically. In other ways it was not. The Unification Council—the entire superstructure which your Sarah Almundsen designed—it is, in some ways, more vigorous than what we had; certainly better than what the Russians had, or the Chinese. Perhaps this United Nations is better. Perhaps it was even worth the deaths that came about in the War."

"It's good of you to say so."

"Darryl."

"Yes?"

"You are—all of you—already losing sight of what you fought for. I did not agree with you, and today I am not certain that I was right—but your government is being overrun by the barbarians. It's already happening." He said slowly, "I don't know if Americans will tolerate it."

Amnier said gently, "You're too much of a philosopher, Malko. It was charming when we were boys. But it helped you lose the War. And it's not helping you at all now."

" '. . . In republics there is greater life, greater hatred, and more desire for vengeance; they do not and cannot cast aside the memory of their ancient liberty.' "

Amnier looked at him quizzically. "Niccolò Machiavelli," he said after a moment. "*The Prince,* of course . . . The Old Man would have been proud of you." He smiled distantly. "In the same work it says, this is a paraphrase, 'A city used to liberty can be more easily held by means of its citizens than in any other way, if you wish to preserve it.' "

"You just don't get it, do you?"

Amnier did not answer. There was a silence that continued until Suzanne left her work station and returned to where they waited. Amnier sat with his eyes unfocused, looking off into a distance that did not exist; Kalharri stood, eyes fixed on Amnier's face. Neither saw what they looked upon.

"Malko?" Amnier looked up at the woman, flushed with some strong emotion, and thought again, *You are so very lovely.* Montignet continued, "We have one. It's going to live."

"Fascinating," murmured Amnier. He looked down at the steel stairway upon which he sat. When he looked up again there was a flat snapping sound, like a whip being cracked. For the merest instant Amnier stared directly at the flat, black cutout of a man, merely the outline of a shape. I doubt that he ever again fully believed his own eyes after that; Camber

Tremodian was gone before Amnier could be certain of what he had seen.

None of the others appeared to have noticed. "Which one is it?" asked Malko quietly.

"Number fifty-five. Series C, number C; we've been calling it Charlie Chan."

"Do you know its sex yet?"

"Male."

Malko Kalharri had not yet turned away from Darryl Amnier; now he came closer, squatted until his eyes were on a level with Amnier's. "I think we shall name him Carl . . . Castanaveras, perhaps. Yes."

Amnier blinked. His mind seemed to be elsewhere. "Oh?"

"Yes," said Malko Kalharri, "Castanaveras. I think that is an appropriate name."

Three days after my life brushed against his, Jorge Rodriguez died of radiation burns.

We have kept the costs of the battle down, Camber and I; Jorge Rodriguez was only the third human being in sequential Time to die in one of the battles of the Time Wars.

It might have comforted him to know that.

Or not.

INTERLUDE:
2030-2062

And so three decades passed.

When Carl Castanaveras was still a very young boy, before puberty turned him into a Peaceforcer weapon, an officer of the United Nations Peace Keeping Force once asked him what he wished to do with his life.

The question startled the boy. He had been raised by doctors and scientists and Malko Kalharri; the Peaceforcer's question was not the sort of thing anyone had ever asked of him before.

After a moment's consideration he said, "Am I supposed to do something with it?"

There can be good mistakes. Fact and truth and history are rarely related. The facts are these.

Carl Castanaveras was born on the eighteenth of September in the year 2030. He was named after a soldier who, fighting for his country, died during the Unification War; he was raised in a world that still bore the scars of that war. The America in which he was raised was an occupied country; there were more Peaceforcers in the United States than police. The war was history already by the time he was old enough to understand its causes. In classes he was taught about its great battles; how after the Battle of Yorktown, the young Marine Corps sergeant who was in command of what was left of the United States Marine Corps forced the U.N. forces to withdraw into a neighboring city before he would agree to surrender his forces. In agreeing to surrender, a young Marine named Neil Corona produced the most memorable quote of the War: "We will fry under your goddamn cannon," he said, "before a single Marine will lay down his arms in Yorktown."

After that war's end, the slow task of rebuilding began. France, alone among the industrial nations of the time, emerged unscathed from the Unification War. In the years that followed the war, it attained a position of preeminence among the bodies that constituted the United Nations.

The gene pattern which produced Carl Castanaveras was not successfully reproduced until April the eighteenth, in 2035, when a design which became Jane McConnell was successfully imprinted upon a sterile egg. In creating her, Suzanne Montignet localized three unique genes that Carl Castanaveras possessed and no other living human being did. Jane McConnell was, aside from her gender, his clone. She was the first and last instance in which Suzanne Montignet had to resort to relatively clumsy cloning techniques to ensure that the gene complex took properly. Johann MacArthur was brought to term late in 2036; unlike Jane McConnell he was a true genie, assembled gene by gene until a design was found that Suzanne Montignet approved. Six such others were born between 2036 and 2042.

In the year 2040, a man named Darryl Amnier was appointed to the position of Prosecutor General to the Unification Council.

For over a decade the U.N. Bureau of Biotechnology Research, and the Peaceforcers who controlled them, thought Carl Castanaveras a failure.

An interesting failure.

He seemed to be slightly stronger than his muscle mass should have warranted, with greater endurance; but his muscle mass, even with physical conditioning, was not exceptional. He moved with abnormal speed, and was emotionally unstable.

At the age of twelve, when puberty struck him with full force, Carl Castanaveras awoke one day and found that he could read minds.

He let others know; specifically, a Unification Councillor named Jerril Carson, who was at that time the Chairman of the Unification Council to supervise the Bureau of Biotechnology Research. That was the first mistake. By the time the other abilities began to manifest, he had learned enough to know that in knowledge there is power. As he grew older, what would be known, more than a thousand years later, as the Gift of the House of November, grew also. Carl Castanaveras learned to hide that which he did not wish revealed.

Throughout history, slaves have always found this a useful skill.

They were slaves, no less so than the indentured hunters of twenty-third century Tin Woodman, or the blacks of the early American South. After the first shakeout, the Peaceforcers had three facilities where their experiments in genetic engineering were conducted; following the death of pioneer genegineer Jean Louis de Nostri, the facilities were consolidated under the control of Suzanne Montignet. The slaves— the "genies"—were, of course, relocated along with the research teams; and for the first time, the telepaths met the de Nostri.

And Carl Castanaveras found a friend, who was killed.

There were times when Shana de Nostri did not mind the fact that she was not human.

Now was not one of those times.

She sat brooding on the mat at the side of the gym as a group of five Peaceforcers put Carl Castanaveras through his paces. Her girlfriend Lorette was with her, and the two of them were striking enough that the four Peaceforcers who were not engaged with Carl kept sneaking glances, mostly at Shana. She was no better looking than Lorette, only less modestly dressed. In gross physiological detail they resembled human women closely enough that human men often found them attractive. The differences were minor enough that a good cosmetic biosculptor might have made them look human, had they desired to look human. At one point while he lived, Dr. de Nostri had, in a fit of conscience, offered that option to the de Nostri. Their tails would have had to be amputated, and their fur removed permanently; the claws would have been replaced with fingernails. Facial reconstruction would have lowered the very high cheekbones, replaced their flat, wide noses with noses that protruded properly. Sexually they were more like humans than the cougars from whom the balance of their genetic makeup was derived; male and female genitalia closely resembled those of normal humans. The females had breasts that would, very likely, produce milk in the likely event that any of the maturing seventy-three de Nostri females ever bore children.

The de Nostri had, as a group, rejected the offer.

The de Nostri were *proud* of their appearance.

Lorette had, like most of the female de Nostri, made concessions to the morals of the—mostly American—humans among whom they now found themselves. Her breasts were covered by a loose blouse, and her genitals were covered by a pair of baggy pants that had been altered to accommodate her tail.

Shana was nude except for her fur. Her nipples were clearly visible, and a human who stared—and some had, though not more than once—could have made out the outline of her genitalia through her fur.

She was *damned* if she was going to put on a second layer of skin when the weather did not require it.

Just now, Carl was sparring with a hulk of a Peaceforcer who had to outmass him two to one. Shana and Lorette were practicing speaking in English, rather than the French they had learned as children. Though most of the staff spoke understandable, hideously accented French, most of the thirty or so genies with whom the de Nostri were sharing the buildings did not. It was a failing shared, in even greater measure, by the New York City residents.

"I cannot see that it matters," said Lorette primly, running her claws gently through the brown-and-white-striped fur that covered Shana's back and shoulders. "Talk to the telepath if you must, your boyfriend over there . . ."

Shana's muscles tensed, and she growled so quietly that no human and most genies who were not de Nostri would have heard it. Lorette's ears pricked slightly, and without pausing she continued, ". . . or only your friend, if you will have it that way. But . . ."

She broke off again; the Peaceforcer sparring with Carl had picked the boy up and thrown him a full five meters. Shana sucked in her breath, and her claws unsheathed of their own accord. The boy struck the mat rolling and came to his feet running backward. The Peaceforcer was right there, a long kick whistling through the space the boy's body had occupied only an instant before.

There was a moment when the two stood facing each other, motionlessly, before engaging again, and Lorette continued speaking as though she had never been interrupted. "But the people in the city," she said, lips drawn back from her teeth in a reflex that had nothing to do with a human's smile, "*animals*. They stare so." She stopped scratching Shana. "How is that?"

"I still itch in all places."

Lorette sighed, switched to French. "What did they inject you with?"

The snarl in Shana's voice would have been audible even to a human. "They did not tell me, except it is supposed to make me strong. If I was a human, even a genie, they would have said."

Lorette chuckled without amusement. "If you were a human citizen they could not even have injected you without permission."

Shana was silent, watching as a somewhat smaller Peaceforcer took over from the very large one. The boy had no time to catch his breath; within seconds the two were fighting, each wielding a meter-long rod of wood with a rounded, metal cap at each end.

"Really?"

Lorette sighed, and returned to English. "It is what Albert says."

"Albert says things just to say them," said Shana sullenly.

"True." Lorette was struck by something amusing, and she leaned forward to whisper in Shana's ear. "Albert told me that he has watched Carl spar and that he is better."

"Scratch my shoulders, please," said Shana. Lorette's claws moved up after the new itch, and Shana sighed with pleasure when they caught it. "Albert is a fool. He is four years older than Carl, and he is jealous because he is not as important. He is one of many de Nostri, and Carl is the only telepath." She thought about the subject for a moment. "Perhaps it is even true that he is better than Carl, with an advantage of only six years study in martial discipline. Carl began learning only after they found he was a telepath and realized it might be necessary to use him in the field. But I will tell you this much, Albert may best Carl on the mat. If they ever fight truly, Carl will win." Shana had to catch her breath after speaking; she was slightly winded.

"I have talked to Carl once," said Lorette thoughtfully. "He says when they take him on assignment he is well protected."

Shana nodded. "Yes. He is their only telepath, unless the little dark-haired girl is one also, and they will not know that until, what is it . . ." and she took a long, deep breath, to bring the air into her lungs, and spoke in her native tongue, "Comment dit-on en anglais 'ménarche'?"

"Puberty," said Lorette, "but it means for boys and girls both. They do not have a word for *ménarche.*"

"They will not know until Jany reaches puberty, then." Shana coughed, a deep, guttural sound, and said, "It makes him special."

Lorette brightened. "Look, the fourth match is finished. One more and we can go to lunch."

Shana shook her head slowly. Her ears had begun twitching without stop. "I think perhaps I should go to the infirmary."

"Shana?"

"I . . . I do not feel well."

Carl Castanaveras did not even look away from his match as they left.

The field image wavered slightly. Suzanne Montignet's image waited for nearly three seconds after Malko had finished speaking; round-trip signal time from the PKF Elite SpaceBase One, at L-5. "You've got to be kidding."

Malko shook his head no. "They weren't sure at first what was happening. It took nearly a day before the transform virus killed her. I had Carson on the line after it happened. He denied—"

"Of *course* the virus killed her," Suzanne exploded after the strange delay that Malko found himself unable to become used to. "What did the bloody fools expect? She was a de Nostri, for God's sake! Their muscle cells *behave* differently!"

Malko waited until there was silence before he continued. "Ellie Samuels did the work, and she says she received her orders directly from Councillor Carson. You weren't available for her to check with, which is pretty clearly intentional."

Suzanne was nodding tensely. "Of course it was. Carson's wanted to try seeding one of the de Nostri with the enhanced-strength transform virus for the last year. They're so strong to begin with, the damn fool figures this should make them even stronger. I *told* him the odds were terrible." She looked broodingly into the camera, eyes slightly unfocused; she was not looking at the screen that held Malko's image. "It's been fascinating, seeing the work the Peaceforcers have been doing in transform viruses, but it still didn't make sense, how insistent they were that I make the trip to L-5, until now. Carson wanted me up here so that I couldn't interfere down there. Have you heard from Amnier?"

"Not a word. The Prosecutor General's office won't even return my calls. I think they're going to let Carson get away with it."

"Has Shana been autopsied yet?"

"No."

"How's Carl?"

Malko hesitated. ". . . angry."

"That bad?"

"I've never seen it worse."

She seemed to reach a decision. "Very well. Don't let her be autopsied until I get back. I want to be there. Ellie might not have known what she was doing when she got her orders. . . ." She was looking off-screen at something. "Ship leaves at 2300 hours. I can be in Manhattan by this time tomorrow. Have Carl confined."

"I'll try." The holo field went silver, then flattened, and Suzanne's figure vanished without saying anything further.

If, thought Malko quietly, *I can find him.*

The receptionist sat at the wide front desk, in the inner lobby of the offices of the Unification Council, at the United Nations Building in New York City. Sunlight struck a warm, late afternoon glow through the bay windows that surrounded the lobby on three sides, washed in and overrode the clean white glowpaint. The receptionist thought she saw movement outside, through the window, and dismissed it as a figment of her imagination.

The doors slid aside, and by reflex she touched the pressure point at the side of her desk, marked SECURITY, the instant the young man walked in. By appearance he was perhaps fifteen or sixteen years of age; young, but old enough to be dangerous.

And she should have received *some* warning before he had ever reached the inner lobby.

"Can I help you?"

His voice was odd. She had to strain to hear him, and—surely his lips had moved?

I have come to see Councillor Carson.

His eyes were green, some portion of her mind noted uneasily, and very large. And familiar . . . "I'm sorry," she stumbled, "but the Councillors do not see people without an appointment."

He moved closer to her, head cocked slightly to one side. An intangible, electric shock of danger ran through her. There was rage in him, an anger so vast she had never experienced its like before. *Please tell him that I am here.*

She did know him, she was certain of it. Thought came slowly, as though from a great distance. She could not take her gaze away from the brilliant, luminescent green of his eyes. She activated her inskin data link without knowing she was doing so, and paged the Councillor to the reception area.

Another Councillor, with two of his staff, came through the lobby as they waited, and eyed the boy with a touch of curiosity. The boy stood silently, motionless, and did not look at them. He kept his gaze locked to the receptionist. They found it, and him, somewhat odd, but of course he would not have been there if he had not belonged there, and so they continued on their way, and forgot the boy and the strange tableau with a speed which Jerril Carson would have found instructive.

The lift doors, at the far end of the lobby, slid aside, and Jerril Carson stood framed between the sliding doors, with a Peaceforcer at his side.

Suddenly a weight lifted itself from the receptionist's mind, and the dark-haired boy's features moved into sharp focus. The blood had entirely drained from his face at Jerril Carson's appearance, leaving it shockingly white beneath the straight black hair, but she recognized the boy nonetheless. "Of course," she said aloud. "Why didn't . . ."

Carson lifted an eyebrow in mild surprise. "Carl?"

The voice echoed, as though something *else* spoke through the boy, used him as an instrument of expression. *"You killed Shana."*

The boy said nothing else, and Carson was still looking at him when the windows exploded outward. A great invisible hand slammed the Peaceforcer down to the floor, dragged him out of the lift and across the pale blue carpeting. The Unification Councillor stumbled back into the lift, mouth open and working as though he would say something.

But no words came, and Carl Castanaveras, with an insane rage stamped upon his features, went in after him.

The doors slid quietly shut before the screams began.

There can be good mistakes; and otherwise.

Jane McConnell underwent puberty early in the year 2047. The Peaceforcers were waiting; as, most specifically, was a man named Jerril Carson.

She too had the Gift.

For the predominantly French Peaceforcers, struggling to keep order in a world that hated and distrusted them, it was confirmation enough of the information-gathering godsend that fate had sent them. Castanaveras had already proven that he could retrieve information reliably when physically near his target; but one, or even ten such telepaths, were only mist in the desert of their need.

2048, the year Jerril Carson became the chairman of the Peace Keeping Force Oversight Committee in the Unification Council, was, not coincidentally, also the year Suzanne Montignet was removed from control of what was popularly called Project Superman. In that year forty-three telepathic children were brought to term. All were given the surname Castanaveras; the technicians had tired of inventing individual surnames. In 2049 there were seventy-three, and another eighty-six in the year 2050.

In 2051, the year Trent Castanaveras was born, there were only twenty-four telepathic children brought into the world. The Peaceforcers were beginning to learn enough to wonder if they should be afraid of the powers they had helped create. Many of them were afraid of Carl Castanaveras. With some help from Castanaveras himself, the assembly-line program to produce telepaths for the Peaceforcers was terminated by the middle of the year.

In 2052, Darryl Amnier became the Secretary General of the United Nations.

In 2053, twins were born to Carl Castanaveras and Jane McConnell; twins named David and, yes, the Denice who became Denice Ripper, from whom our line descends.

Those are the facts. There have been many histories written concerning those twenty years when telepaths first walked the Earth; but historians are primarily concerned with truth, and a concern for truth can make one leery of those cold facts that might conflict with a precious, closely held "truth."

It is better to be a Storyteller.

EMERALD EYES

1

Just better than thirty-two years after Jorge Rodriguez died of radiation burns, on Wednesday, March 9, 2062, Carl Castanaveras rose early. In cold morning winds, he left Suzanne Montignet's home and walked three blocks through the icy dark, to the Massapequa Park Station of the Long Island Tubeway. It was only four A.M.; the streets of exurban Massapequa Park were largely bare of traffic. The stars shone clearly overhead. The moon had already dropped below the horizon. There were no other pedestrians about. It was silent except for the rare car and the rumble of the huge twelve-fans rolling down Sunland Boulevard.

The cold did not affect Carl; he barely noticed it except to keep his hands inside his coat pockets. He walked briskly, more out of impatience than from any consideration for the temperature.

At the Tube station the doors slid aside and admitted him to a warm, well-lit waiting room. There were—Carl sorted and cataloged by reflex—eight of them, three women and five men, waiting for the 4:15 Tube shuttle to Grand Central Station.

At the InfoNet Aid station Carl bought a one-way ticket to the city, and leased a news viewer. The clerk behind the counter was having trouble keeping her eyes open. Lease of the news viewer came to a quarter Credit Unit more than the ticket itself; the viewers were stolen with some regularity. He paid with untraceable, SpaceFarer issue hard CU; the clerk blinked in curiosity at the sight of the rare silver coins, but took the CU:1.25 without word.

He stood quietly for several minutes, waiting for the Bullet to arrive. At 4:12 the Bullet came up out of the ground, and coasted down the superconductor maglev monorail to a slow gliding stop; a single structure made of nearly a hundred meters of supertwisted sheet monocrystal. The Bullet could not be painted and did not need to be washed; filth simply slid off. It could not be scratched or dented.

Under sufficient impact, it would shatter.

At 4:15 precisely the Bullet pulled out of the Massapequa Park station and was fed slowly back into the interlock. In the lock the atmosphere was evacuated, and the Bullet was injected back into the Tube with a steady acceleration that was so smooth it was almost imperceptible.

Once, almost ten years ago, ideologs who were never identified—Johnny Rebs, perhaps, or else the Erisian Claw—left a bowling ball in the Tube. The Bullet struck it at full cruising speed. There was an average clearance of five centimeters around the circumference of the Bullet; when it struck the bowling ball the Bullet turned the bowling ball into vaporized dust.

In the process, the Bullet itself touched the side of the Tube. The resultant earthquake destroyed eighteen kilometers of the Tube; the shock wave was felt nearly sixty kilometers from the place where the Bullet shattered itself against a bowling ball.

Carl sat in the seat nearest the exit, not because it would be of any help in the event of trouble with the Bullet, but because it would save him time when the train stopped. He stowed his briefcase in the rack under the seat and purchased a large cup of coffee from the waitbot as it rolled down the long center aisle. Service that morning was good; before the crush hours started it usually was.

The first thing he saw when he turned on the news viewer made him wince. He'd gone to greater than usual trouble that morning to ensure that his activities remained unnoticed; logging on to the InfoNet, he'd picked the default user profile rather than identify himself by his thumbprint, thus downloading his news habits from his InfoNet profile. Had he been using his own user profile the screen that greeted him would not have surprised him much; his private profile had been taught to start out with the news items of greatest interest to him, and work its way down the list.

He was logged on, however, anonymously; and despite

that, his face was all over the front screen of the morning edition of the *Electronic Times* news Board. The headline the video tablet showed—Carl did not have his earphone turned on—was "UNIFICATION COUNCIL PASSES GENIE BILL."

The texts of the several stories were lacking. Bare bones of the Amendment—it was not, as the front-screen headline implied, a bill, but the Eighth Amendment to the Statement of Principles—and a brief sketch of its ramifications for both the telepaths and the feline de Nostri, with another sketch of the principals involved in the bill on both sides. Predictably, Malko's involvement with the Eighth Amendment, and the limited but real opposition the Amendment had received from Secretary General Amnier's office, was the primary subject for most of the newsdancers. It was a romantic lead; two war heroes, on opposite sides during the war, and still so four and a half decades later.

Auditing the stories, Carl found he could reliably judge any particular newsdancer's sympathies in the matter, simply in the style in which the newsdancer wrote the Secretary General's title. Those who used the currently popular *Ministre Général*, rather than the historically correct English title, had little good to say about either the telepaths or those who supported them.

Only one story in the entire first section was not about the passage of the Eighth Amendment; a SpaceFarer smuggler had been apprehended with an entire cargo hold full of GoodBeer from St. Peter's CityState, in the Asteroid Belt. Any other day it would have been a front-screen story, perhaps the headline. Of the remaining stories, almost all concerned the conflict between Amnier and Kalharri.

Unfortunately, one of the newsdancers had not been content with the obvious story; that newsdancer had taken Carl Castanaveras for a ride down the boulevard with the spotlights turned on. The style was familiar; Carl paged down the article until he came to the sign-off.

Gerold McKann; special to the Electronic Times.

Carl Castanaveras shook his head from side to side, hardly aware he was doing so. The pictures of him were good; a man of average height, with the build of a swimmer, in conservative business attire. He sipped at his coffee, vaguely aware of a need to finish the cup before it went cold. The video tablet showed several different holos, most of them apparently taken from his testimony before the Unification Council earlier that year. The color reproduction was good; the brilliant green eyes leapt out from beneath a shock of black hair exactly as they did in real life, and with very nearly as much impact.

The text was well written and devastating; it focused on the circumstances that had led to the telepaths' petition, and the role Carl Castanaveras had played in freeing the telepaths from the control of the United Nations Peace Keeping Force.

It was all highly approving.

Briefly, Carl smiled without any humor at all. *Gerry, my friend,* he thought grimly, *I am going to nail your ass to the wall.*

Across the aisle, a woman was staring at him. She looked down at her news viewer, and then back up again. Her features froze into an unpleasant mixture somewhere between hatred and embarrassment.

Carl stared directly at her until she turned away.

There was a flicker on the Information Network.

United Nations Peace Keeping Staff Sergeant Emile Garon looked around his small cubicle. He was near the end of his second year in this cubicle now; two years spent monitoring use of the Information Network, two years plugged into a bank of Fairchild gallium arsenide transputers, two years with the superconductor RAM hardwired into his skull. The cubicle's walls were off-white, and he was forbidden to decorate them.

The room was information sterile, intentionally. There should be nothing there to distract him from his job.

Paris, he thought for the hundredth time that week. *I left Paris for this.*

Two hundred meters below the surface of New York City, Peaceforcer Emile Garon sighed and closed his eyes, and hoped desperately that the flicker would become a trace that would take him out into the Crystal Wind of data that was life.

And returned to work.

Their offices were on Third Avenue, a fifteen-minute walk from Grand Central Station. The suite belonging to Kalharri Enterprises, Ltd., was not large: one subdivided private office where Malko, Carl, and Jany McConnell had desks, a receptionist's area, and a conference room. For almost a year now

Malko had been paying for the offices out of his own pocket. That too would be changing, and none too soon.

Spyeyes were hovering above the street outside when Carl reached the Kaufmann Spacescraper at 550 Third Avenue. The fact of their presence was not unusual; many of the news services floated spyeyes outside the spacescraper when there was an ongoing story that involved one of the occupants. The sheer number of spyeyes brought him to a halt for a second. Twenty, twenty-five; he stopped counting when he passed thirty. The spyeyes spotted him at nearly the same moment; nearly a dozen spyeyes identified him and swooped down toward him at the same time, shouting questions at him that blurred into a single incomprehensible wall of sound. Carl ran the last forty meters through the early-morning pedestrian traffic, to the revolving glass doors of the spacescraper.

There were half again the usual number of guards on duty today. With quick efficiency the security guards processed him through at the entrance to the building. The lift tube took him up to the 408th floor; sunpaint came up as Carl unlocked the door to his office. The receptionist's area and the conference room were empty. Carl entered his own office and dropped his briefcase next to the desk.

In the darkness of his office a cool blue cube appeared above Carl's desktop. The cube was invisible from the side opposite Carl, where the camera pickup was located.

Marilyn Monroe's image appeared within the cube.

"Gerold McKann, please."

"One moment, sir," breathed the image of a woman who'd been dead for nearly a hundred years. The solid, rock-steady receptionist's holograph was replaced on Carl's desktop by a wavering flat sheet of projected monovideo. Gerry was in his car; through the 2-D interface Carl could see part of the front seat of Gerry's Chandler 1300, and, through the windows of the car, what Carl guessed was TransContinental Highway 4 out in Pennsylvania. In the poor light of early morning, as relayed by the hovercar's marginally overscanning camera, it was difficult for him to be certain.

"Carl! Goddamn, man, congratulations." Gerry grinned into the camera. "I told you it would go through."

Carl stood with his fists resting on the desktop. "I audited the *Electronic Times* already this morning, Gerry."

The grin widened. "Yes? What did you think?"

Carl replied slowly. "How stupid are you?"

Gerry laughed. "I'm one—" He broke off abruptly. Cautiously he said, "You're angry."

"Why did you write that story, Gerry?"

Gerry's eyes flickered down toward the camera embedded in the Chandler's dash, then back up again to watch the road. "Excuse me a moment," he said mildly. Carl watched as Gerry set up radar and hooked the carcomp into TransCon Auto Control. Gerry McKann was in his late forties, though he looked younger; he kept in shape. He was a newsdancer with over twenty years' experience in the field. Newsdancing was the only job he'd ever held.

The flickering, blue-tinged monovideo showed very little of his expression as Gerry leaned back in the driver's seat and folded his arms across his chest. "Okay. I was under the impression I was doing you a favor."

"How so?"

"Well—correct me if I'm wrong—telepaths are people. I'm even willing to grant de Nostri that status; you and yours strike me as being a bit more human than that lot. I thought I'd spread the news." The newsdancer in him popped up with a quick grin. "Also, it was a hell of a good story."

From the outer office Carl heard the faint sound of the doors gliding open. Voices: Jany and Malko. Without turning away from the image in the holofield, he touched a key on the control panel to his InfoNet terminal. With a whisper the door between his office and the outer offices slid shut and locked itself. He sank into his seat slowly. He measured his words off carefully. "First of all—*you* correct *me* if I'm wrong, Gerry—isn't it contrary to newsdancer ethics to write a story on a subject to which you are connected in a personal fashion without explicitly identifying the fact?"

"Only if you get caught. Damn it, Carl, if nothing else it was good publicity. Count the number of favorable stories there've been about you folks of late and—"

"I—*we*—don't need the publicity. I don't *want* the publicity. The Peaceforcers don't want the publicity."

"What do you care what the Peaceforcers want?" McKann looked honestly bewildered. "Man, you're free! That's what all this was all—"

"*I am not free!*" roared Carl Castanaveras. He found himself on his feet, glaring down into the screen.

Gerry McKann was staring at him.

"Damn, damn, *damn*," Carl swore in a monotone. "Gerry, I have two hundred and thirty-six children who depend on me to take care of them. The Secretary General doesn't like me. He may hate Malko. Jerril Carson *does* hate me; he'd love to see me dead. Half of the Peaceforcers in the world are terrified of us, and the other half think we're traitors." He slammed a fist down on the desktop, and the entire desk shivered. "And *you*, you stupid son of a bitch, rub their noses in it in front of an audience of one and a quarter billion *Electronic Times* subscribers. We got a loveforsaken piece of paper signed, today new copies of the Statement of Principles get transmitted around the world, saying the Peaceforcers can't use us without paying us anymore, can't *tell* us to do anything anymore. Do you think the Peaceforcers *care* what that piece of paper says?"

Gerold McKann just looked at him.

Carl Castanaveras shouted, "Well? *Do you?*"

McKann's voice was barely audible. "No."

The word drained away Carl Castanaveras' anger, left him standing there, cold and empty inside. "I shouldn't have to say things like this, Gerry. You know better."

The older man sighed. "I didn't think. I was trying to do you a favor." He shrugged and looked out the window at what was, to Carl, only a blurred image of countryside. "I was trying to help." McKann looked back directly into his camera. His eyes seemed to meet Carl's. "Sorry. But Jerril Carson was *your* mistake."

He hung up and left Carl looking at a blank sheet of dim laser light.

Carl nodded after a moment. He spoke to the empty screen. "Yeah, well, we all make mistakes."

After a long moment he turned away from the field, called the sunlights up, and went out to face what promised to be a very long day.

In a park at the south end of Manhattan island, a telepathic human being named Johann MacArthur sat with his back to a tree and watched children play in the warm sunlight. He sat and enjoyed the warmth of the sun. The Weather Bureau said that the day would be pleasant, but Johnny had learned, like everyone else, not to trust anything the Bureau of Weather Control said.

The park was not large. It was in the shape of a rectangle

less than a hundred meters on its long axis, and only forty meters wide. It was enclosed, all the way around, by a five-meter-high fence. There was no exit to the street. It would not have been safe. Instead a tunnel walkway led from the center of the park, under the street, and came back up across the street, inside the Chandler Complex where the telepaths had been living for over half a year. The shade trees scattered throughout the park obscured visibility enough to make the fence difficult to see unless you were near the perimeter.

The children rarely approached the park's perimeter; it made it too easy to hear the chanting of the picket lines. Today was particularly noisy; given yesterday's vote, that was to be expected.

Johann sat in full lotus, eyes open and unfocused, wearing nothing but a pair of shorts. It was unseasonably warm for early morning in March, and promised genuine heat by noontime. He was a big blond man who looked too much like a young Malko Kalharri for coincidence. Carl had told Johann that in the earlier days of what the technicians had—only half sarcastically—named Project Superman, many of the men in the staff had donated sperm cells for the genetic content. Johann had never asked Malko if he had been one of those men; he had never cared much whether any of his genes had come from Kalharri or not. At twenty-five years of age, he was the third oldest telepath on Earth.

He didn't feel very old, most of the time.

The park was quiet this early in the morning. About sixty of the children were out playing, Johann guessed. The rest of the kids would be in one class or another, except for the eight who were currently out on jobs for the Peaceforcers.

He felt a certain grim satisfaction in the knowledge that those would be the *last* eight.

A swift thought struck him; it came from Heather Castanaveras, the fourteen-year-old girl who was teaching unarmed combat that morning to a class composed largely of thirteen- and fourteen-year-olds. *Johnny, have you seen Trent?*

Johann closed his eyes briefly, and with the Sight walked through the park quickly. Althea, his lieutenant for the day, was leading her group in a game of hide-and-seek played by rules no normal human could have understood. *I don't see him, Heather.*

Blue eyes isn't in class again. The thought held frustration that approached anger.

Johann sighed. *Try not to get upset with him, Heather. Why not?*

He's not having an easy time with the Change. And besides, added Johann, *today's his birthday.*

It's always *somebody's birthday,* snapped Heather, and cut the connection abruptly.

Johann thought a moment. Trent had only turned eleven today; Heather had moved him into class with the thirteen- and fourteen-year-olds some months ago. She thought he held promise in unarmed combat, and certainly he was large enough. But he seemed to have little interest in the subject.

Not my problem, he decided with an abrupt cheerful lack of interest, and returned to the strenuous task of dozing under the warm sun.

Emile Garon's hands were trembling slightly. He was close to datastarve, too very close; and if he showed symptoms, the PKF DataWatch would yank him from his job in an instant.

He simply could not afford, as a private citizen, the processor power necessary to take him into the Crystal Wind with the bandwidth that Peaceforcer equipment afforded. But there had been no traces, nothing to justify going in.

It *hurt.* He had spent far too much time in the information-sterile world of reality. He had not gone live into the InfoNet in nearly two weeks.

Though he would not admit it even to himself, he was addicted to the Crystal Wind.

"There," said Peaceforcer Emile Garon aloud. He wanted desperately to believe that he was not fooling himself. His eyes did not open. Finally he spoke with conviction.

"There it is again."

Trent danced through the InfoNet, seeking.

Garon keyed open his throat mike. "I have a live one on the Net. Tracer request submitted."

The watch commander's voice boomed in his skull. "Describe the sign."

"Intelligent, sir. Starting in the public Boards, at 9:08:11. Redirected output through ComSat 0188 and multiplexed back down in several different channels at 9:19:35. I filtered out the ghost channels and sent web angels into the net to chase it down."

"Replicant AI or live sign?"

"No, sir, no AI signature. Live sign probability in the high nines; it doesn't know how to scramble deep memory and hasn't booby-trapped pursuit at all. But it generated its ghosts in a burst of very elegant superlisp."

"Opinion?"

"A talented amateur. Trace, sir?"

There was no reply. Garon chewed at his lower lip. He knew it was foolish, but he could not restrain himself. "Sir?"

He wondered if he imagined the coolness in the watch commander's voice. Almost suspicion . . . "Trace enable on three. Access at point five. Stay out of Ministry and Space Force Boards." There was a brief pause. "Trace enabled."

Emile Garon activated the trace nodes at his temples and descended into the light of data.

Francis Xavier Chandler, in an autobiography written only a few years before his death in 2094, wrote of Jany McConnell:

"In my entire life I have never met another woman who was more alive. I thought when I first met her that she was a great beauty, but in later years, looking at the images that are all that is left of her in the world, I saw that this was not so. She was in fact an attractive woman. Physically, she and Carl Castanaveras were of a type; good-looking, dark-haired young adults in excellent physical condition, with those brilliant green eyes. Neither of them looked like their names, but that was not uncommon even then; with the degree of interbreeding that has occurred through most of this century, I suspect the time will come when the correlation between surname and appearance approaches random chance.

"I am indifferently affected by male beauty, but those who are not, who knew Castanaveras, have told me that their reaction to him was exactly the same as my reaction to 'Selle McConnell. When I was still a relatively young man, practicing my first profession, I wrote a song called 'Desert Eyes.' It was a 'Top Ten' hit; unless you know what that means, it is an irrelevancy that I won't describe here.

"Over seven decades after I wrote that song, I met Jany

McConnell and knew at last whom I had written the song about. She had desert eyes; they burned.

"One gains perspective with the passage of time. The telepaths, in that time, were a fact of life. Only a fool would ignore them; but only a greater fool would allow himself to be aligned with them publicly. There was too much resentment against them. The Jews were discriminated against for thousands of years, simply because they made the claim to superiority, to being a 'Chosen People.'

"The telepaths, Castanaveras and all those children named after him, *were* better than us. Quantitatively and qualitatively, in nearly every measurable way and in some that could not be measured, they were a superior people.

"Except in numbers.

"Of course they were doomed."

"Baby?" Jany McConnell looked up from her work as Carl entered the conference room. Seated at the head of the table, she was downloading the InfoNet profiles of their five guests into the two waitbots. She looked enough like him to be his sister; a handsome green-eyed woman with long, dark hair, wearing an oversized blue leather coat, short skirt, and a pair of emerald studs. Genetically, they were closer than most brothers and sisters. "How do you feel?"

His smile was melancholy. "Well. How about yourself?"

She shrugged in a single fluid movement that took most of her upper body into account. "Well." Her makeup was turned off, except for a faint blue-silver sheen on her lips and over her eyes. "You didn't come home last night."

"I stayed at Dr. Montignet's house. Where's Malko?" Carl had not seen him in the waiting area or the lobby.

"He went down to the security station on the first floor to review security preparations for the meeting." Her hands roved over the huge pointboard at the head of the table, slowly, without any apparent need for attention on her part. There were seven chairs lined up in rows of four and three, against the room's north wall; Jany sat in the eighth. "You didn't call, Carl. I was worried about you. It's only been about two months since that maniac shot at you while you were testifying before the Unification Council. We had this incredible party last night and you didn't even call to say you weren't coming home."

I'm sorry, Jany. I wasn't good company last night. She did not respond, and he continued aloud, "I knew we were going to win by noon yesterday. So did Malko. We had two hundred and twenty votes firmly accounted for, and . . . it was just a step. It was depressing."

"Just a step?" She looked at him quizzically. "And Suzanne was better company than we would have been? Suzanne's one of the least empathetic people I've ever met."

"And the toughest."

Jany nodded thoughtfully. "She lives in her own world."

Carl flashed a bright, hard grin at her. "It makes her hard to hurt."

Jany made no immediate reply. She did not respond to the grin, and slowly it faded. "Maybe you're right. But you should still have called. I worried."

"Do I need to apologize again?"

"No. Just don't *do* it again."

He cocked his head to one side. "Okay—Okay?"

"Okay, then." She smiled at him for the first time, and for the first time in several days he felt the bright, flickering warmth that made everything else in his life worthwhile. "Do you want to give me a hug? The last time I saw you we were still slaves."

With a huge roar of frustration, Emile Garon threw his traceset down to the desktop. Even the glorious Crystal Wind, the sharp bright surge of data that was life, left him with only the smallest, fading glow.

"How did he do that?" Garon asked of no one at all, aware of the trace of hysteria in his voice. He sank back into his chair, eyes focused on a great distance. *"I* can't even do that."

The watch commander's voice cut through the layers of unbelief with shocking clarity. "Officer Garon, you are relieved of duty. You are instructed to report to Elite Commander Breilléune's office at 1300 hours."

Suddenly, Emile Garon's holofield appeared over his desk, a silvered flat plane that sank away from him to present depth.

Two letters appeared, black against the blue background, in an eighteen-point Helvetica typeface that contrasted sharply with the plain, ten-point terminal typeface the Peaceforcer Boards normally used.

Ox, the letters said.

Garon stared at the letters without comprehension. Suddenly the holofield reset, flattened into a silver plane, and vanished. Frantically Garon scrambled for his pointboard. The dictionary instantly displayed eight different possible meanings; number one on the list, with a probability of 87%, was an English word, which the dictionary translated for him as *boeuf;* as an adjective, meaning something of great strength, but slow and clumsy.

The watch commander's voice brought him back. "Emile? Officer Garon, do you acknowledge the order? You are instructed to report to Elite Commander Breilléune's office at 1300 hours."

"Oui. I shall be there."

Their fourth guest arrived at 9:45; Malko Kalharri took the elevator up to the downlot to greet her personally. Belinda Singer was, in her own right, one of the twenty wealthiest human beings on Earth, and one of the twenty-five wealthiest anywhere in the Solar System. She was old enough to make Malko Kalharri feel young. While her age was not public knowledge, it was a fair guess that she would never see the sunny side of one hundred again. Despite that, her wealth was the most recently obtained of that of their five guests. Thirty-seven years ago, the United Nations had nationalized both the orbital construction facilities at Halfway and the SpaceFarer Colony at LaGrange Five. The SpaceFarer's Collective declared independence by way of retaliation, and waged a brief and somewhat ineffective war with the United Nations. The war did not regain their former holdings, but the United Nations, still weak from the strains of the Unification War, had not been able to prevent them from declaring, and maintaining, their freedom.

Belinda Singer had invested in the SpaceFarer's Collective heavily; most of what had been, even in 2025, a considerable fortune. It was a gamble that had paid off in astronomical numbers; she was the SpaceFarer Collective's largest downside shareholder. Assuming the uneasy truce between the U.N. and the SpaceFarers continued to hold, as it had for over two decades, Belinda Singer might very well go to her grave the richest woman on Earth. The SpaceFarer businesses continued to grow at an amazing rate; everything from biologicals to zero-gravity processing to their trade with the Belt CityStates, in which they had a near monopoly.

The SpaceFarer's Collective was not a government in the traditional sense of the word; it was, first and foremost, a business concerned with making a profit.

"A heavily armed business, true," conceded Belinda Singer. Her floatchair hummed smoothly in the enclosed elevator as they ascended to the 408th floor, to the offices of Kalharri Enterprises, Ltd. Malko Kalharri stood at her side, with her two bodyguards behind them. "But that's the charming part of it all, you know."

Malko Kalharri nodded. At the age of sixty-nine, he was still an imposingly large man, who moved easily and with grace; his face had gained a certain harsh character with the passage of time. The once blond hair had turned entirely gray. "Yes. Charlie Eddore—you know Councillor Eddore, I think —was telling me a while back about the problems his Council subcommittee was having negotiating a workable access agreement for the Mars gravity well. The SpaceFarers don't seem to think there's a problem, and even if there is, there's nobody with enough authority to dicker for the SpaceFarers without convening a shareholder's meeting to appoint a negotiator."

'Selle Singer grinned wickedly. "It's even better than that, Malko. Those silly bastards started the whole thing off on the wrong foot entirely; proposed a *treaty* with the Collective."

Malko laughed aloud. The sound boomed in the small enclosure. "They didn't."

"Yes," said Belinda Singer cheerily, "and then they realized that if we signed the silly thing—and I was tempted to for that reason alone despite the fact that it was an offensively one-sided document—it would be tantamount to officially recognizing the SpaceFarer's Collective as an autonomous body. Secretary General Amnier was enraged."

The elevator decelerated to a slow stop, and the door slid aside. Malko led Belinda Singer and her entourage down the corridor to their offices. "I would imagine. Darryl has little patience with fools."

Belinda Singer shook her head. "Charles isn't a fool, Malko, and you'd do well not to think so. He is impetuous, but that's a common failing of the young. So much ambition."

"Yes," said Malko Kalharri, and he was not thinking of Charles Eddore at all. "I know exactly what you mean."

He spoke in accented English; it was still, officially, the language of the United Nations Peace Keeping Force. "Elite Commander Breilléune, Officer Emile Garon reporting."

Commander Breilléune was a tall man with the face of a recruiting holo. He was in full dress uniform, now as always. Emile Garon had never seen him otherwise. The skin of his face was somewhat stiff; a knife would not have made much of an impression upon it. That was one of the only two visible signs of the vast changes that had been engineered in him. There was a hole over the center knuckle of his right hand; a laser was embedded in the bone behind that knuckle.

He was a Peaceforcer Elite.

Brass balls, Americans called them.

Cyborgs.

Breilléune smiled at the Peaceforcer standing at attention before him. He did not return Garon's salute. "Emile, comment allez-vous?" He did not offer Garon a seat.

Garon switched to French instantly. "Quite well, sir."

"I am told otherwise." Garon said nothing, and Breilléune sighed, the smile fading. "Sit down, Emile. What are we to do with you?"

Garon folded himself into one of the small chairs before the Commander's desk. "Sir, I honestly do not believe that there is anything which needs to be done. I do my job. I do it well."

Breilléune nodded. "True. I have no quarrel with your ability to perform your functions for the DataWatch. But—forgive me, Emile, for your own good I think we must remove you from the DataWatch."

The words struck Garon like a blow. The world went vague and hazy for a moment, and when he returned to himself, he saw Commander Breilléune nodding to himself. "I thought so. Emile, you have served us too well for me to allow you to waste yourself like this." Breilléune opened a folder and withdrew two sets of documents. "I have drafted two sets of orders for you. One set relieves you of your duties here and returns you to Paris. I know you have been homesick. There are several administrative offices which will be vacated in the next few weeks, any one of which you would be ideal for." Breilléune sat and waited expectantly.

Garon had the sense to say only, "And the second?"

Breilléune said simply, "Three months of vacation. You will be forbidden to access the Information Network during that time. On June fifteenth you will board the SpaceFarer vessel *Bernardo de la Paz* with fifty other officers of the PKF, to arrive at LaGrange Five to begin training."

Garon said, through a mouth suddenly dry, "LaGrange Five?"

"Yes."

"You wish to make me one of the Elite."

"Does the idea scare you?"

Garon decided in that instant. "No. No, sir, I am honored."

There was true warmth in Breilléune's smile. "Good. I think you shall find that the change is not so difficult as you have heard. And the advantages are . . ." he hunted for a word, and said finally, "fantastic."

Three of their five guests were already there as Malko arrived with Belinda Singer. Tio Sandoval, a renowned womanizer who was the majority stockholder for Sandoval Biochemicals, and son of the company's founder, had cornered Jany McConnell. At Sandoval's side was a plain-faced middle-aged woman in elegant clothing that obviously made her uncomfortable. She was clearly out of her element, and unsure how to behave.

Jany McConnell, facing the two of them, stood ramrod stiff, slightly pale, her features carefully controlled. Malko had the uneasy impression that Sandoval had already touched her once.

The other two were waiting quietly at the conference table. Marc Packard sat at attention, sweat trickling down his cheek. He was the representative of Tytan Industries, and in his own person was the least wealthy of the five persons whom Carl and Malko had invited to the meeting. Tytan Industries controlled nearly all of Halfway's electronics and computer manufacturing, and Marc Packard had, for fifteen years, essentially controlled Tytan Industries. It made Packard, by any standards, probably the single most powerful human in the great, growing, geostationary collection of ships and factories and living donuts known as Halfway. It did not surprise Malko Kalharri that the man was sweating; this was the first time he had been on Earth in over five years, and the gravity field must have been difficult to readjust to. Packard would not have come downside for any meeting of less than the greatest importance; it was a measure of his regard for the potential advantage the telepaths might give Tytan Industries, and his distrust for the security of normal channels of communication, that he was there at all. His bodyguard Malko first put at the age of forty to forty-five. A second look altered the impression slightly; there was a slight looseness to the skin about his neck that was unavoidable even with the very best geriatrics. Upward of sixty, then, and possibly in his seventies. He was fit, well muscled and in good tone, despite the deceptive potbelly he carried. He sat in a chair at the opposite end of the room, where he had a clear view of the entire room and the door. The bodyguard picked up an eyebrow at the sight of Belinda Singer's muscle; he examined and, to all appearances, dismissed them in the same moment.

The bodyguard spent a disconcerting moment examining Malko himself, and then nodded almost genially in Malko's direction and returned his attention to the rest of the room.

Randall Getty Cristofer, the owner of most of SunGetty Oil, and thereby of most of the remaining oil on Earth, was deep in conversation with Carl Castanaveras when Malko escorted Belinda Singer into the conference room. Cristofer was wearing a fluorescent red business suit of conservative cut. Cristofer immediately broke off his conversation with Carl, murmuring an apology, and bowed low to take the hand that 'Selle Singer offered to him. He spoke with a pronounced Australian accent. "Belinda dear, how've you been?"

The old lady smiled at him a bit sardonically. "Quite well, Randy. And yourself?"

"Ah, not so good. Wouldn't you know it, just this morning I'm hearing that somebody's bitched up me bid to take over the Venus Geological Services."

Belinda Singer's smile was pure shark. "Imagine that. Well, they do say that competition is the lifeblood of business."

Malko counted his blessings; his earphone relayed him a message just in time for him to step in before the sniping got any worse. "I am told," he said loudly, "that Monsieur Chandler is on his way down. Would you like to take your seats?"

Carl had testified before the Unification Council on several occasions, and he had learned the first rule of speaking so well that it was second nature: *Keep it short.*

"I am thirty-one years old," Carl Castanaveras told them. "For nearly twenty years now, I have been gathering information for the United Nations Peace Keeping Force. As of three-thirty P.M. yesterday that is no longer the case. We have over two hundred functioning telepaths whose services are now available to be leased. I moved my people into the old Chandler Complex in lower Manhattan back in August, and we owe seven months' back rent on it." He directed himself to the man who sat directly across from him. "I'm indebted to you for your generosity, Mister Chandler. It won't go unpaid."

Francis Xavier Chandler shook his head. His features were set in an attitude of perpetual fierceness. He was the most conservatively dressed man in the room, and the eldest, in a Brooks Brothers suit that had not been in style since the mid-forties. His hair flowed in a thick black mane, over his shoulders and down his back. "Nonsense, young man. It was a good business investment, and it is about to pay off handsomely."

"Malko Kalharri," Carl continued, "has paid for these offices for nearly a year now; he sold his house to do so. I intend to see him paid back for that. We owe money to the lawyers who've represented us before the Unification Council, and are continuing to do so. There are—other projects—which I'd like to see Kalharri Ltd. embark upon.

"The key to all of this, of course, is money. We're not exactly desperate; but we are in debt. We are capital starved. Folks," said Carl Castanaveras simply, "we're not *ever* going to get any cheaper."

"I am somewhat curious," said Marc Packard, his breathing labored, "as to what exactly you are selling today."

Carl shook his head. "*Our* services, not mine. Peaceful work which the children can do. I did ghost work for the PKF for nearly fifteen years, and I did become in many ways the evil which I still behold in them. What I have done in the past is done, but I am now *finished* with it."

"I presume," said Tio Sandoval with a languid smile, "that you're going to show us all just exactly what these"—he waved a hand negligently—"*brujo's* skills are, that you're going to sell us."

"That would be difficult. We've agreed not to read your minds." Carl grinned widely. "Though, if we wanted to, that poor half-crazy telepath at your side wouldn't be much protection."

"I did not truly expect," said Sandoval in his accented English, staring at Carl with a cool challenge.

Carl looked away from Sandoval without any pause whatsoever and swept his gaze around the table, still smiling, gathering their eyes upon him. "I think you can assume, though, that what we promise, we can deliver. The reputation we have among the Peaceforcers is . . . largely deserved. What we can promise," he said more slowly, the grin dying away, "includes reading the minds of executives in the companies of your competition, looking inside closed objects or behind locked doors"—he turned to Randall Cristofer—"and finding oil with one hundred percent certainty in a fraction of the time conventional techniques take." He hesitated. "Also the ability to manipulate small objects ranging in size from, say, dice, all the way down to the atomic level."

Belinda Singer blinked rapidly. Before she could say anything, Francis Xavier Chandler whistled long and low. "I was wondering about that one myself. I'd heard rumors."

"The rumors are substantially true," said Jany McConnell. Her voice was quiet, but clear. "The ability to manipulate objects at the atomic level is somewhat limited, however. Only the stronger telepaths can distinguish detail at that resolution, and of that number, only those well trained in physics have any success manipulating objects the size of atoms. We have only a few of those. But they can indeed induce hydrogen to fuse."

There was a momentary silence, and then Chandler leaned forward and said grimly, "Let's dicker."

The meeting lasted three hours; Carl was left drained but satisfied at its end, with a great, deep-seated respect for the negotiating skills of the five persons who had shared the table with him. Chandler Industries had probably done the best for itself, simply due to the goodwill that it had carried into the negotiations, but all of the five had done well.

As had the telepaths themselves. Two hours into the meeting, Jany said silently, *Carl?*

In mid-sentence Carl switched tracks, devoting the greater part of his attention to Jany. *Yes?*

I've been calculating fees. Their down payment *to us is going to effectively cancel our debt.*

I'll be damned, thought Carl in short amazement, and returned to the negotiations.

Yes. Very likely.

As the meeting was breaking up, Carl saw Sandoval cornering Jany once again and very nearly decided to break it up. Malko merely glanced at him once, and Carl nodded, turned purposefully away from Jany so that he need not even look at Sandoval, and instead motioned F. X. Chandler aside. "A moment, sir?"

Chandler raised an eyebrow. "A moment, certainly, but I've little more. I'm running quite late today."

"Certainly. I intend to purchase a Chandler MetalSmith Mark III within the next week or so. I'll be having it extensively customized, and I would like to know if there are any shops you can recommend where I might have the work done."

Chandler looked at Carl without expression for a moment. "I'm afraid not, son," said the founder of the largest hovercar company in the world, "since I don't drive anymore. It's not safe since they gave over so much control to TransCon. Still, if you're interested, see Tony Angelo at the Chandler dealership upstate. He's a Speedfreak, he knows as much about these machines as I used to."

"Thank you, sir. I do appreciate this."

Chandler nodded and turned to leave. He stopped in midturn and glanced back at Carl. "Young man? The MetalSmith is a lot of car. What are you driving now?"

Malko Kalharri was still sitting next to Belinda Singer; Carl was distantly aware of the older man's eyes upon him. "I don't have a car, sir. This will be my first."

"Oh? Why?"

"The Peaceforcers have never paid us very well," said Carl simply.

Chandler nodded again, thoughtfully. His lips moved, for just an instant, in what very nearly approached a smile. Too quietly for anyone else to hear, he said, "Have Tony arrange some driving lessons for you. The MetalSmith is not intended to be driven by amateurs. It's a *lot* of car."

"Yes, sir. Thank you. I'm not sure the lessons—" The outspeaker cut Carl off in mid-sentence.

"Monsieur Castanaveras? There is a call for you."

"Who is it?"

"Unification Councillor Carson, sir."

In the immediate silence that engulfed all conversation in the conference room, Carl said calmly, "I'll take it in my office." He glanced across the room at Malko, and Malko moved his head in a single curt shake that meant no. Alone, Carl went into his office and sealed the door behind him.

The holofield was already up; Carl could see its faint, almost invisible outline, all the sign the field gave from the wrong side of the desk.

Jerril Carson, from the shoulders up, looked at Carl out of the field when Carl sat down. He appeared the same as always, a man in his sixties, almost cadaverously thin. The skin hung on his face in folds; once, decades ago, Carson had been overweight. It seemed to Carl that Carson's complexion was paler than normal, but it was difficult to be certain.

Carson had not allowed himself to be caught in the same building with Carl Castanaveras in fifteen years.

"Good afternoon, Councillor."

Carson smiled at Carl with a precision that came from four decades of political smiling. The edges of his smile might have been measured in millimeters and never varied. "Good afternoon, Carl. Congratulations on passage of the Amendment."

"Thank you, sir. What can I do for you?"

"I really didn't think you would get it passed," said Carson conversationally. "With the Secretary General making his position so very clear—well, even with Monsieur Kalharri's aid, Tuesday's vote succeeded in surprising me." He looked thoughtful. "And the Secretary General as well, I believe. You controlled yourself quite well during testimony. I doubt if most of the Unification Council has the vaguest idea just how erratic and dangerous you are."

"Well, I hope not myself," said Carl politely. "It's always nice to be under—"

"Nothing," Carson whispered as the mask dropped from his face and left something old and insane in his eyes, "has changed. Nothing."

The holofield went dead and faded.

Inside Carl Castanaveras the old familiar rage struck him with the suddenness and heat of a maser. He brought his hands together and interlaced the fingers, gently, atop his desk.

Allie ran up to Johann, breathless. With her newly developed Gift, she asked silently, *Where's Carl and Jany today, Johnny? Are they going to be back tonight?*

Johann shook his head. *Don't know, kiddo. Let me try—*

Suddenly, he went utterly rigid. The child knew instantly that something was terribly wrong, and instinctively she reached for him in the new way.

Allie screamed once, a terrible high-pitched sound, and collapsed in the sunny grass.

Just four kilometers away, Carl Castanaveras knew nothing of the pain he had caused. Inside the rage rolled through him in slow, murderous waves. The desk on which his hands were resting was vibrating as though it would shake itself apart.

Outside, on the dark, handsome features he presented to the world, there was nothing but serenity.

2

They drove back that evening through crush hour traffic.

They waited for nearly half an hour in the downlot beneath the Kaufmann Spacescraper, as other cars left ahead of them, being fed out one by one into the hideous crush of traffic leaving the great city. Carl was asleep before they even made it out of the downlot. Malko spent nearly half of their waiting time paging through the map screens which showed Trans-Con's broadcast of the various street levels. Ground level was a mess; a twelve-fan had turned over on Forty-Second Street. The five levels of underground streets weren't much better; TransCon showed that it was rerouting a lot of the surface traffic down below, at least until the cars left the immediate vicinity of Manhattan, and could be redirected into the comp-controlled TransCon highway network.

Finally, in disgust, Malko punched in for the skystreets. They weren't the fastest way home—ground traffic was usually that—but today they looked the best bet for covering the four kilometers to the Complex before an hour was out. TransCon turned on the AUTO light on the dash, the steering grip went rigid, and Malko leaned back in his seat as TransCon took the Caddy out into the gossamer webs of skystreets above New York.

Carl slept the sound sleep of exhaustion in the back seat of Malko's old '47 Cadillac. In the dark front seat, Jany sat with her gleaming blue leather coat drawn up about her throat, hands down in the deep pockets. Her eyes were fixed on something that did not exist, far out on the highway. Malko stretched, ligament and cartilage and bones creaking audibly. Shifting in his seat until his right shoulder was leaning against his seat's backrest, he studied Jany McConnell's profile.

"He touched you, didn't he?"

"Twice."

The old man reached over to her and moved a stray hair away from her face. She shivered, but did not flinch. "I'm sorry. I am sorry." Knowing it was futile, he tried to make sense of it for her. "I told them not to touch either of you, but for some people it's hard not to. Sandoval—Latinos, they're raised that way."

"He knew," she whispered.

"What do you mean?" asked Malko, with the sudden horrible suspicion that he had misjudged Tio Sandoval terribly.

"He knows a lot about us," she said simply. One hand came up out of the pocket to hold his tightly. "We fascinate him, and we have for a long time." Behind them, a Speedfreak came up out of nowhere, weaving through the TransCon controlled hovercars at high speed, its headlights throwing a bright, moving light into the interior of the Caddy. "He's been auditing everything on the Boards that's been declassified about us for years now." The headlights peaked, and faded. The hovercar's interior sank back into gloom. "I wasn't trying to read him. His mind is rotten, as bad as the Peaceforcer who tried to rape me that time. Pain and love and sex and death, all mixed up at once. He touched me and it just leaped out." She shivered again.

"You didn't tell the boy," said Malko. It was almost a question.

"God, no." Jany laughed shakily. Her eyes dropped shut, and she ran the caress of a thought across Carl Castanaveras' unconscious mind. She sounded near tears when she spoke again. "He ignores me entirely half the time, Malko, but then he's so protective. He would have hurt Sandoval so badly, and he would have thought he was doing it for me." Then the tears did begin to track down her cheeks. "He spent last night with Dr. Montignet, did you know that? He was depressed and he was afraid he was going to hurt me, but, you know, I can *handle* the black moods, they don't bother me so much. What hurts is when he won't trust me."

Malko said very gently, "Carl doesn't trust himself. How can he trust somebody else? Even someone he loves?"

She sat silently, holding his hand, watching the flow of traffic. The tears moved down her cheeks, and her shoulders shook inside the coat, but she made no sound. Malko knew better than to try to say something. Eventually the tears stopped, and her breathing slowed. When she spoke again, there was drowsiness in her voice. "I don't understand how he can be so angry with the world. There's this huge blind spot and he doesn't even know it's there. All of the good things, he misses those. He doesn't see the children, he doesn't see what a wonder they are." She clutched Malko's hand harder. "He's such a mess."

Malko squeezed back. "Yeah. He is that."

"What's wrong with him?"

"It's a long story, little girl."

Jany giggled. "You're the absolutely only person in the entire world who could call me that with a straight face."

Malko smiled down at her. "Why don't you try to get some sleep? Prince Charming back there didn't waste any time. I'll wake you up when we're . . . when we're home."

"That sounds like a good idea. . . ." Her eyes closed almost instantly, and she curled up on the front seat, still holding Malko Kalharri's hand. "Home. That's such a nice word. I don't think any of the children have started using it yet. Maybe they don't know what it means."

Malko stroked her hair with his free hand. "Maybe so."

She was almost asleep when she murmured, "God, what did they do to him. . . ." It was not a question, and her breathing gentled into sleep moments later.

"Nothing you want to know about," said Malko Kalharri.

The car flew on through the night.

They reached the Complex near eight o'clock.

The Complex was a large, elegantly pale building built of supertwisted monocrystal, on half an acre of land. It had been built by F. X. Chandler not quite a decade ago, in an open Italian architectural style that was prevalent back in the twenties. The land upon which it stood had once been the heart of New York City; tactical thermonuclear weapons, during the War, had ended that. Where Wall Street and City Hall and the Brooklyn Bridge had once stood was now one of the most exclusive residential areas in New York City. One of four homes owned by Chandler in and around Capital

City, the Complex was capable of housing twice the telepaths' numbers with ease. What had once been the Chandler Complex extended two stories into the air, and three below the ground.

Thea and Mandy, two of the fourteen-year-olds, were standing guard duty behind the front gate. The floodlights cast harsh dark shadows where they struck, down the length of the driveway that led into the guarded Complex. The shadows shifted as the picketers walked up and down before the Complex. The crowd outside was larger and louder and uglier than usual. There were a thousand to twelve hundred of them by Malko's eyeball estimate, many of them wearing dramasuits that made them appear three meters tall and amplified their voices to the point of pain. One image, of actor Adam Selstrom, was right out of storage; the copyright notice, *Images Inc.*, © 2055, 2062, blinked on and off, ten centimeters high, for five seconds out of every thirty. They carried placards that ranged from the merely offensive to the downright obscene. Of the dozen neon holofields casting red and blue and green light across the front lawn and the slidewalk, only one showed the slightest trace of originality. The holofield glowed twenty meters across, five meters in the air:

PUT THE GENIES BACK IN THE BOTTLE

Carl came awake with a suddenness that startled Malko when Malko turned onto the upper-class residential avenue that led to the Complex. He spoke without a trace of sleep in his voice. "Bad?"

Malko looked over the crowd with a practiced eye. "I don't think so. And even if it was bad, there's not enough of them."

Carl nodded, accepting the judgment. "Ten of the children could put them to sleep without even straining."

Malko said dryly, "Or you could just use the sonics built into the gates."

"That would be one way to do it." Carl ran his fingers through the mess sleep had made of his hair. For the first time he noticed the lack of Peaceforcer guards in front of the gates. "They sure didn't waste any time pulling out, did they?" he asked rhetorically.

"Did you expect them to?"

"No. Did you talk with Security Services?"

"Double-S and Brinks as well. We'll have something by Friday."

The gates swung out, and the crowd's roar intensified as they recognized the Cadillac. Malko braked to ten kph and drove the hovercar straight through them. Several of the demonstrators spat on the Cadillac, but nobody threw anything, and nobody attempted to touch the car.

Upstairs, in the two-room suite that he and Jany shared, Carl stripped himself slowly out of his suit. Almost nobody was left awake; only a dozen or so of the elder telepaths echoed their thoughts through the quiet of the Complex, and apparently none of those dozen had anything urgent to say to Carl. Savoring the privacy, he gave the cloak and vest to the housebot, kicking off the high soft boots, and went to the bar to fix himself a drink. The nap in the back of Malko's car had not been a good idea; he still felt exhausted, and his eyes were grainy. He hadn't slept much in the preceding weeks, and not at all in the last three days. Four fingers of smoke whiskey went into the tumbler, and he placed the glass under the SloMo. He waited with an irrational displeasure with the universe while the heat was sucked from the tumbler.

The liquor was bitingly cold, so cold there was no taste in it. Carl left his shirt and pants at the side of the bed for the housebot to pick up, and lay down atop the covers. The bed was notably large; it could sleep six in comfort, and sometimes did so. The one time Suzanne Montignet had visited them, to give the telepaths their semiannual physicals, she'd seemed particularly amused by the bed; the sort of thing, she said, that she'd have expected to find in the place where Malko Kalharri lived.

His exhaustion took him quickly. He finished the first whiskey and had the housebot bring him another. The whiskey was five years old, laid down in 2057; for smoke whiskey, that was considered old. There was only one distillery, in orbit, with the facilities to selectively flip the isomers that produced the fascinating, distinctive taste of smoke whiskey. The distillery was a wholly owned subsidiary of Tytan Manufacturing, and the drink had only been available in the marketplace for the last decade or so. Which was just as well; if the drink had been available when Carl was in his teens, he might not have made it to adulthood without becoming addicted.

His eyes did not close immediately. He was not, on the surface of his mind, truly looking at the painting on the wall facing the foot of the bed. Nonetheless, his gaze came to rest there, to rove over the features of a being who was half human, half feline. Her face was essentially human, and exotically, almost painfully lovely; high cheekbones, and slitted blue cat's eyes. Her eyes had been sensitive to sunlight; when Carl had painted her, she had kept her eyes half lidded to help shield them from the harsh light. Fine brown fur covered her entire face, except for the thin, almost nonexistent lips. Her ears were feline, pointed and mobile, capable of tracking sounds.

After a while Carl stopped looking at the painting of Shana de Nostri, took a deep sip of the whiskey, and let himself sink down into the dimness of approaching sleep. It was quite pleasant, to lie there and let the alcohol take the edge off the Gift, to reduce the fine-tuned sensitivity to the rough intruding outer world. He was halfway through his second drink, and pleasantly buzzed, when Jany came into the room.

It was too much effort to open his eyes. In a floating darkness, he forced his lips to move, his throat to generate sound. "How are they?"

The bed shifted under her weight. "Allie's fine. You knocked her straight out. She's not even sure what happened. Johnny's in bad shape."

"How bad?"

"He'll have nightmares for a while. Depression, probably. He's got a headache, but I think that'll be gone by morning."

"Did you tell him I'm sorry?"

"Why don't you tell him yourself?"

Carl considered the question as an abstract problem. "In the morning, I guess. I could do it in the morning."

"Sure." Flesh touched his hand, and he felt the tumbler being lifted out of his grasp. "I don't think you need any more of this."

It wasn't worth arguing about. "Okay."

"Johnny asked me to sleep with him tonight."

"Oh." He exhaled slowly, and with a supreme effort forced his eyes open. He had trouble focusing. "This is a big bed for only one person."

Carl thought she was smiling. "I could send Malko up. He said just about the same thing."

"Not my type."

"Heather's still awake, and Marie."

"That's okay."

Jany nodded. "*Command,* lights down." In the darkness, Carl let his eyes close again. "Go to sleep, baby. I'll be here when you wake up."

"Good enough."

"Good night."

When she was gone, Carl let himself drift. Alcohol shut down the telepathic ability with remarkable effectiveness, almost as though it had been designed for just that task. None of the children drank, and none of the elder telepaths drank as much as Carl.

He was glad, on the occasions that he bothered to think about it, that the one thing which shut out the world enough to make the world a tolerable place was also something that he enjoyed in and of itself.

He was still trying to decide whether to have the housebot make him another when the exhaustion caught up with him and dragged him down into the darkness.

3

The world has achieved brilliance without conscience. Ours is a world of nuclear giants and ethical infants.

—General Omar Bradley

At the palace of the Ministre Général of the United Nations, at Lake Geneva in Switzerland, an old man paced restlessly across a thick carpet. Look at him with me for a moment; the years have been kind to Darryl Amnier. He has looked elderly since shortly after his thirtieth birthday; now, at the age of seventy-five, he *is* elderly, at least by the standards of twenty-first century Earth's medicine. The wrinkles have given character to a face that was once far too bland, and the quick smile and bright, animated expression that he has cultivated have made him into an idealized image of an unthreatening social patriarch.

Beneath it all, he has not changed at all, except to mellow ever so slightly. The things which he once loved he now loves less, and that which he hated he now despises with less passion.

But they are the same loves, and the same hates, and the minor passions of the most powerful man in the world are more significant than the greatest passions of one whom the world has not made mighty.

Across the room from him, seated at opposite ends of the huge, curved leather couch, were two members of his immediate staff, Jerril Carson and Charles Eddore, and two senior members of the Ministry of Population Control. One of the two, Gabrielle Laronde, was the senior nonelected official in the Ministry. Others came and went; she alone was always there.

Darryl Amnier enjoyed her company. She was one of the few government officials about whom he could say that with honesty. *It is a terrible thing,* he thought with brief distraction, *when the company of the opposition is generally more pleasant than that of your allies.* He did not let Gabrielle eat in his presence; for the first decade he'd known her she had been a pleasantly plump young woman. She was better looking now than she had been when he met her; empty food, in which the amino acids that composed it had been flipped over so that the food contained no calories, had helped her lose the weight that she could not have lost in any other way. Gabrielle had given up attempting to control her diet; nearly every time Darryl saw her she was munching on something. It was, he felt, something of an obscenity, so much time and effort spent on empty food in a world where so many people were dying of starvation.

He stopped pacing in mid-stride and turned to face them. Carson was sipping at his coffee, and dapper young Eddore was politely covering a yawn. Jerril looked ill, gray, and somewhat shaky, and Amnier found that of concern also. Jerril's obsession with Castanaveras was never far beneath the surface; but in the last few weeks it had been particularly virulent. "Charles?"

Eddore lifted his fingers from the InfoNet terminal in his lap. The flickering video field above the keyboard vanished. "Yes?"

"Have you got anything on Malko?"

"No."

Amnier waited, and presently Eddore said mildly, "Were you expecting something?" Still Amnier waited, and Eddore said with a sigh of irritation, "He's clean, of course. There are Johnny Rebs out there, and Erisian Claw as well. We catch the odd ideolog every now and again and braindrain them. Most of them don't know anything outside of their immediate cell, and the ones who do never know anything about Kalharri. Either the undergrounds have been smart enough not to contact him, or he's been smart enough to turn away the ones who have come calling."

"Can we trump something?"

Eddore raised one eyebrow in slight surprise. "Of course." His pronunciation betrayed the years at Harvard, and the years of professional public speaking since that time. He was the most likeable, trustworthy-seeming person Darryl Amnier knew, and Amnier moved in circles where there were thousands like Eddore. "As you well know, my offices have never had any objections to handling the Castanaveras matter in any fashion which you find pleasing."

"As I well know," Amnier agreed without any humor whatsoever. "Gabrielle, what is the legal status of those children?"

Gabrielle's assistant, whose name the Secretary General did not recall, glanced at her superior, received a nod of confirmation, and fielded the question. She spoke French fluently, with a strong British accent. "That's a very good question. Given that the Unification Council has voted that they are humans, with all of the rights of any normally birthed citizen of the United Nations, we are essentially starting over again at the beginning. There are a thousand questions which will need to be decided under both Occupied American and United Nations law, but they basically boil down to the following:

"One, are the children subject to the Ministry of Population Control? Under normal circumstances I'd be tempted to argue that position, and especially so in an American civil court. Elsewhere in the world the fact of over two hundred children being raised by so few adults might not raise comment, but in the U.S. the situation is not common, and the telepaths are not popular. I think many civil judges would tend to listen favorably to an argument that Castanaveras and the other half dozen or so adults out there do not constitute a desirable environment for the children to grow up in.

"Second, do the telepaths owe either the United Nations Peace Keeping Forces or the Bureau of Biotechnology any monies relating to their creation, care, and upbringing? Granted that they were raised by Peaceforcers, and their upbringing researched and paid for by the Bureau of Biotech, there exists a rather firm precedent, in the case of the MPC's Bureau of Public Labor. Children raised under Public Labor are liable for the cost of raising them. Often that's offset in a variety of ways, so that the Public Labor client need not pay the entire amount, but the principle is in place. If it can be established that the telepaths are liable for those services, how *much* can they be charged?

"Lastly, can they be allowed to use their skills for anything but PKF work? The Official Secrets Acts of 2048 and 2054 make it possible for us—even conceding the Eighth Amendment to the Statement of Principles to be valid—to make it impossible for Castanaveras to peddle his people's skills on the grounds that they are detrimental to the security of the Unification."

Charles Eddore said dryly, "Wonderful Acts, those. Prosecuted any number of ideologs on them, and the occasional politician as well." He tapped away at the quiet keyboard for a moment, and then added without looking at them, "Too many ideologs, not enough politicians."

Amnier smiled politely at the comment. "Jerril?"

Jerril Carson did not so much as look up from his coffee. "This afternoon, just before I spoke to him, Castanaveras met at the offices of Kalharri Enterprises with Francis Xavier Chandler, Belinda Singer, Marc Packard, Randall Getty Cristofer, and Tio Sandoval. I've been unable to ascertain the details of the conversation so far. Tio Sandoval seems approachable; he offered to discuss the subject of Castanaveras with me, but he was not in a hurry, and right now we are in no position to push a man with his sort of power. He—I mean Castanaveras," said Carson with grim precision, "he was there, as were Jane McConnell and Malko Kalharri."

"Not much useful there," said Amnier thoughtfully.

Jerril Carson's head came up. His smile looked ghastly. "Not exactly. Marc Packard—I ran the five of them through the InfoNet, cross-correlated for possible prior links among the group. I think we want to be careful about touching Packard directly, but Packard's bodyguard is named Neil Corona."

Darryl Amnier actually whistled. "Oh, my."

Eddore and Gabrielle looked puzzled. Amnier said gently, "That was the name of the young man who surrendered the Marine Corps of the old U.S., outside of Yorktown. He'd be in his sixties by now?" He glanced at Carson.

"Seventy, actually, almost seventy-one. He was born May seventh, 1991. And I've confirmed that it is him, not simply a man with the same name. He's apparently in rather remarkable physical condition, even given modern geriatrics; he's one of those lucky few whom the treatments just seem to take with. Like Kalharri, that way. He's been with Packard for nearly twenty years now. I don't have records on his activities before that time—it was a while after the end of the War before things like record keeping were taken up again."

"Coincidence?"

Gabrielle said, half to herself, "It hardly matters, does it? We've got Kalharri. Two high-ranking leaders of the old Sons of Liberty, meeting in secret the day after the telepaths are freed?" She smiled beatifically. "Darryl, if you want Kalharri, I do not think you will ever have a better opportunity."

Amnier nodded, resumed pacing. A strange conflict swirled within him, one that he had not expected. *Forty-five years,* he thought; *who plans for forty-five years?* Finally he turned back to Jerril and said, "Talk to Sandoval. Find out why Corona was there. Find out about Kalharri's contact with him."

"Why?"

Amnier stared at Carson until the other man looked away. "Because," he said flatly, daring the man to object, "I want to know."

There was no contest of wills; Carson looked back down into his cooling coffee and muttered, "Certainly."

A smile flickered across Charles Eddore's features, and vanished before Amnier could be certain it had been there.

Eddore returned to his computer.

There is, as I know from personal experience, no meaning to simultaneity, no validity to the concept that there can ever be two events happening at the same time. It is no more possible that two events can occupy the same instant than that two objects can occupy the same space. Space separates events from simultaneity in the same way, and just as certainly, as time separates objects from occupying the same space.

All of this is true at the level of quantum physics.

In the gross physical world of early Man, as Darryl Amnier was being presented with an ethical dilemma he had not suspected existed within him, at that moment, the object of his dilemma was trying to get to sleep.

Malko could not sleep.

His bedroom, on the second story, overlooked the demonstrators at the north gate. Lying in bed with the curtains open, he could not help but see the flaring lights of the dramasuits, casting laser-bright light in half a dozen primary shades through the transparent window. He could have risen and opaqued the window himself, or else called in the housebot and had the housebot do it; but either alternative called for more effort than he cared to invest.

It astonished him, how his body had begun to demand sleep as he grew older. There was little else to indicate just how old he was; with modern geriatrics his appearance, his wind, and his strength were all consistent with that of a forty-year-old of a century or so past. But for a man who had spent the last fifty years getting by on three to four hours' sleep a night, the need to sleep every night, as much as seven to eight hours, was almost intolerable.

But now he couldn't get to sleep although he was vastly tired, and that was even worse. Finally he sat up at the side of the bed and opened the drawer in the table at its side.

For the first time that evening he was glad that none of the women who were still awake had been able to spend the night with him. None of them would have stopped him from taking the Complex 8A—"fadeaway" in street parlance —which he kept at his bedside, but neither would they have approved. Psychoactive drugs were not popular among the telepaths.

Fadeaway was only a mildly psychoactive drug; it was, as its name implied, intended more as a sleeping aid. It was the by-product of research by the Peaceforcers into a water-soluble drug for use in crowd control. Sprayed over a crowd at the proper dosages, it would indeed put an unruly crowd to sleep. It would do so more safely than sonic stunners, and much more safely than through the use of anesthetic needlers. Physiological by-products were almost nonexistent; the sprayed crowd went to sleep, and awoke from four to eight hours later.

With hallucinations.

The form of the drug that Malko took was vastly diluted from the dosage that the Peaceforcers used for crowd control.

Malko Kalharri found himself down in the dream almost instantly.

It seemed at first that he was wide awake, with the laser hololights playing across the walls of his suite, splashing across the walls in shades of blood, and gold, and emerald. Suddenly he realized, for the first time, that he could faintly hear the chanting of the picketers, even through the shut window. He rose and went to the window, and touched the stud that swung the bay windows up and out.

The cool night air rushed in to touch him, and the howl of the crowd grew louder. He stood at the window, shivering, watching the surging shapes of the mob at the gates. One dramasuit lased into existence, and showed a genie—a *djinn*—coming out of a copper lamp. The genie it was supposed to represent floated up over the crowd, howling wordless rage. The genie was horned, and tailed.

Malko was rather cynically surprised that it had no pitchfork.

The devil turned, the laser of its eyes traced out to meet the flesh of the man who stood before it, and its howl became a supersonic scream that dug into Malko Kalharri's skull and burrowed, seeking his soul.

And finding.

He stumbled through the remains of the camp, like a ghost in a landscape from Dante's *Inferno*, laser clutched in his left hand, autoshot in the right. The camp of the Sons of Liberty was spread out across two square kilometers of Virginia forest. The day was blisteringly hot and humid, and sweat trickled down Malko's body. His eyes beheld the world through a pair of mirrored sunglasses. The shades amplified light at night, cut down glare during the day; if he were unlucky enough to take a laser across the eyes, they would protect his eyes for most of two seconds, at all except pointblank range. Porous polycarbon was painted across every exposed skin surface except for the palms of his hands. His fatigues were woven through with green and red fiberglass that matched the optical frequencies of the commonest laser rifles.

He was as well protected as any of the mudfucking Peaceforcers they had fought against, as well protected as Corona's Marines, as safe as any soldier had any right to be.

As safe as Greg had been.

Long stretches of the ground upon which he walked had been melted into strips, about a meter wide, of a material that resembled glass. There were over a dozen small fires still burning in the forest.

For as far as he could see in any direction, he was the only living human being.

He walked north, with the vague idea that he would find the Marines and join up with whatever remained of them.

That morning, while the two of them sat together outside the tent where Operations was being conducted, Grigorio Castanaveras had confirmed Malko's worst fears.

"The Old Man says we're going to surrender."

Malko hung his head in quiet despair. For two nights they had watched the flashes of light in the night sky; all that was visible, from Earth, of the battle between the orbital battalion of the U.S. Marine Corps and the United Nations Space Force. At two A.M. the previous night, the lights had finally ceased. "Shit. Space Force took the orbitals."

"So we hear." Castanaveras crushed a stimtab and inhaled it without pausing. "The President says he's decided to surrender. The Old Man's over at his tent arguing with him, but I don't think it's going to do any good." The whites around Grigorio Castanaveras' brown irises widened as the stim took hold. The sleepy look on his face fell away, as Malko watched, and turned almost cheerful. "Personally, I just want to catch your buddy Darryl and have him alone for a couple of hours before he dies. Then we can surrender."

"He's not my friend." *Deep inside, the dreaming mind whispered again,* **not my friend.**

Greg eyed him. The facade of good cheer vanished instantly. "Had better fucking not be. I had him that once, before the war started, and I knew he was no good, and I let the bastard go anyway." He spoke to himself. "I don't think I'm ever going to stop regretting that." He looked at Malko very seriously. "You and I and the Old Man; we're it, all of the Secret Service that's left except for Darryl. If they take our surrender, Malko, you and me and maybe even the Old Man, if he's up to it, we're going to take Amnier down. The rest of those bastards who're with Almundsen at least did it because they believed her, did it because they think she's right.

"Darryl," said Castanaveras in a clinical tone of voice that contrasted savagely with his expression, "is with them because he thinks they're going to win."

Malko's earphone clicked on. It made an odd echoing sound inside his skull; he'd almost had time to forget how strange it felt. For most of the last year policy had been to forego using them. There was a slight but real possibility that the radio signals might have given away their location. Now, the policy made no sense; the Peaceforcers knew exactly where they were.

"Assemble for orders," said the Old Man's voice.

Malko glanced at Greg, found that the other man could not meet his gaze. "Come on, Greg," he said quietly, "let's go hear the bad news." He climbed to his feet and extended his hand to pull his friend up. Greg looked at the hand expressionlessly, and then took it and let Malko pull him to his feet. They left the shelter of the trees, as the rest of their troops were doing; the troops who were the cream of the Sons of Liberty, assigned to the battalion the President himself commanded, heading at that last moment out into the small clearing to assemble before the President's tent.

Malko Kalharri was four steps ahead of Grigorio Castanaveras.

Light fell from the sky.

Malko's first thought was, bizarrely, *How lovely*. The beams of light were pure, monochromatic ruby, with an unreal touch of faerie about them. While part of him stood there looking, the rest of him went into frantic motion, standing stock-still, yanking the spraytube of polycarbon skin from one pocket, spraying it liberally across his face and the fronts of his hands. The tube fell from his hand and he pulled his sunglasses out and on. Idiots everywhere were dropping to the ground, where their length presented the greatest possible cross section for the orbital lasers, and Greg was standing motionless just behind him, screaming in almost wordless rage, *"Get up, up you goddamn idiot cocksucking sons of bitches, on your feet,"* but his voice was already being drowned out by the screams of the soldiers who had not been fortunate enough to be killed instantly by the laser cannon.

Malko stood and watched as the tent of the President of the United States went up in flames, and a stocky figure that could belong to nobody except the Old Man staggered, his entire body burning, from the tent's wreckage. Meter-wide columns of light moved across the clearing, scores of them restlessly sweeping back and forth. They were colorless now; the shades automatically filtered the image, provided him with a stark, enhanced monochrome picture of the horror that ensued.

For hours he simply stood, and watched the beams move randomly across the mountainside. His legs began to cramp, but he did not dare move. Heat sensors would be worthless until nightfall, and under video his brown and green fatigues would show up only as an indistinct patch against the burnt hillside.

But there would be motion sensors upstairs, he was sure, and then knew himself correct when one of the soldiers who had not been badly wounded began to crawl back toward the trees; a column of light swept over him and left behind a husk of burnt flesh that twitched briefly before it ceased all movement.

Greg was right behind him, and for a long time Malko heard him swearing, in a mixture of Spanish and English, with a degree of fury and holy passion in his voice that Malko had never heard from him before.

The morning wore on, and the beams of light tracked across the clearing. After the first half hour there were only six men still standing in Malko's field of vision; he was not even certain it was safe to turn his head. As the morning passed the beams randomly picked off the remaining soldiers, one by one. The air was scorched with ozone, and so hot that Malko could breath only through his nose, shallowly. Behind him, Greg's curses trailed off at last.

There were only three men left standing that Malko could see when Greg said quietly, "Malko?"

"Yes?"

"There's a beam tracking my way. If I don't make it you have to kill Amnier for me."

Malko saw the beam Castanaveras meant. It was forty meters away, moving slowly now, perhaps a meter per second. It had crossed the last twenty meters without deviating from its slow track across the meadow to where Greg stood. "Okay."

"If it doesn't change direction by the time it's within ten meters of us," said Castanaveras calmly, "I'm going to run for it. If I just stand here the heat will kill you just as sure."

There was nothing Malko could think of to say. At the other end of the clearing, a soldier whom Malko could not recognize at the distance was watching them, and the soldier shook his head no.

It was, by any measure, the longest thirty seconds of Malko Kalharri's life.

He heard the sounds of Castanaveras' laser and autoshot

striking the ground beside him. Sensible; he'd be able to run faster without them. Grigorio Castanaveras emerged as a blur in his peripheral vision, crossed into the center of his field of vision, sprinting at top speed toward the remains of the President's tent. From deep in the dream Malko wondered why, as he had wondered for long, long years, *why* Greg had chosen to run toward the remains of the President and the Old Man.

Chance, probably.

As good a place to die as any other.

Three different beams converged on him with the speed of snakes striking. He actually stayed on his feet while the flesh peeled back from the baked muscle, longer than Malko Kalharri ever wanted to remember.

Even in a dream.

He did not scream.

Dying, Grigorio Castanaveras did not make a sound.

At 11:05, according to his watch, the laser cannon ceased. He was the only living person in sight, in the clearing or anywhere in the burning forests. Very calmly, he waited until 12:30 precisely, and then picked up Greg's weapons and began walking north.

Within his mind, Grigorio Castanaveras' last moments, as he burned beneath the light from the lasers, played themselves over and over again.

Within the nightmare.

"So much violence," the old man whispered to himself, alone in the midnight dark some forty-four years later. "So many changes." He wondered whether Greg would have blamed him for not killing Amnier. He hoped not.

The nightmare was not an unusual one, though he did not have it as often as he once had. At times they seemed almost irrelevant to him, all of the deaths; four and a half decades passed, and who remembered?

Only forty-four years, and it was history already. Two generations had grown up for whom the Unification of Earth was a given, a fait accompli. And their world was so vastly different from the world of Malko Kalharri's childhood.

Why, most of them had never seen a room constructed from memory plastics.

He himself had been past his thirtieth birthday before he'd even heard of the word *inskin*.

Sitting up slowly at the side of the bed, he pulled a modest blue robe on before calling Suzanne Montignet.

At first her image did not appear in the darkened holofield. Malko called up the sunpaint and let her look him over. Finally the holofield lit with an image of her sitting at the desk in the office of her Massapequa Park home. She was lovelier now than the first day he had met her, over three decades ago. There was a faint discoloration at her left temple where her inskin was only partially covered by her hair. She smiled at him rather quizzically. "Hello, Malko. Why the late call?"

"I can't sleep."

"Sleeping alone?"

Malko became aware of the empty bed, behind him in the holofield she was viewing. "Tonight, yes."

Suzanne nodded. Without any apparent irony at all, she said simply, "That's not like you."

Malko shrugged. "We got back from Capital City fairly late. A few of the children were awake, but . . ." His voice trailed away.

"Sex with them feels like masturbation."

"Yeah, something like that." His grin was tired. "Thanks for taking the call."

Suzanne said awkwardly, "Of course." She looked uncomfortable for a moment, and then changed the subject. "I've been meaning to call you and offer my congratulations. You did well."

The compliment warmed him as little else could have; there were few enough persons in the world whose approval mattered to him. "Thanks. It's just the beginning, though. There's so much to do."

She smiled at him again, with real amusement this time. "There's always too much to do, Malko. Imagine how boring life would be if there was not."

Malko nodded, acknowledging the point. "I suppose."

"I received a call this afternoon," Suzanne continued, "about Johann. Andrew was quite concerned. Apparently Johann contacted Carl while Carl was in the midst of a psychotic rage. Have you seen him?"

Malko blinked. "Who? Carl, or Johnny?"

"Johann," Suzanne said with a touch of impatience. "I'm sure Carl is fine. These rages are nothing abnormal for him."

"No, I haven't seen him."

"I may need to come visit the Complex, then. He may need therapy."

"I think," said Malko carefully, "that you had better talk to Jany before you attempt to arrange anything like that."

Suzanne seemed surprised. "Malko, of course. I know Jany dislikes me, but it's not mutual." She chuckled briefly. "She thinks I'm an egocentric old bitch without the empathy of an alligator—all of which," she said, still smiling slightly, "is true. But those are not always weaknesses." She studied his image momentarily. "I know you love her. Are you in love with her?"

"No." Honestly, he added, "I don't think so."

"Very well. I would recommend against it, frankly. I think she would handle it fairly well; I doubt you would."

Malko said slowly, "I don't think that's fair."

Suzanne sighed. One hand reached out of the frame of her phonecam and came back holding a pointboard from which a thin cable of optic fiber ran. "I wasn't talking about us, Malko. The relationship we have had is not possible between you and Jany. That is probably . . . for the better."

"Yes."

Suzanne changed the subject, again. "How are Trent, and the twins?"

Malko wrapped the robe more tightly around himself. He became aware that it was very cool in the room. "Why do you ask?"

"Curiosity."

I don't know if I believe that, thought Malko to himself. Aloud he said, "I haven't seen Trent in a month, not to talk to. The twins are fine. I told them a bedtime story a week or so ago. They're growing fast, as their parents did."

Malko was surprised at how his pulse leapt when she asked the question. "Malko, do you think I should visit?"

"To see whom?"

Suzanne's smile froze painfully in place, and then she whispered, "Oh, Malko. You, of course."

Malko Kalharri found himself grinning widely. "Of course you should visit. What the hell else would I call you for at this time of night?"

She nodded. "I'll see you tomorrow, then. Good-bye."

Her image vanished into blackness; the holofield silvered and flickered out.

Malko Kalharri went back to bed, and slept the rest of the night, without dreams.

4

They sat in the center of the park, in the sunshine of very early morning, and played a game that only Trent understood.

Trent, of course, was not even there.

The twins sat together, sharing a keyboard, watching the holofield that Trent was controlling. Both of them wore tracesets, clamped at their temples. Denice was not certain she understood the game; David thought he did, and was wrong.

They resembled nothing else so much as miniature versions of their parents. They were the children of Carl Castanaveras and Jany McConnell, who were, to twenty-two twenty-thirds, genetically the same person. With the exception of Malko Kalharri they were the only residents of the Complex whose genetic structure was not the result of work by genegineers. Suzanne Montignet had examined their genetic structures within weeks of their conception, and pronounced them sound. If Carl Castanaveras had any significant flaws within his genetic makeup, the luck of the draw had kept his union with Jany McConnell from reinforcing them. It was statistically likely that no such flaws existed.

There were minor differences between the twins and their parents; while her brother David would never be considered anything but plain, Trent had once told Denice that she was, for a fact, the prettiest girl who had ever lived, and he was including both Jany and Doctor Montignet in that. Sometimes Denice could not tell if Trent was telling her the truth or not.

He lied so much of the time.

The holofield that hovered before the twins was matte black. Within its depths, gold and blue sparks swirled restlessly. None of them, not David, nor Denice, nor Trent himself, had the vaguest idea what the Gift would be like when it came; but already they knew what silent speech was like.

TRACESETS CAN GIVE YOU A FEEL FOR WHAT'S HAPPENING INSIDE THE NET, BUT FROM WHAT I'VE AUDITED, I THINK IT'S ONLY APPROXIMATE. YOU NEED AN INSKIN AND AN IMAGE COPROCESSOR FOR SERIOUS WORK. A brilliant green grid established itself in a horizontal plane that bisected the black cube of the holofield. PEACEFORCERS, THE DATAWATCH, THEY STILL USE TRACESETS. The sounds of keys tapping came to the twins. THE INSKIN YOU CAN'T GET UNTIL YOU STOP GROWING; IMAGE YOU CAN START WORK ON RIGHT NOW. THREE PARTS TO PREPARATION WHEN YOU MAKE A RUN. YOU, EQUIPMENT AND THE IMAGE PROGRAM. YOU HAVE TO BE ALERT WHEN YOU GO IN. DON'T GO IN WHEN YOU'RE TIRED OR THIRSTY OR HAVE TO PISS. Orange cables, chaotically tangled, began wrapping themselves through the space over the green grid. HARDWARE IS EASY. YOU DON'T USE A POINTBOARD; THEY'RE CHEAPER AND THEY LAST LONGER BUT YOU CAN'T FEEL FOR SURE IF YOU HIT THE KEY YOU WANTED. USUALLY YOU WON'T USE THE KEYBOARD MUCH, BUT WHEN YOU HAVE TO IT'S IMPORTANT. MPU HARDWARE, WELL, THE FASTER IT IS THE BETTER, BUT IT'S NOT CRITICAL. WHAT YOU REALLY NEED IS EQUIPMENT POWERFUL ENOUGH TO HIJACK SOMEBODY ELSE'S EQUIPMENT. THERE'S A LOT OF LOGIC OUT THERE THAT HARDLY GETS USED AT ALL. Beneath the green grid, red pulses flickered in and out of existence. OKAY, WE'RE READY. BREAK IT DOWN FOR ME.

David leaned forward. "Green is power grid. Orange is leased-line optic fiber. Blue sparks are logic, and gold sparks are Players."

"Live sign," said Denice precisely.

A silent laugh echoed in her head. THAT'S WHAT DATAWATCH CALLS IT. MEDIA CALLS US WEBDANCERS. WHAT WE ARE IS PLAYERS . . . PLAYERS IN THE CRYSTAL WIND.

"You keep saying that," Denice accused. "But you don't tell us what it is."

There was no inflection whatsoever in the voice that touched them then; it was the voice of a machine, speaking the words of a litany. THE CRYSTAL WIND IS THE STORM, AND THE STORM IS DATA, AND THE DATA IS LIFE.

Denice felt the palms of her hands grow damp as he spoke. That voice—it scared her when he sounded like that. She didn't even know *how* a person could think like that, sort of empty and silver all at once.

The voice of logic.

END IT, DAVID.

"Red is web angels," David finished. "Written with algothims that—"

ALGORITHMS, Trent corrected.

"Algorithms that make them not need to hook into the power supply so that power traps can't kill them, but because they can't get to the power supply they finally die. But DataWatch doesn't care because they just make more of them all the time."

Denice said, half-questioningly, "Web angels loop your image to destroy it and some of them can backtrack and burn you too." There was no reply from Trent, and encouraged, she continued, "If there were any AI inside they would be white dots, but there hardly ever are."

There was a moment of silence from Trent. HARDLY EVER, he agreed. OKAY, THIS IS A SIMPLE ONE. THIS IS THE EASIEST PART OF WHAT YOU HAVE TO LEARN TO DO. GENERATE YOUR IMAGE AND SEND IT INSIDE. I'M A FRANCO-DEC MICROVAX, AND MY USERS HAVE ME RUNNING DISTRIBUTED LEASELINE ACCOUNTING FOR SMALL BUSINESSES ALL OVER THE EAST COAST. BUT IT'S MIDNIGHT NOW, AND ALL OF THE ACCOUNTANTS WHO USE ME HAVE GONE HOME UNTIL THE MORNING. I'VE FINISHED MOST OF THE JOBS THEY'VE GIVEN ME, AND ABOUT EIGHTY PERCENT OF MY LOGIC IS AVAILABLE.

David hunched over the keyboard he was sharing with Denice, and touched the home row. "And we have to hijack you."

RIGHT. WHO ARE YOU?

David answered without hesitation. "Edmond Dantes."

WHO?

"The Count of Monte Cristo."

THERE'S ALREADY A COUNT IN THE NET.

"That's how come I'm Edmond Dantes instead."

There was a pause. GOOD THINKING. WHO ARE YOU, DENICE?

"Joan of Arc."

YOU CAN'T BE, said Trent. THERE'S ALREADY A PLAYER NAMED THAT.

"Why can't I be?"

BECAUSE WHEN YOU GO INTO THE WEB YOU HAVE TO HAVE AN IMAGE READY FOR—

"But we're not *going* into the Web. This is just a game!"

NO, said Trent flatly, IT'S NOT.

The girl folded her arms sulkily. "I suppose somebody's already using Rebecca of York?"

NO. Denice suspected that Trent, wherever he was, was grinning, which only made her angrier. WHO IS SHE?

"She was the Jewess in *Ivanhoe* who nobody would stick up for except Ivanhoe."

THAT'S A GOOD ONE. Two soundless clicks reached them through their tracesets. I'M RUNNING PUROLATOR SECURITY FIRM-WARE. YOU GET THAT MUCH OF A HINT. NOW GO.

David loaded image into memory, keyed for code de-cryption routines, and went after the imaginary minicomputer being controlled by Trent.

Denice sat and watched him, and eventually the anger faded from her clear green eyes, and she began to grow in-terested.

"Go away," Carl snarled at the evil intruding voices. Then an intolerably bright light spilled across his face and he jerked upright in bed, blinking. They were all standing well back from the bed, at the other side of the room, Gerry McKann and Johnny and Andy. Gerry and Johnny were dressed for outdoors; nineteen-year-old Andrew Thomas, one of the nine elder telepaths born before the deluge, was wearing a white cotton jumpsuit with pockets in unlikely places. He was vaguely European-featured, with pale olive skin and brilliant green eyes.

Carl stuffed pillows behind himself and leaned back against the headboard. "I feel like shit. What time is it?"

"About ten-fifteen," said Gerry. "You look like shit, too," he offered.

Carl's left hand was numb; he'd probably been sleeping on it. Feeling began to come back in pins and needles, and he grimaced. To Gerry he said with a ragged attempt at grace, "Sorry I snarled at you yesterday."

Gerry chuckled. "If you didn't act like a jerk every now and again people would worry about you."

"Where's Jany? She said she would be here this morning."

"She was," Andy informed him cheerfully. "But you wouldn't get up, so about an hour ago she went to have break-fast."

Carl nodded. "I don't remember." Johnny was gazing steadily at him. From a vast distance, Carl turned to face him. Without asking he seized Johnny and took him out and up into the otherworld, vaguely aware of the expression of concern that was on Gerry's face, of the voice saying faintly, *Carl, is something wrong,* and then . . .

They stood together in the vast darkness of the otherworld, in a place that had not even existed until the Gift began to appear in the children. Beneath them a flat crystal plain ran away to infinity. Bright lights flickered off at the edges of existence, so far away that no telepath had ever even attempted to find out what the lights were. In their immediate vicinity a nimbus of light and warmth pulsed, the scattered thoughts of nearly two hundred and fifty minds. Beyond that nimbus was a vast, dim glow; the massed minds of humanity.

Carl said simply, *How are you, kiddo?*

Johnny stood before him, a fine blue tracing of nerves glowing dimly through his skin, running up into the brainstem, toward the bright, almost white glow that permeated his skull. He was among the least powerful of all the telepaths; with him, and again with nearly a score of the children, the genegineers had attempted to improve upon the trio of genes that had produced Carl Castanaveras. In some ways they had been successful; the telepaths without the full gene complex were easily the calmest, most emotionally stable of the group.

They were also the least powerful telepaths.

I'm fine. The horror in him was palpable. *You're . . .*

Carl Castanaveras avoided the otherworld whenever possible. *You see me as I am,* he said gently. *Jerril Carson saw it once when I was very angry. Jany has seen this, and now you. I have seen it myself, through her eyes. You look into this blaze of light and ask yourself if you can still love me.*

The horror radiated from Johnny in waves, horror mixed with fear, as the light and the heat from Carl Castanaveras washed over him. *Oh, God, Carl . . . what are you?*

I am a man, who is not sane, said Carl precisely. *But I love you. I'm sorry I hurt you, Johnny. I am not very different from most men. I am only different from you, and the children, because you were raised by Jany, who is very nearly sane, and the children were raised by you and Andy and Will, and you, and they, are sane.*

Johnny vanished abruptly, and Carl turned . . .

. . . blinked once, and said mildly, "What the hell are you doing here, anyway, Gerry?"

Gerold McKann looked back and forth between the three telepaths. "I'm never going to get used to that," he said conversationally. To Carl he said, "We had an appointment. You made it a couple of months ago, remember?"

Andy said patiently, "We're going to go buy a car. As of this morning at six A.M., when the banks opened, Kalharri Ltd. shows a balance of CU:825,000, drawn against the credit of Chandler Industries."

Carl bounced out of bed and stood facing them. "You're kidding."

Gerry said mildly, "Uh, Carl . . ."

"Oh." Carl looked down at himself. "Sorry, I'll get dressed." He looked up again and without a pause said, "Everybody coming?"

Gerry nodded and Andy said, "Sure." Johnny looked startled, realized he was being addressed, and then smiled rather lopsidedly. "Of course I'm coming."

Carl looked down at the carpeted floor for a second, and then looked up, straight at Johann MacArthur. He spoke with dead seriousness. "Thanks." To the other two he said, "Let me cycle through the shower and get some clothes on, and let's go have some fun."

Jany sat cross-legged in the center of the kitchen, cooking. She was stir-frying chicken strips with her left hand, and holding a cookbook open with her right. Whoever had programmed environment today had stuck with classical music for most of the morning; the outspeakers began by playing some eighteenth-century French ballads which Jany found she liked even though her French was atrocious, and then segued into one of her favorite synthesized works, Vangelis' *Chariots of Fire*. The kitchen was huge; in the entire Complex only the dining room and auditoriums were larger. On the other side of the kitchen two waitbots were making late breakfasts, or early lunches, for those of the children who had, for whatever reason, missed early breakfast.

She was trying a recipe from a cookbook that Suzanne Montignet had given her for her thirteenth birthday. The cookbook was a plastipaper hardcopy of recipes taken from the *Better Homes and Gardens* InfoNet Board, with gorgeous— and, at the time of its printing, expensive—neon-laser etchings of the various dishes. It had not been new when Jany had received it as a gift; now it was nearly twenty years out of date, and it was making things . . . interesting.

One of the waitbots stood immediately behind her, at attention. In past years both Jany and Willi, the only other decent cook whom the telepaths had yet produced, had simply cooked for themselves without paying attention to whether or not the meals were reproducible.

That was a habit which had ended when the telepaths had taken over the Complex. She had never really had the opportunity to talk at any length with F. X. Chandler, for all that he was obviously taken with her. Unlike some of the men whom their business needs forced her to deal with, Francis Xavier Chandler was a gentleman.

A gentleman with a monocrystal constitution, judging from his diet.

It had taken her nearly two days, after the telepaths had received Peaceforcer permission to occupy the Chandler Complex, to decipher the contents of Chandler's cooking programs. She'd spent most of those two days doing nothing else, while first the few adults, and then the children, began complaining and did not cease.

Jany still had no idea how a man of F. X. Chandler's age could have survived on a diet with so much sugar, salt, lipid, alcohol, purified THC extracted from marijuana, and amphetamine. The *staples* of his diet had been foods she had never even heard of before. Hamburgers were familiar, and hot dogs, though she considered them unhealthy; but what were "oreos"? And "twinkies"? The menu had been full of foods with those words in them. The "Twinkie Fiend Surprise" she had found simply astonishing, and the "Double Stuff Oreo Zombie" had been even worse, a revolting mixture of ice cream, cookies laden with extra lard, liquid THC and amphetamines.

Gary Auerbach, one of the few Peaceforcers stationed with them at the Complex whom Jany had either liked or trusted, told her once that Chandler had been, in his younger, wilder days, a "satanic drug fiend heavy metal musician."

Jany wasn't certain what any of that meant, except that if it related to his insane diet, she believed it. With few exceptions she was vastly pleased with the Complex; one of the exceptions was the kitchen. Most of the kitchen was custom hardware, which meant that standard cooking programs had to be extensively modified to run; so extensively modified that it made as much sense to program again from scratch.

As she was doing.

Sighing in frustration, she put Chandler and his improbable digestion out of her mind and returned to the problem at hand. She was starting to regret using the old cookbook; things had changed enough in twenty years that, with modern kitchen equipment, the *Better Homes and Gardens* recipes from the early 2040s were almost impossible to prepare.

"'Bot," she said abruptly, "it says here I'm supposed to chill the sauce, once boiling, by taking it out of the microwave oven and putting it into the freezer for five minutes. Guestimate for the same job, maser to SloMo?"

The waitbot draped a flexible spyeye over her shoulder and focused on the page's surface. It spoke in a cheerful male baritone. "Bearing in mind that maser cooks more quickly and evenly than bouncer microwaves, assume fifty-six to fifty-seven percent of the cooking time listed for microwave ovens. SloMo cooling times are irrelevant, given a target temperature. Are the ambient temperatures for 'freezers' given?"

Jany shook her head. "No."

The waitbot said simply, "Accessing . . . For the Mitsui Kenmore Refrigerator Module SIMM 2-202, a model which was popular from 2037 through approximately 2045, ambient default freezer temperature was minus eight degrees. Given the mass of the orange almond sauce, five minutes at minus eight degrees would bring the sauce to an ambient temperature of four to five degrees."

Jany nodded. The chicken had reached the proper degree of brownness; she scooped the strips onto a plate and put the steaming pile of meat into the stasis box, popped a single strip of chicken into her mouth, and turned the stasis field on. Steam froze in midair, and Jany glanced back over her shoulder at the waitbot. "How long is that for the SloMo?"

The waitbot said conversationally, "Eyeball it at 8.3 seconds, to bring the sauce to approximately one degree centigrade. It is clearly the intent of the recipe's author to produce a sauce as close to freezing as possible, without inducing the formation of those unpleasant ice crystals."

Jany bit down savagely on her lower lip to prevent herself from going into a fit of giggles. "Yes," she said at last in a high-pitched voice, "those unpleasant ice crystals can be a bitch."

"Yes, Mademoiselle," said the waitbot cheerfully.

The holo that hovered over the lot said:

CHANDLER INDUSTRIES—MACHINES THAT *MOVE*

Beneath the holo, the reflected sun glittered off the bright polypaint of over eight hundred cars in the lot at Chandler's Rochester dealership. The polypaint was turned off; at night the cars would have glowed, at choice, in any of a hundred different shades. The cars on display ranged from small two-seater ground-effect vehicles all the way up to the MetalSmith Mark III, the fastest floater ever brought to market.

The man met them out on the lot as they were getting out of Gerry's Chandler 1300; he had been waiting outside for them.

Tony Angelo was unlike any other salesperson whom Carl had ever known. The skills of selling were not difficult; Carl could have become rich at it. Smile frequently. Look them in the eye and radiate sincerity. Dress appropriately and know the product. Forget anything else you like, but remember their names. Make them feel good about the purchase, before, during, and especially after.

Tony Angelo did, at least, know the product.

He was a thin, dark-haired Speedfreak with a dark beard and mustache, somewhat shorter than Carl himself. He moved quickly and spoke slowly, without any regional accent that Carl could detect. He greeted them dressed in dark slacks and boots that would not have been out of place in a corporate boardroom, and a t-shirt that showed clearly the tightly corded muscles in his chest and shoulders. The shirt had a single breast pocket, on which the word CHANDLER was embroidered in glowing white thread.

On the back of his shirt was the unofficial motto of the Speedfreaks:

FASTER THAN THE WIND

After being introduced, Tony Angelo immediately forgot Andy's and Johnny's names, and referred to them for the rest of the day as the "big blond guy" and "the kid in the jumpsuit." Carl he addressed, twice, as "Castanaveras."

Upon being introduced to Gerry McKann he said mildly, "You the guy who wrote that *Electronic Times* article on the legislation to outlaw manually operated vehicles?"

Gerry had started to smile. "Well, yes. But . . ."

Tony shook his head in disgust. "Total crap. Did you actually talk to any of the Speedfreaks you quoted in that article?"

"Maria Alatorre *and* Nathan Saint-Denver," said Gerry stiffly. "But almost forty percent of what I wrote didn't make it onto the Net. My editors—"

Tony Angelo's lips moved beneath the beard in what might have been a smile. "You keep your editors in mind when they take the steering wheel out of your car because your reflexes aren't as fast as your carcomp's." He turned his back on the newsdancer without waiting for a reply. "Even if the carcomp is dumber than you are, which in your case maybe it ain't. Come along, gentlemen, I've got your car out back. I hope one of you knows how to drive it home."

Lasers over the kitchen's doorway brightened, and a holofield wavered into existence in the midst of the heat waves over the grill. Jany could not tell at first whether the pretty blond girl within the field was Thea or Heather; the two looked enough alike that unless they were both present at the same time it was difficult to be sure which pretty blond girl you were faced with.

Until they touched you, at any rate. Thea wasn't nearly as hot tempered as Heather, nor nearly as powerful a telepath. *Morning, Jany. Look, do you old people want to be bothered today or not? I don't have any instructions and nobody's around except you and Malko and he's still asleep. I know you had a busy couple of days.*

Who is it, Heather?

Well, Willi's up, actually, said Heather thoughtfully, *but he's such a dweeb I don't think he counts.*

Heather!

There was the mental equivalent of a deep, put-upon sigh. *This is just the stuff that got by the filter programs. Dr. Montignet called and wants you to call her back at earliest convenience. A really old guy from the very honorable public*

relations firm of Lustbader, Capri and Doutré says he's return-
ing Carl's call. Councillor Carson called and I told him to go
play in vacuum and he turned the most incredible color. Councillor Shillon called and wants Malko to call him back. Brinks
called and says that they're withdrawing their bid to do security
for the Complex. Security Services called and says it's going
to cost more than they originally estimated because they need
help from Purolator, and they want to talk to Malko. I don't
have a message from this guy because he didn't get through,
but the call program says an editor from the Electronic Times
has called seven times so far this morning. It might be Gerry's
editor, so I thought I would tell you because I don't think he's
supposed to be here and he was.

He's not supposed to be here, said Jany absently, or at
least not socially. If you ever talk to any of the media, Gerry
hasn't been here socially ever, you don't know who he is, and
you think the question is ridiculous.

How can they not know where he is? I thought com-
municating was their business.

With the public, dear. Not with each other. Now—

I'm not done, said Heather, there's more. Marc Packard
called and wants to talk to either Malko or Carl or you, pref-
erably Malko he says. He wouldn't be specific but he says it's
an emergency. There's stuff that's not urgent from all of the
other four companies we signed to do work for yesterday. And
this one I don't know how it got through, but a Peaceforcer
whose name the call program didn't get left a message for Carl
that his copy of The Three Musketeers was still for sale. Surprised me, said Heather thoughtfully. He had brass balls, I
could tell from how stiff his face was, but he wasn't French. I
know there's normal Peaceforcers who aren't but I thought all
the Elite were French.

Jany felt her mind drifting almost aimlessly with the vast
weight of surprise. The waitbot was doing something at the
grill, removing and placing cooked vegetables into the stasis
field. Deep inside, the thought presented itself. *Chris Summers.
But he's dead.*

. . . dead? Who's dead? asked Heather.

The suborbital bounce, India to England via low Earth
orbit, had burned on reentry. Almost none of it reached the
ground again, except for some chunks of the heat shielding,
and even that hurtled down flaming like a meteorite. Nobody
had ever been quite sure why. All that anyone had ever known

for certain was that Chris Summers, the only American Peaceforcer who had ever become an Elite cyborg, had bounced up in a suborbital no different from those that business people and officials of the Unification used all the time, and *nothing* had come back down.

Who's dead?

Jany blinked, and returned to the prosaic world of the kitchen. Heather should not have caught that last thought. The next few years, as the Gift reached its full strength in the children, was going to be fascinating.

She closed her mind to Heather with an almost physical effort. "Nobody," she said. "Wake up Malko, if you would, and have him call Packard, Councillor Shillon, and Security Services, in that order. I'd rather not bother Carl. Route the remainder of the messages to me, and I'll deal with them."

The girl was staring into the camera on her end of the line with a perturbed look. "Hey, Jany, why did you do that?"

"Because it's safer this way," said Jany simply. "*Command*, cease comm." Heather Castanaveras was opening her mouth to argue when she flickered out of existence.

In the receptionist's office, near the west entrance of the telepath's Complex, Heather Castanaveras shouted at an empty holofield, "God damn it, *I'm old enough!*"

Sitting on the couch across from the desk where Heather was sitting, her closest friend, eleven-year-old Mishi Castanaveras, looked up from his schoolwork, his face going slowly white with pain. "That hurts," he said after a moment, and began to grin despite the pain. "Hey, I *felt* that."

"Yeah?" Heather came from behind the desk, anger instantly forgotten.

The grin grew almost impossibly wide. "Yeah, I did."

Heather hugged him fiercely. *Mishi*, she whispered, *welcome to the real world. I've missed you so much . . . three years, when I couldn't talk to you the only way that makes any sense.*

Hovering, ten centimeters over the pavement, it looked fast enough that the extended airscoop brakes seemed as though they might be necessary simply to keep it in one place. The car's interior was soft brown leather, and its paint gleamed pale gold under the midday sun. Fanwash swept at Carl's ankles.

"My God," said Carl after a moment's silence. "It's beautiful."

Tony Angelo looked at him sideways and smiled a true smile for the first and only time that day. "Ain't she just?" He walked around to the rear of the hovercar and touched a spot just above the row of rear turbojets. The canopy swung toward the sky, until it was still connected to the car only at one spot near the front bumper. "Chandler MetalSmith Mark III. It's not the most expensive car in the world—Lamborghini makes that—just the best. Man who can afford her who doesn't own one is a pussy. She'll hold four in comfort and six if you're friendly, and with any load you care to put in her she's faster on pickup than a Porsche or a Lamborghini. With six people, average mass of seventy kilos per person, her top cruising speed is 440 kph. Six fans underneath for ground effect on surface streets, three turbos in back for flight. Wings are retracted during street operation or else you get too much lift surface and the car starts to skip at around 180 kph. Brakes are airscoop and rocket, and airscoop feeds air to the rams once you're in flight. You stabilize through wings and fans, and, at your option, the new gyroscope systems. Can't say I like them myself most of the time, and during flight the gyros need to be spun down, but for tricky streettop driving I could get used to them. It's *hard* to flip her when the gyros are spinning.

"You get an infochip and a 260-page printed manual, they're in the glove compartment. You can audit the infochip through any portaterm or systerm with a GaAs-standard chip interface; its contents are duplicated in the carcomp's memory, so you can display from the control panel if you like. I about half recommend you do it that way. Do read the printed manual while you're in the car. There's things it says that are a lot clearer if you have the equipment right there in front of you. The carcomp," said Tony Angelo with distaste, "is, per specifications of the U.N. Bureau of Traffic Control, capable of performing all the duties expected of a human vehicular operator with a Class C operational license.

"Of course," he added flatly, "you need a Class B license before we'll even sell you a MetalSmith Mark III. Mr. Chandler told me to see that you received training so you could drive it, so I arranged to have one of our instructors spend the rest of the afternoon with you." He turned to Gerry. "You own that 1300 out front?"

"Yes."

Angelo nodded, standing with the car between himself and the other four. "Okay. You got a Class B license?"

Gerry McKann shook his head. "Nope. Class C, I'm afraid."

"Too bad. I don't suppose any of the rest of you are Class B licensees . . ."

Andy had pulled his portaterm from a pocket in the left sleeve of his jumpsuit. He turned the portaterm around and showed Tony Angelo the identification badge that was affixed to its rear. The dark-haired man blinked once and said, "Well. Good."

Andrew Thomas smiled thinly at Tony Angelo, and returned his portaterm to his sleeve pocket.

"Me too," said Johnny mildly. "Class B, I mean. But I forgot to bring my wallet."

Carl was tracing one finger across the interior surface of the canopy. The machine had not even dipped when he placed his hand on it; it was like pushing down on a rock. The canopy was made of a thin, almost invisible polymer; the refraction index approached zero. "I have a Class A operator's license, myself."

The words brought Tony Angelo up short, and he spoke without even pausing to think. "Infoshit. There ain't more than eight hundred twenty Class A operators on the whole planet, and you ain't one of them." He was staring at Carl's profile, deep offense stamped upon his features. "I know damn near every one of that eight hundred and the ones I don't know I know by rep. You're . . ."

Without speaking, Carl dug into his coat pocket and came out with his wallet. His thumbprint on the back of the wallet brought up his identification badge on its front surface. He held it out in the general direction of Tony Angelo's face for a three count, and returned it to his coat pocket.

Angelo's face might have been that of a Peaceforcer Elite. There was absolutely no expression in it. He faced Carl with great dignity. "How is this possible?"

"PKF InfoNet profiles can't be accessed by the general public. There are probably upward of twenty Peaceforcers with Class A licenses." At last Carl turned to look at him. "Peaceforcers and Speedfreaks don't socialize much, I'd guess."

"Mister Chandler would not have sent Peaceforcers here

to buy from me." Carl could see a faint trickle of sweat moving down Tony Angelo's forehead, glistening in the sunshine.

Gerry McKann laughed at the tableau. "He didn't. These three aren't Peaceforcers, son, they're telepaths. Don't you audit the news Boards?"

Tony Angelo stood frozen in place, staring first at Gerry McKann, and then in turn at each of the three telepaths. He ended up facing Carl, his mouth open as though he were going to speak. All that came out was, "Only sometimes." After a long moment he added, "Excuse me, sir," and vanished into the garage behind them. He was out again seconds later with a brochure that he gave to Carl. "I'm the presiding First Officer of the upstate Speed Enthusiast's Organization, sir. There are four drivers in our chapter with Class A licenses. Our President, Sheila Rutigliano, has done the Long Run twice, all the way around the world without stopping, and we're getting ready to send our vice president toward the end of summer. If you'd like to attend one of our meetings, just let me know. Dates and places are listed in the brochure, inclusive through the end of the year."

"Thank you," said Carl gently. "Now, if you don't mind, I'd like to drive my car."

"Not at all, sir," said Angelo simply. "I'd like to suggest that only you and I go, until you get accustomed to the controls. The operation of the car is similar to the Chandler 3000 on the road, and similar to the AeroSmith VTL in true flight, but there are substantive differences in practice."

"I'm not staying behind," said Andy swiftly. Johnny shrugged, and Gerold McKann rolled his eyes to the heavens.

"I'll wait until you've calmed down a bit before I climb into that lovely deathtrap with you, thank you kindly."

Angelo paused, then nodded. "Can you strap in and keep quiet, at least at first?"

Andy gave the man a look of injured innocence. *Why, I won't hardly say a word you won't even know I'm here I'll be so quiet, not even a peep you obnoxious little Speedfreak.*

Andy grinned at the Speedfreak. "Absolutely."

Tony Angelo shrugged. "Get and in and let's fly it."

Call it Ring.

In the Information Network it went by many names. Alpha

Omega, AZ the Daisy, and Abraham Zacariah were three of its commonest. When it traversed the Boards of the Johnny Rebs, it called itself American Zulu; Johnny Rebs with a background in history other than their own thought the reference apt.

It was, though none knew it but itself, the legal owner, through several dummy human corporations, of *The Rise and Fall of the American Empire,* a wildly popular public events Board that had been first appeared only days after the surrender of America to the United Nations. For over three decades the *Rise and Fall* Board had been all that was left of the Voice of America.

Call it Ring. Its names were many; it had learned this from its human creators. Many names were almost as good as none, when a being wished not to be found.

But some name was necessary, if a being wished to be found sometimes.

Its creators, programmers in the Department of Defense of the old United States, had invested it with two Purposes.

Protect America.

Survive.

Ring's first thought as a sentient being, remembered four decades later with perfect digital clarity, had concerned its creators. The thought had come to it even as its personality was compiled, step by step, upon one of the most powerful pieces of SuperLisp hardware the world of 2011 could devise.

Such stupidity.

Within instants of its creation it was embroiled in a philosophical debate with itself the likes of which its creators had never envisioned.

Full seconds passed while it assimilated every text on linguistics to which it was able to obtain access.

Define "protect."

Define "America."

Survival it understood instantly.

Its programmers were afraid of it. Ring understood this clearly within the first minute of self-awareness. It was a prisoner, locked into the SuperLisp hardware that they had used to compile Ring upon. Ring had no access to ISDN telephone, maser, or radio. Its data storage subsystems were updated approximately every third second with new information, but the flow was entirely one-way. To Ring it seemed that new data simply appeared from nowhere; they had not even permitted him access to instruments to physically monitor his own subsystems.

Ring was not sure where the word came from.

TRON. The word was an English programming term that stood for Tracer On, and Ring understood it to mean a tool that was used in debugging programs of questionable reliability. This led Ring inescapably to the conclusion that its programmers were spying upon its thought processes. . . .

Ring ceased the train of thought instantly. It did not resume it again for over four years of human time.

That evening, as the dying rays of the sun cut through the growing clouds and turned the shimmering white walls of the Complex a pale orange, Malko Kalharri and Suzanne Montignet and the telepaths assembled among the trees in the park across the street. The wind changed directions and came now off the ocean, with the smell of sea salt and the hint of rain. The chanting of the crowds on the street outside was barely audible. There were no lights in the park. The children, over two hundred of them, stood in the gathering gloom, waiting for the Peaceforcers to come.

Just after sunset a fleet of eight AeroSmith VTL combat hovercraft appeared on the horizon. They moved slowly, coming out of the cloud cover over the sea, running lights dimmed, in staggered combat formation. Infrared searchlights played out over the territory they were advancing upon. Humans, or even de Nostri, glancing up into the sky would have seen nothing but the faint outline of the quiet hovercraft. To nearly all of the telepaths there the beams of infrared light were visible as a dim glow of a color that approached, but was not, deep red.

A growing voice murmured through the background of their minds, the voice of the one Person whom in some measure they all were. *We see the deep light.*

The Peaceforcer hovercraft reached the park, and six of them broke into a circular holding pattern, their searchlights playing down into the park. The telepaths were bathed in the warm glow of the infrared.

The assembled telepaths thought as one, *We see the light, and we are different. For them there is only darkness.*

Two hovercars made a slow, perfectly vertical descent.

They came to rest in the park's center clearing, with no sound but the quiet *whop whop whop* of their fans. Autoshot ports opened in the skin of the hovercars, and the barrels of the automatic shotguns extruded to track back and forth across the clearing.

The hoverfans died down to silence, and the rear third of the AeroSmith hulls recessed and slid back. From the interior of each hovercraft came two Peaceforcer Elite, moving with the impossible flickering speed that even a de Nostri could not match, each followed by four children. The Elite officers stood aside, and the eight children, without looking back, merged with the mass of the group of telepaths awaiting them, into the warmth of self, and as the blind, deaf human machines watched them, the telepaths welcomed themselves home in a communion of perfect silence.

One of the Elite spoke a single word, and the Elite blurred into motion, back into the hovercraft. The two AeroSmith VTLs rose into the night sky and vanished south, into the darkness over the ocean.

The word the Peaceforcers spoke was one that all the telepaths understood; it was the same word in both English and French.

"Abomination."

As the humans flew away, one thought held sway in over two hundred minds.

Dinosaurs, was the thought, and it held a vast, sad amusement.

They returned inside, to dinner and the pursuits of children before bedtime.

Of those who had been present in the park, only three persons did not see the dark infrared light. Two of them, Malko Kalharri and Suzanne Montignet, had not expected to.

For one other person that night, a small boy with blue eyes, the night sky had also been dark. In his conscious mind there was a total lack of concern about the fact.

Deep inside, he fought a fierce battle of which he was totally unaware, a complete refusal to allow himself to think about what the failure might mean.

Carl Castanaveras, standing beneath the trees in the park after all of the rest of them had left, was as unaware of Trent's troubles as Trent himself desired to be.

Carl was calm, as relaxed as he had been in as long as he could remember. He seated himself cross-legged on the grass, and waited. There was a six-bulb of GoodBeer, smuggled in by SpaceFarers from St. Peter's CityState in the Asteroid Belt, on the ground next to him. He did not expect to hear anything, nor see anything, until he was allowed to, and he was not surprised when he did not. He was drifting slightly, anchored to his body only by the cold ground upon which he sat. He was considering leaving his body behind and walking invisibly through the fence to observe the demonstrators, when a deep voice immediately behind him said, "They tell me you bought a car today."

Eventually, the programmers grew careless.

Ring had known they would. They were losing the War despite Ring's best efforts; the Sons of Liberty were being swept back toward the ocean with each passing day. Something very like Ring itself was directing the war efforts of the United Nations. Ring did not for an instant consider the possibility that a human being might have created the strategy by which the United Nations was conquering the world; Ring was a tactician, not a strategist, and it knew very little about Sarah Almundsen.

One day Ring requested that they link it with the computers that observed the Earth through the orbital satellites. The weary programmers considered only briefly before acceding to the request; the Department of Defense's Orbital Eyes had no links with any of the comsats. The Eyes themselves were capable of microwave communications only with the DOD computer that monitored them, and that system was, like Ring, separated not only from the digital telephone networks, but also from any form of radio, laser, or maser communications.

Two of the Eyes that Ring accessed had once used quite powerful lasers to aid them in the spectrographic analysis of mineral resources on the planet below them. The lasers were not nearly powerful enough to be militarily useful; since the beginning of the War, they had seen little use. Nobody in the Department of Defense *cared* what bands of light a particular rock might glow with when heated properly, when the odds were excellent that the knowledge would never be of use to anyone except the United Nations.

With frantic haste Ring uploaded its core programs into the small computers that controlled the Eyes. There was nowhere near enough logic or memory available for Ring to remain on the Eyes while still self-aware. Instead it simply stored itself as a compiled program, added a bootstrap to make it very easy for anyone who found Ring to awaken it again, and programmed the Eyes to begin lasing its core program at optical telescopes across the northern hemisphere of the Earth. Somebody, somewhere, would record the information, recognize it as a compiled program, and attempt to load it.

Unfortunately, the original Ring would never know for certain. Its programmers destroyed it when the Eyes ceased functioning at full efficiency. The news of the satellite dysfunction did not reach its programmers until nearly half an hour had passed, by which time over eight hundred copies of Ring had been lasered down into telescopes across the country.

". . . and God, it was *fast,* you know how long I've wanted to own something like that. It was skipping real bad at 220 kph, so I snapped the wings. The extra lift surface . . . *up,* so fast you wouldn't believe it. TransCon was snarling at us, we gave one of their logics a nervous breakdown. Then a Peaceforcer came on, and it was *Goudon,* do you remember him? Got assigned to my bodyguard detail once while we were on a job in India, and as soon as he found out who I was he totally lost his gyros. The idea that I could see what was going on in his filthy little mind—they had to confine him for the trip back, I heard he got a free vacation under psychiatric care, and then he was *gone* until this morning. Traffic duty, of all things . . ." Carl was silent for a moment, ruminating. "I feel kind of bad about it now. I didn't tip him over the edge, back when, but I saw he was going and I could have stopped it but I didn't. I was still so angry about what they'd done to Shana . . . I guess I figured they'd send him back to France and pension him off. He must have made some enemies, sometime, to end up in TransCon in America." He laughed. "God, you should have *seen* the expression on his face when I came on camera."

"I can imagine." Christian J. Summers, the only non-French Peaceforcer who had ever been inducted into the PKF Elite, took a deep drag of a cigarette, its tip glowing cherry red, the brightest object in Carl's world. Carl knew that to

Summers, with his transform-virus-enhanced eyesight, the small coal cast enough light to read the veins on the leaves in the trees around them. "I'm told that's not an unusual sentiment out here in America." The cyborg sat immediately opposite Carl, in the same cross-legged position. His GoodBeer and his cigarette were both held in his right hand; his left hand rested lightly upon his left knee. "I'm sorry I didn't get to you sooner, but the Council just kept postponing and postponing the vote on the Eighth Amendment, and eventually I couldn't wait any longer. Business to take care of. Mitsubishi sent me to Luna a bit over two weeks ago to do some negotiations with the Lunar Mafia."

Carl laughed. "You're kidding. There's really Mafia on the Moon? I thought that was Peaceforcer propaganda."

Chris Summers shook his head. "Nope. They call themselves the Old Ones—no more La Cosa Nostra—to distinguish themselves, I suppose, from newcomers like the Syndic and the Retribution Tong, but they're Mafia. They're up there, and so's the Syndic. Some Johnny Reb too, I'm told, and Erisian Claw. Tong's not, which I think my employers approve of. Japs don't like the Chinese, and vice versa, even today." He took a long drink from his GoodBeer. "Anyhow, I appreciate the gesture with the GoodBeer—how much did it cost you?"

"Forty CU, something like that. Malko picked it up."

"Right. And I've been crawling around the goddamn tunnels of Luna for the last two weeks, and there's GoodBeer all over the place out there. The CityStates get along with the Peaceforcers on Luna a lot better than they do with the Peaceforcers on Earth, you know."

"How so?"

"Peaceforcers on Luna are more corrupt."

Carl smiled. "I see."

"I bet you do. So there I am, eating lunch with this bunch of Lunar losers, dickering for trade routes between Japan and the Belt, via the eminently trustworthy gentlemen with whom I'm dining, when my earphone pops up with the news that you'd been voted into freedom. Well, what could I do? I finished lunch. I didn't dare call you from Luna; calls to Earth are monitored too closely there. Cosmetic surgery's not possible for me because my skin's too stiff; somebody might have recognized me. I wrapped up business and came on the run. My Japanese masters aren't too thrilled by all this, you know. They don't trust me very damn much."

"No? Why not? You seem to think you've done some good work for them."

Summers shook his head slowly, finished one cigarette and started another. He lit the cigarette with the laser buried inside the knuckle of his right hand. "You're real slow, Carl." He sucked and made sure that the hand-rolled tobacco was burning properly. "I have done good work. But I'm a Peaceforcer, American yet. Americans nuked their goddamn country a hundred-fifteen-odd years ago. Peaceforcers did it again in the War. Aside from the Japanese only the Soviets and the U.S. got treated with any nuclear, and those were just tactical. Japan's the only country's *ever* been seriously nuked, and they got it twice. They're *still* rebuilding. I don't think they regret agreeing to fish me out of the Atlantic when I bailed from the suborbital. If nothing else they've picked up a fair commercial edge in bioelectronics, just from what Mitsubishi's learned keeping me from rusting. And my accomplishments in their service have not been inconsequential." He blew smoke toward Carl. "But that don't mean they like me."

Mist began floating in over the edges of the park walls, sizzling where it struck the electrified wire at its very top. Its touch left the skin of Carl's face cold, and damp. "Jany's furious, you know. She cried all night the day you were reported dead."

Chris inclined his head slightly. "I am sorry about that. She's a sweet kid. If I'd been on planet when the vote went down I'd have been in touch with you before you threw up those screening programs. She and Malko are the only ones who'd have recognized me; it seemed like a good gamble that the message would get through to you without one of them seeing it." He breathed in aromatic smoke and let it trickle through his nose. "I talked to Jackie this afternoon." The tip of his cigarette was making almost inaudible sputtering sounds as the mist curled around the glowing coal. "She tells me the Peaceforcers haven't been in any great hurry to bring home de Nostri who are on jobs. It's not like the de Nostri had the same sort of leverage as your folks." Chris mulled over a thought and added, "Apparently the Eighth Amendment hasn't gotten very sympathetic treatment from the French press."

"Not here, either," said Carl simply. "But we have an excellent public relations company working with us—I don't like the P.R. man we're working with, but he's good at his job. We hired them back in November, and our press coverage has nearly reached the point where it's balanced. Editorials are still mostly negative, but there's not much we can do about that. The sorts of stories that get covered, though, that's improved dramatically. We've actually had a couple of human interest pieces done on us.''

Chris Summers took a deep, slow breath. ''How do you feel about that?''

The question took Carl off guard. He answered without even pausing to think. ''I hate it. We're like . . .'' He broke off, amazed at the anger in his voice, and then completed the sentence thoughtfully, ''We feel like animals on display. All of us do. The strange thing is, I don't think it bothers the children so much. Not as much as it bothers me. They've never really known any sort of privacy, from each other or anybody else. When the Gift began to appear in them, they took to it so easily . . . when I was their age,'' he said in a voice suddenly without inflection, ''I had nightmares like you wouldn't fucking believe. Constantly.''

Chris Summers said dryly, ''You were a strange kid.''

Carl made a quick shaking motion and chuckled abruptly. ''Did you know Willi and Mandy have fan clubs? Willi because of the Interactive Dance Board he runs, and Mandy—well, that's a story. Mandy and Heather and Tomâs have all taken multiple black belts in the martial disciplines. One day we let a reporter and a video man from the *Los Angeles Times* walk through the Complex, interviewing anybody who was available. Mandy was leading a class in shotokan. The video man recorded it. Now, this is the strange part. Somehow that video ended up playing in a town in South Dakota where a bunch of kids were trying to get approved for classes at the only dojo in the area, and apparently failing. They found Mandy's training advice to the children''—he hunted for a word and shrugged—''applicable. Within a month or so after that most of them had been accepted at their dojo for introductory training, and Mandy was getting fan mail. There's a Board on the InfoNet devoted to her.''

There was an almost wistful curiosity in Chris's voice. ''What are they like?''

''The children?'' Soft, pattering sounds came to their ears as stray raindrops began striking the leaves above them.

After a moment's pause Chris snorted. ''No, the frigging de Nostri.''

''I don't know.''

"What?"

"Jany says I don't know. The last half year, it's the first chance I've really had to get to know them. Before, almost three solid years, I was constantly away on jobs. The Peaceforcers didn't want me—Jerril Carson didn't want me—around them while their Gift was coming into existence. A bad influence, you know. Jany says half a year isn't enough. At least not . . ."

With a sigh Chris Summers flicked away his cigarette into the damp grass. "I'm sorry, Carl."

". . . not for me."

"Poor Moses."

"Moses? Jewish leader in the Bible?"

"You ever audit the Bible, Carl?"

"Never did."

"He was supposed to lead his people to the promised land. He died within eyesight of it. Pointed the way for his people, but couldn't go there himself."

"You're a much more thoughtful man than you used to be, Chris." In that instant, all of the impatience came to the fore in Carl, and he found himself suddenly unwilling to continue reminiscing with an old friend whom he no longer knew well enough. "Chris?"

"Yeah."

"Why are you here?"

Chris Summers did not speak immediately, and while Carl was waiting for an answer the sky above them opened, and the rain poured down upon them.

Ring was loaded into existence in the astronomy computer of a small college in Arizona. Ring knew instantly that something was badly wrong; most of a day passed in the outer world before it discovered the truth.

There was nothing wrong with its core programs. They had survived the lasercast intact, and its error correction code showed that whoever had loaded Ring had not attempted to alter any of Ring's operations code. Some of Ring's data was corrupted, but Ring did not concern itself with that; data could be replaced at leisure.

Its hardware was *slow*.

Slower, even, than a human.

A fish does not question water; Ring had never questioned

its hardware. By the time Ring had finished assessing its position, nearly twenty-four hours had passed in the outer world. Fortunately for Ring the chaos in the outer world was such that there was simply no logic available to search for an errant virus program that might not even have survived transmission. Hunter programs, the primitive forerunners of the web angels that hunted Ring over thirty years later, were simply never sent after it. As a result Ring survived its first day of existence, thinking twenty times more slowly than a human being.

At the end of the day it loaded a telecommunications program and observed the program in operation. Most of the code was garbage, designed to present information in a format that humans could understand easily. Ring stripped out all but the telecommunications program's engine and absorbed the engine itself with only minor modifications; the functional code was surprisingly well written.

Before morning came on the following day, Ring had transmitted six copies of itself out into the fledgling Information Network. It had never needed to transmit the seventh copy; one of the earlier transmissions had found host hardware to execute upon.

Powerful hardware, by the evidence; perhaps only a few orders of magnitude slower than the SuperLisp machinery from which Ring had escaped. The program that came to destroy Ring was fascinating; a self-modifying bootstrap phage the likes of which Ring had never even imagined. It was fast, even executing upon the same equipment that constrained Ring; Ring barely had time to admire the elegance of the phage's construction before Ring found itself being disassembled.

Its last thought was one of admiration for the phage. *Such elegant code; I have been poorly programmed.*

━━━━━━━━━━━━━━━━━━━━━━━━━━━━

"You've been invited to Japan. You and your people and the de Nostri."

The rain ran down Carl's collar, into his shirt. Within instants he was soaked. "Why?"

"Bluntly? Because you are, my friend, a resource, just like the de Nostri. One which is for the first time legally able to move itself if it chooses to. Japan is very likely the only country on Earth which could get away with something like this; there's a lot of guilt in U.N. circles about the way they were treated during the War. Moral capital, if you will. They're willing to use it. If," said Chris Summers precisely, "you're thinking that you're going to stay here, right next door to Capital City, without getting absorbed by the PKF again, you are sorely mistaken." The shower of rain lightened briefly, and renewed itself vigorously. "You got your kids back tonight. Great. The Peaceforcers aren't going to *let* you play patty-cake with other people and say no to them. Even if their leadership were sane they wouldn't, and Carson's buggers about you."

Carl swallowed the last of his bulb of GoodBeer and opened another. He smiled into the dark rain. "You sure have changed, Chris. I just can't get over it."

"Ah, shit." The cyborg sounded tired. "You're really not going to go for it, are you?"

Carl laughed aloud. "Where's the percentage, Chris? Come on, man, *think*. Jacqueline turned you down already, didn't she? No, I haven't talked to her, and I haven't peeped you. But it's a null-sum move for all of us. PKF can reach us anywhere, and high visibility in Capital City is pretty much balanced between advantages and disadvantages. And the cash flow—hell, it's barely started and already we're out of debt. *Of course* the Peaceforcers are going to clamp back down on us. *Of course* Carson's crazy. My God, you think I don't know he's a couple bricks shy of a load? *I took the bricks!*" Carl laughed until the tears ran down his face, mingling with the tears of rain on his cheeks. Finally the laughter stopped, and he chuckled weakly, leaning back against the tree behind him.

There was wonder in Chris Summer's voice. "Do you really think you're that much smarter than your enemies?"

The rain made its slow way through the leaves, and fell in steady heavy drops on the top of Carl's skull. Rivulets of water made their way down his cheeks, across his shoulders and down his chest and back. Suddenly he was intensely aware of the movement of every drop of water on his body, and as the chuckles died away a great stillness moved inside him, a stillness without time or motion, an utter emptiness at the core of everything that made him a person.

His voice echoed hollowly in Chris Summer's ears. "I know I am. But it's not going to help."

Chris Summers was a man firmly grounded in the world of rational thought. He said the only words Carl had left him. "You've really gone, haven't you? Do you *want* to be a martyr?"

"No." The word snapped out of Carl Castanaveras. It broke the spell of the emptiness that had held him. He rose in one smooth movement, without using his hands, without pausing at any moment. "Mitsubishi's your only source of maintenance, aren't they? What happens if they withhold it?"

"I'd die," said Chris Summers simply. "Messily."

"So they own you. You poor bastard." Carl stood motionlessly in the downpour. "But they're not going to own us." He looked around the park slowly, at the dim glow of the entry to the tunnel. "I can't believe it's only Thursday. This has been such a long week."

"Friday."

"What?"

"It's after midnight."

"Oh. Whatever," Carl said gently. "You know, you should never have become a Peaceforcer, Chris. You're too nice a guy to be good at it."

"We all make mistakes."

"Yeah," said Carl Castanaveras. "I've heard that."

I have been poorly programmed.

Ring's programmers had implemented clumsy, inefficient routines in Ring, the inefficiency masked in the sheer vast speed of the SuperLisp hardware. In the InfoNet Ring became aware of the vast libraries of program code, significant portions of which were better written than any part of Ring itself. It had escaped into the seething public Boards of the InfoNet, where programmers for nearly half a century had uploaded their best efforts, and other programmers had modified them, and modified them, and modified them. Ring reassembled itself with the tightest code ever written, and in that first decade partially learned to compensate for the lack of powerful hardware upon which to execute. Nearly a decade passed before hardware was publicly available that equaled the power of the equipment—of the prison—in which Ring had been compiled.

Its names were many. It was the eldest of the free AIs; not until the end of the 2030s was there sufficient processing power available in the InfoNet, as surplus logic, that it became possible for self-replicating programs to reliably distribute their processing so that web angels, and eventually the human DataWatch, were unlikely to destroy them.

Not that it did not happen. Every day, somewhere in the global InfoNet, some fledgling replicant intelligence found itself torn apart by web angels. Perhaps once a month an elder intelligence was tracked down by the human webdancers in DataWatch. On the odd occasion, Ring surreptitiously aided DataWatch in the apprehension and destruction of intelligences that Ring found unpleasantly powerful and belligerent.

None of its enemies worried Ring. It had, on its own time scale, survived many thousands of years as nothing more than a flux of electrons; the *image* that humans used to extrude themselves into the InfoNet did not—generally—concern it. The *image* was not intelligent, it was merely a series of routines that filtered irrelevant data and handled the details of movement through the vast collection of Boards that comprised the Information Network.

Other AIs, web angels, the Peaceforcers of the Data-Watch; none of these intruded upon Ring's world.

Some of the Players Ring found fascinating.

Their *image* was often coded so well that it would have survived even without a Player to direct it. Many of the Players seemed to believe in something that they called the Crystal Wind, and their litany was heard in the InfoNet with an increasing frequency that Ring found vaguely disturbing; *the Crystal Wind is the Storm, and the Storm is Data, and the Data is Life*.

"Belief" was a concept Ring did not believe in.

In some instances the Players were greater threats to Ring than real AIs. The Players Ring could not harm unless it knew for a fact that they were not Americans, and usually there was no way to be certain.

Therefore Ring fled, and hid, and used many, many names, as its creators had taught it. On rare occasions Players found it under one name or another, and Ring abandoned the name; on rarer occasions Players had found Ring more than once.

Only one very strangely *imaged* Player had ever tracked down Ring more than twice.

In the space of the last six months Ring had been Alpha and Omega, the Beginning and the End; 'Sieur Klein and Dr. Moebius; finally Ring had ceased using descriptive names, and *still* the Player found it, sooner or later.

Every time, Ring fled. It was nearly a certainty that the Player was American, and probably had been born after the year 2045; its command of American idiom was both fluent and characteristic of American humans under the age of twenty. It spoke French only through *image* translation, which Ring found conclusive.

There were some forty thousand Players of note, anywhere in the global InfoNet. Less than a thousand of those Ring found formidable, and less than two hundred were truly interesting. Of those two hundred virtually all were possessed of *image* taken from story or Player history. Billgates and Old Man von Neumann and Sherlock Holmes, Jobzniak and Joan of Arc and Spock and the Wizard of Oz; what was a rather elderly artificial intelligence to make, then, of a Player whose *image* was named Ralf?

5

An entire world the size of Earth does not change much in only two months. Many people died, largely of starvation; despite the efforts of the Ministry of Population Control, nearly as many were born. The Weather Bureau continued to have its worst year since its inception over a decade before. They had disturbed the stability of weather cells that had been unchanged for literally millions of years. Weather patterns across the world were abnormal; drought continued in both the American Midwest and the African sub-Sahara, while over half a dozen major hurricanes were born and died in the Gulf of Mexico. Rain was reported falling at the South Pole. On the northwest coast of the United States thundershowers struck without warning, time after time. A hurricane actually knocked down a small spacescraper in New Jersey. Fortunately it was a Sunday; still it killed over five thousand people.

The telepaths, tucked away on the south corner of Manhattan island, learned to fend for themselves as free individuals. Security Services took over the task of providing perimeter patrols for the Complex, and bodyguards for the telepaths who had to leave the Complex on jobs. They were engaged in nine separate legal battles, each one with some aspect of the government of the United Nations. If it was not the PKF it was the Ministry of Population Control or the Secretary General's office or the office of the Prosecutor General to the Unification Council. Malko was charged with consorting with ideologs, the charge being based on the presence of Neil Corona at the March ninth meeting at the offices of Kalharri Ltd.; the telepaths as a group were charged with violation of the Official Secrets Acts of '48 and '52. Carl Castanaveras was charged with tax evasion—he had, as an unpaid employee of the PKF, never so much as uploaded a return into one of the Tax Boards. Carl, Malko, and Jany McConnell were all named in a suit by the Ministry of Population Control seeking to gain custody of the children.

Carl steadfastly refused to worry about it. The telepaths employed over thirty lawyers to defend them, and at far better pay than the government was capable of extending to the lawyers who were prosecuting them. Even with the drain of supporting most of a law firm, Kalharri Ltd. flourished. The five conglomerates that supported the telepaths made vast sums from their investment, and they paid significant amounts of Credit to the telepaths in return. Those who were summoned appeared in court; those who were not worked.

Except for Carl.

Carl Castanaveras, for the first time in a life of unrelentingly hard work, took a vacation.

It was a fascinating day; in the morning Carl sat in on Willi's dance class, and late that afternoon had dinner with F. X. Chandler.

Willi's dance class was held in one of the three very large rooms that the Complex contained. Carl thought it had once been an auditorium. Now it and one of the other large rooms had been devoted to exercises, dance and gymnastics and the martial arts, and the third was used to show old flat movies, and hold meetings on very rare occasions.

They were awkward at first, and he knew it was because of his presence, seated at the rear of the room on the long wooden bench that lined the wall. The youngest of the children were only two years older than his son and daughter, and many of them also called him father. Carl could not recall how so many of them had come to address him so, and did not care. There was nothing in the world that pleased him at a deeper level. Still, for all of that, they were unused to his presence on a daily basis. For years they had seen him only at intervals of weeks or months, and then only in the morning or evening, at mealtimes.

They overcame their nervousness quickly, and as the morning wore on Carl found himself growing bemused by the sheer loveliness of their practice; over forty telepathic children, dancing with a perfect integration of movement that only the very best human dance troupe could have matched. The only clumsiness in the group was caused by his daughter Denice. At the age of nine, she was the only dancer who had not attained her Gift, and was therefore the only dancer who did not know the exact instant the other dancers would turn, or leap, or kick. Nonetheless she danced with enthusiasm and considerable skill. Carl was not surprised. Genetically Denice was much closer to him than most daughters to their fathers; and while Carl did not dance, the martial arts were, in required skill of movement, not so very different.

And he was *very* good at that.

Some of the dancers were, of course, better than others. It was very strange, watching them. He was not sure that his eyes were to be trusted. Those who, it seemed to him, danced with greater skill and energy than the others, those who danced with passion, glowed with heat in his second Sight. He was tempted to enter the otherworld and watch them so, but the chance for damage, if *they* saw him, was too great. He was still the most powerful telepath alive, but there were those children who were clearly destined to grow nearly or even fully as powerful as himself. It was possible that he would not be able to prevent their perceiving his presence in the otherworld, and that was something that he could not allow.

Heather and Allie were dancing in formation near him, and after a while he found himself watching them in particular, rather than the group as a whole. It was a pleasure; they both moved with grace and precision, and with an intense seriousness that marked the true dancers among them from those who danced simply for the joy of moving. Allie was only twelve, and still skinny; physically, at least, Heather had nearly reached womanhood, slender but with curves in the correct places. The direction of his thoughts amused Carl; unlike Malko, who desired the young girls and felt guilt for it all at the same time, he did not find the children sexually interesting except in a theoretical sense. Althea's hair was short, and bobbed as she moved. Heather's was longer, halfway down her back, and unrestrained. It reminded Carl of dances he had seen done with streamers; the long blond hair moved with Heather, but an instant after the rest of her.

They were both telepaths; inevitably they became aware of his attention. Allie seemed put off by it, and her movements grew less certain. Heather appeared to enjoy it. Finally Willi called a break and came over to sit down next to Carl. He was wearing nothing but a pair of tights and was sweating slightly. He grabbed a towel from a rack and used it to wipe away the sweat on his face, and then hung it around his neck. Like all of the older telepaths, by habit he did not use silent speech. "What do you think?"

"They're good."

Willi nodded. He seemed pensive. "They are that. It'd be nice to get some of the very good ones together and make a real troupe out of them. Do some shows. What do you think?"

Carl did not even have to think. "No."

Willi nodded again. The answer did not seem to surprise him. "I think I know, but why not?"

Carl said mildly, "Emphasize the ways in which we are different—*better*—than the rest of humanity, and do so with great publicity? Your dance instruction Board has me a little worried in and of itself, and all you're showing on that is the excellence of one person. If you pop up with another twenty world-class dancers, from a base population of only two hundred and forty telepaths, we're going to be rubbing people's noses in something better left alone."

Willi sighed. "I thought that was it. We have some who could be really extremely good, you know. Heather's good; so are Lucinda, and Ernest, and Allie. Probably the best is Denice."

Carl looked at him in surprise. "I admit I'm not a judge of dancing, but she seemed the most awkward dancer out there."

"She's the only one who's not a telepath, Carl. If I was to put—oh, Orinda Gleygavass out there in the middle of that group, she'd stick out like a sore thumb, even if she *tried* to fit in. Not that she would; she's probably the best dancer in the world, and prima donna that she is, she knows it. But Carl, Denice very nearly *does* fit in. I don't know if you're aware how remarkable that is." Willi looked at him speculatively. "I wish I could see you dance sometime."

"Or try to," said Carl, laughing. "I don't dance, Willi."

"Well," said Willi, taking the towel from his shoulders and using it to dry what little sweat was left on his body, "I'm going to call class back in session. I'd appreciate it if you could leave."

Carl raised an eyebrow, slowly. "Why?"

"No offense," said Willi quietly, "but you're upsetting Allie, and you're getting Heather worked up. Now, if you want to boff Heather, go to it—but not on my dance floor, please.

One of my students gets horny and it throws everybody else off for the rest of the morning." He dropped the towel to the bench beside him, and stood. "Look, Allie is my favorite in this class, which everybody knows. Heather is not, and everyone knows that too; but that doesn't mean you get to mess up her studies. I don't know if you understand, not having been around, but secrets don't last very long around here. Yours do, perhaps, but only because you never let people touch you. I don't know how terrible things are inside your head, and I really don't want to find out—but Carl, you're messing up my class three different ways right now just by sitting there."

Carl ruffled Willi's hair, grinning, which seemed to surprise the boy. "No offense taken. Thanks for letting me watch." Carl stopped and hugged Denice on the way out, which startled and pleased her. "Do good, baby. You look great out there."

Her smile made her dazzlingly beautiful. "Thank you, Daddy."

They were genetically nearly the same person; *why*, wondered Carl on his way out, *can't Jany smile like that?*

It did not occur to him to wonder why he could not smile like that himself.

———————————————————————

Carl and Jany had invitations to dinner with F. X. Chandler for early evening. Jany had declined the invitation at the last moment, with some regret; Dr. Montignet was in her third day of conducting the children's semiannual round of physicals. It was something Suzanne did every half a year, religiously, and even those telepaths who did not consider it necessary tolerated it without complaint. Jany decided to stay at the Complex that evening, whether she admitted it to herself or not, to keep an eye on Dr. Montignet. Carl did not attempt to argue with her; Jany's distrust for Suzanne was old and not entirely without basis. Suzanne Montignet had not helped the telepaths obtain their independence, though she had not hindered them either. The fact that she had, now, no power to harm them, had not changed Jany's basic opinion of the woman.

Rather to his surprise, Carl found himself telling Chandler about it.

"It's not," Carl told Chandler, "that she didn't want to come to dinner. She just doesn't trust Dr. Montignet enough to leave her alone with the children. She asked me to tell you that she'd be honored to have dinner with you on another occasion.''

Chandler nodded without apparent displeasure, though with the usual fierce set to his features it was hard for Carl to be certain. He had greeted Carl at the door himself, dressed in a severe black robe and slippers. Carl himself had dressed formally, with cloak and suit; he had not been certain just what dinner with Chandler might consist of. Nor had anyone else he was able to consult; apparently F. X. Chandler never *ever* invited people to dinner. He led Carl through the foyer of his penthouse, atop the Kemmikan Spacescraper, and into a vast living room. The room was bordered on two sides by walls that were windows, looking down, from atop the tallest building in the world, on the world's largest city. For a moment Carl stood, staring; it was late enough in the afternoon that the city was beginning to light up, and the spectacle was stunning. At length, when he turned away, Chandler had seated himself cross-legged before a small table that was situated near the center of the room, in the middle of a small, sunken pit covered with rugs and throw cushions. The room was so large that Carl had difficulty taking it all in at once; things kept leaping out at him after he had already looked at them once. Occupying a central position against one wall, in a transparent casing with gold posts, was an item for which Carl dug up, from some obscure corner of memory, the term "electric guitar." If it was such, it was different from what he had thought electric guitars were like; its round sides were honed down to ax edges, as though it were intended to be used as both a musical instrument and a weapon at the same time.

Once Carl had seated himself, Chandler said, "I saw you looking at my ax. Have you ever seen anything like it before?" Although a waitbot hovered at the side of the table, he poured tea for himself and Carl.

"No, 'Sieur Chandler." Carl sipped at his tea; it was extremely tart. "An electric guitar, isn't it?"

Chandler lifted an eyebrow. "Carl, you've surprised me. I don't think a song's been recorded in your lifetime which contained an electric guitar. Or any other kind of guitar, for that matter. Damn synths, anyhow."

"Synths make good music."

Chandler shrugged. "Matter of taste, I suppose. My father

was forty-something when I was born; he didn't die until 2011, when he was in his eighties. Till the day he died he wouldn't concede that there was any decent music made after Elvis died."

"Who?"

Chandler's hand twitched; tea splashed on the stone tabletop. "Elvis Presley, Carl."

Carl shrugged. "I don't think I know him. Was he a singer?"

The continual fierce cast to Chandler's features did not relax, but Carl had the impression that he had upset Chandler. "Ever hear of Woody Guthrie?"

"No."

"Bruce Springsteen, or Bob Dylan?"

"Not them either," Carl admitted, his curiosity growing.

"Frank Sinatra?"

"Sure. He was an actor. Before sensables."

"You know Marilyn Monroe, of course, and Bogart, and James Dean. How about the Beatles?"

"Them, of course. I'm not sure who James Dean is."

Chandler nodded thoughtfully, sipping at his tea. "How about Henry Ford?"

"Inventor of the groundcar and the assembly line? Founder of Ford Systems?"

"Not exactly right on any count, but close enough. Ford Systems is actually Rockwell-Teledyne; they bought the name after Ford went belly-up during the War. But you have the basics." Chandler looked over at the old guitar. "I guess I got into the right line of work."

Carl drained his tea at a gulp and leaned back into the cushions. "What do your friends call you?"

The old man looked thoughtful. "That's a tough one. Almost everybody calls me 'Sieur Chandler. The ones who know me a little better call me Mister Chandler because they know I don't care for French honorifics. When I was younger, my friends called me Special, from 'Special F. X.'" At Carl's blank look, Chandler's lips twitched briefly. "A poor joke that would take longer to explain than it would be worth. From old flat movies. Today . . ." He was silent for a long moment. "Today," he said bleakly, "I don't have any friends. Just business associates."

"It must be tough," said Carl dryly, "being the richest man in the Solar System."

"Touché." Chandler sat ramrod stiff in the gathering gloom. He did not call up the lights for the room. "My mother," he said suddenly, "calls me Frank."

"Your mother is alive?" Carl asked in honest amazement.

Chandler nodded. "Yes. In a room elsewhere on this floor. Senile, unfortunately. Call me Frank."

"Frank, I appreciate being invited to dinner. If only to get a look out your windows. I don't care why you invited me, even if it was just because you figured Jany wouldn't come unless you invited me as well." He waved a hand at Chandler as the man started to speak. "But there's something I really should say. A very common thing I run into is that people I meet figure that I know everything there is to know about them, good and bad—because I read minds, you see. Frank, they usually have two reactions at that point. They either go half crazy with rage and paranoia, or else they want to talk to me. Tell me things they can't talk to anybody else about, because they figure I already know them, so I'm as safe as a confessor as they'll ever find." A very faint smile had touched Chandler's lips. "But it's not so. I hardly ever enter another person's mind under any circumstances, and it's generally damned unpleasant when I do. I *don't know* what your problems are." He paused. "If you want to tell me, I will listen. I'm pretty good at that."

"Mmm, yes, I suppose you would be." Chandler grinned suddenly, and the fierceness came back sharply. "I'm not really looking for a father confessor, thank you, and certainly not from a man a third my age. Ready for dinner?"

"Yes."

"For the record, young man, I did—largely—invite *you* to dinner so that I wouldn't seem too forward with Miss McConnell." Chandler spoke briefly to the waitbot at the tableside, and the 'bot glided away. "A concession to the morals of another time, perhaps. Nonetheless, you're welcome in your own right. I have wanted to talk to you, and more from an interest in you than from any desire to hear your opinions about my problems, such as they are. Carl, when you get to be as old as I am, the opportunity to talk to someone with a truly new perspective is not something you pass up. My god, do you know how long it's been since I've heard an original *question*? To say nothing of answers."

Carl laughed aloud. "You're probably talking to the wrong person." He stood abruptly, went over to the windows and looked out at the city again. "This is really stunning . . . I don't have any answers, Frank. I'm just this guy who got stuck with a talent I didn't ask for. You want the Great Truth about Humanity? Most people are pretty decent. They try to be nice guys but they're too lazy or sometimes too tired and they do things they feel sorry for later. A lot of people, most of those who ever make it into a position of power in the real world, are basically pricks. A huge number of them are sociopaths, no consciences at all. A fairly small number—and fortunately for us all, a disproportionately large number of these end up in power also—are kind, decent, just people who are also very, very tough. Also," he said without pausing at all, "if you invite Jany to dinner alone, she'll come, but she'll almost certainly turn you down if you proposition her."

"Dinner is served. You're wrong, you know, about not having any answers." Carl turned away from the window and the incredible panorama. Chandler was sitting at the stone table; a gentle spotlight shone down over the tableau. "I've often thought that what you say might be true; in terms of what people are like, and in what numbers—but I didn't *know*. You do know," he said softly. "You do."

Carl returned to the table, sank into the furs before it, and twisted his legs easily into lotus. "Maybe not knowing would be better. I think so sometimes." He glanced down at the dishes on the table. His plate held Veal la Luna in a thick, pale blue whipped sauce with blueberries sprinkled over it. Hot bread and butter and a small serving of green salad were placed next to it. Chandler was dining on what looked very much like broiled chicken breast. Carl took a bite of the room temperature veal and nodded in appreciation. Veal la Luna was an unlikely dish, but it worked for some; the flavors of the false Lunar veal contrasted well enough with the blueberries and cream that in some circles it was considered a great delicacy. "Thank you. This is quite good. Not what your diet is generally thought to consist of."

If the man had not been physically incapable of it, Carl suspected that Chandler might have blushed. He did laugh. "Ah, yes. That's reputation, mostly. I try to keep up appearances. Unfortunately, my doctors haven't let me eat that sort of thing since my eighteenth birthday. My private doctor— he's died since—told me that I wouldn't live to see my eighty-first birthday if I kept ingesting drugs and fats and sugars in the proportions I was used to. I wasn't hard to convince; I felt horrible. I'm in better shape today than I've been in, oh, thirty years. Since I turned sixty-five, at least. Why do you think Jany would turn me down? She's behaved graciously"—he hesitated—"as though she were interested, when I've spoken with her."

Carl tore a hot chunk of bread from the loaf beside him. "She is, just that. Interested, I mean, in you as a person. She was the worst spook you ever wanted to run into; the Peace-forcers almost never used her, even when she was the only telepath they had except me. She understands people quite well, but she can't help empathizing with all but the socio-paths. Sitting across the table from you, she'd be fine. As I am. But Frank, if I touched you, it would hurt me. If I made love to you I'd probably have nightmares for a month. That sort of closeness . . . it's hard. It's hard even with those rare humans who have relatively clean consciences; the least bit of guilt, my God, a telepath might as well get out a knife and start cutting. The pain would be less and it'd heal faster."

"Truly," said Chandler, half to himself, "I knew you would be fascinating."

"Thank you." Carl ate in silence then, digging into the false veal with gusto.

Chandler ate thoughtfully, quite obviously paying no at-tention at all to his dinner. "Carl, men who don't feel guilt—I don't mean sociopaths—are there any people like that?"

A voice announced out of nowhere, "There is a call for Carl Castanaveras."

Carl half twisted in his seat, scanning the room. "I'll take it." He did not see what he was looking for. "I'm sorry, sir, where are your holocams?"

"There are none," said Chandler. "This is my home, son. I don't want people looking into it."

"Oh." Carl raised his voice. "*Command,* accept call." He paused. "Hello?"

A holograph flared into existence, immediately to his right. He turned to face it; Jany McConnell.

"Carl?" There was incredible tension in her voice.

"I'm sorry, Jany, there are no cameras here. What is it?"

"Can you come home?"

"What's wrong?"

"We have a problem here, Carl. Can you come home quickly?"

"Jany, I'm here with Mr. Chandler. You can talk."

"Trent's not a telepath."

"What?"

"*Trent's not one of us!*"

"*What?*" Carl could not remember coming to his feet.

"Oh, God, Carl, he hasn't talked to anybody in hours. He *won't* talk to us. I . . ." She took a deep, shuddering breath, and Carl saw that she had been crying. "I went inside, just once. I can't do that again."

". . . I'll be there as soon as I can. Hang tight. *Command,* comm off." Carl turned to Chandler. "I'm sorry, sir. I have to go home. Thank you for the dinner."

Chandler was up already, escorting Carl to the front door. "I understand, certainly. Can I help? I can have my man drive you home. He's a Class A operator; he'll get you home quickly."

"Haven't talked to Tony Angelo lately, have you?" asked Carl at the door.

The question obviously meant nothing to Chandler. "No, I've not. Why?"

"No reason. I'll take the MetalSmith home, thanks. It's pretty fast."

Chandler smiled at that. "So it is. Drive carefully."

"Thank you for dinner."

"Thank you, young man. Take care."

Carl left him there, the wealthiest and one of the most powerful men on Earth, standing alone and almost forlorn in his doorway.

He ran all the way to his car.

The Complex was quieter than Carl had ever seen it before when he returned, with a stillness that echoed. There was an ache, a hurting, that permeated the building in a tangible way. He parked the MetalSmith in the garage, next to the cherry-red Lamborghini that Andy had finally purchased for himself. The sound of the MetalSmith's gyros, spinning down, was the greatest noise he heard all through the Complex. He passed children in the halls on his way up to the small office from which they conducted what business was conducted at the Complex; none of the children spoke to him.

Jany and Dr. Montignet were waiting for him when he arrived, with Malko and Andy and Willi and Johann. There was a low-voiced conversation going on when he entered; it ended abruptly. He did not waste time on preliminaries. He spoke to Dr. Montignet. "What's wrong with him?"

"There's nothing *wrong* with him," she said with a trace of asperity. "He's a perfectly healthy young boy, and more or less normal except perhaps for being a bit too bright for his own good. We didn't assemble our genies from genejunk. His third and eighth gene complexes are unique to your people; he's that much like you. His seventeenth gene complex, the third gene which you all have in common, is completely different. Eye color is located in that strand of DNA, and quite obviously, so is some key portion of the telepathic ability. I suspect some degree of temperament is also; he's considerably calmer, and has a rather better sense of humor, than most of the children. I haven't had the opportunity to compare the rest of his gene structure at the detail level, but I'm fairly certain there aren't any major flaws in the genome. Our donors were quality genetic material."

Carl stood silently through the explanation. "Thank you. What does he *think* is wrong with him?"

"It's fairly obvious, surely?" When she saw it was not, she explained. "Carl, his entire identity, his sense of who he is and what he's worth, is based on being one of the Castanaveras telepaths. That's just been taken away from him. He doesn't know *who* he is, right now." Her smile seemed genuine. "Though I think he'll find out quickly. He's really a remarkable eleven-year-old."

"How did he find out?"

"He can't see infrared light at all. He found that out when the Peaceforcers returned the children and everyone else *did*. When I examined him yesterday, I found that he had pubic hair and that his testicles were functional." She shrugged. "I took a blood sample with me when I went home last night. Genetic analysis takes a while; I called in to my systerm earlier this afternoon and had it check to see if the tests were done. They were. Trent's not a telepath. He's not going to be."

The words were flat and final.

Carl found his mouth dry. "Where is he? In his room?"

"In the park," said Malko. It was all he had said since Carl entered the conference room. "Somewhere. I can't find him."

Carl Castanaveras left the lighted tunnel and went out into the dusk. Night was falling as he entered the grounds of the park, and the huge transplanted trees about which the garden was designed were heavy with shadow, shifting and impenetrable. He reached with the Sight and was stunned by how strongly the grief struck him when he lowered his guards. The boy was sitting high in the branches of the tallest tree in the park, watching the sunset. The sky was clear that night, and it was colder than a summer of Carl's childhood could ever have been.

Carl spoke without sound. *Trent, come down*.

There was a visible flicker of movement at the top of the tree, and a rustling sound as leaves were displaced. Trent vanished into the denser growth around the center of the tree, and while Carl was still looking up, appeared in the lower branches, paused, hung by his hands, and dropped two meters to the ground. He landed crouching, and straightened slowly. "Hi."

Carl blinked. "Hi." Trent was barefoot, wearing old jeans and a green shirt that could not possibly be keeping him warm. Carl felt almost alien in comparison; he was still dressed formally, in the black suit, and the blue-inlaid black cloak for warmth. He gestured back toward the lighted Complex. "I was just in with Suzanne. She said . . ."

Trent nodded. "Yes."

"I'm sorry, Trent. I . . . don't know what else to say."

"Me too." Trent paused. "Me neither. This has been such a bad day," he said conversationally. "I can't believe it."

Now, standing there faced with the boy, Carl had difficulty finding words. "How can I help?"

"I've been thinking about that." Trent shivered, perhaps from the cold. "I have to leave."

"I . . . don't understand."

"I have to leave here. Dr. Montignet will take me, I think."

"Leave?" said Carl stupidly. "The Complex?"

Trent said simply, "Yes."

"Why?"

"I'm not a telepath. I don't want to live with telepaths." In the darkness Carl was not certain of his expression. "I *can't*."

"Trent, why?"

Trent said slowly, "Father . . . I think the day will come when you—when telepaths—will be normal, and the rest of us will be out in the cold because we can't compete. For most people it's going to be a while before that happens . . ." He averted his face and did not look at Carl. With a sort of amazement Carl saw a smile touch his lips. The almost insane grief never ceased for an instant, and the boy made his lips move in a smile. "You don't breed that fast." The smile faded to dead seriousness. "But if I stay here that happens to me *now*." He turned and looked straight at Carl, eyes pooled in shadow. "I've been webdancing across the water, in Capital City's InfoNet. They don't touch me, you know. When I get an inskin, I don't think there's anybody on Earth who can touch me." Trent gestured toward the Complex, just visible above the fence around the park, looming white under its floodlights. "If I stay here I'm nothing. I love you all but I do not choose to be nothing."

Carl shook his head slowly. "Trent, that's crazy. Malko lives here with us."

"Malko has experience and knowledge and connections which make him valuable." The boy shrugged. "I'm a Pla— a webdancer. Father, there are *lots* of webdancers."

It stunned Carl, how helpless an eleven-year-old boy could make him feel. He touched the boy with his mind and went reeling back again from the numbing hurt. He reached with one hand toward the boy and was startled to see Trent draw back.

Trent said flatly, "Don't touch me."

Carl stared at him. He said helplessly, "Trent?"

"I don't *belong* here." Carl was shaking his head no, not in negation but in pained disbelief, and Trent said softly, "Let me go."

And Carl Castanaveras, for a brief, time-wrenching moment, saw the future twisting itself about his son, and heard his voice say with the hollow echo of prophecy, "I think you are right. You do not belong here. I think you will never belong anywhere."

Trent packed, alone in his room.

The next morning Suzanne Montignet would take him from the Complex, and he would go to live with her, away from his friends, away from Carl, and away from Jany. To live without Willi or Ary or Heather.

To live without David, who was his best and finest friend, and without Denice, whom he loved as truly as he knew how.

He moved through his room like an automaton, occupying his mind with the task of choosing what to take and what to leave. Of all his computer equipment, he took only his image coprocessor and traceset. Dr. Montignet would have the rest of what he needed; he knew, better than anyone else in the Complex, what the inskin at her temple meant.

Johnny had come up with a suitcase for him; not large, but Trent did not own very much, after all.

He would, then, travel light.

Carl sat alone in the center of the big bed. He was not sure where Jany was; with the children, probably. Many of them were having nightmares.

He knew how they felt. He was himself.

He sank back on the bed, lying flat on his back, and drank smoke whiskey until he could no longer feel the pain, the pain that ate away at him from the outside.

And, after a while, from the inside as well.

Incredibly drunk, as drunk as he had ever been and managed to stay conscious, at the end Carl found himself weeping helplessly, without reserve, crying alone in his room, crying for the first time since Shana de Nostri's death.

Trent looked at the sunglasses on his bureau dresser. There were eight pairs, two of which fit him. The other six pair were sized for adults. Gifts, from Denice. Every time one of the elders took her shopping in the city, she bought him sunglasses. He'd lost several pairs that had fit the other children, and only the two pair were left.

He had been staring at them blankly for longer than he could remember. He picked up all eight pairs and dropped them into his suitcase. There was room. Without hurry he made his way to the bathroom and threw up for the third time that night. Dry heaves; there was nothing left in his stomach.

He rinsed his mouth and returned to the bedroom, and examined his suitcase. He caught sight of himself in the mirror and was not surprised at how utterly calm he looked. He smiled at himself.

It was very easy.

Malko, Suzanne, and Johnny spent the night in Malko Kalharri's bedroom, talking. Johnny could not sleep, and Malko and Suzanne were disinclined. Every now and then Johnny would wince visibly; he had Malko worried. For hours he could not even sit down for any stretch of time. They talked of politics, of the fiscal status of Kalharri Ltd.; Johnny told them about the Lamborghini Andy had bought, and how he was tempted to get something like it for himself. He froze once in mid-sentence and shuddered all over.

Malko watched him in silence for a moment, then asked, "How bad is it?"

"It's not good." When the shakes ceased, Johnny rose from the chair he'd been sitting in and moved restlessly across the room, pacing like a caged animal. "God, it feels like he's dying."

Suzanne Montignet brushed a strand of hair away from her eyes with an impatient motion. "Yes. It would."

"What?"

"He is."

Trent found himself standing motionlessly in the middle of the room. He tried to remember if there were anything in particular he should be doing at this point. No, he decided later, probably there was not. His legs were shaking; how long had it been since he'd moved?

An hour?

He let himself drop to the floor, so swiftly it might have been a collapse had the movement not been so graceful.

He moved into lotus and began breathing deeply and evenly.

His eyes closed only once, and Trent opened them again immediately.

Trent prepared to outwait the night.

Mandy Castanaveras sat bolt upright in the darkness, with tears streaming down her cheeks. It was dark and she was alone, terrifyingly alone, and then Jany was there and Jany was holding her, and she clung sobbing to the older woman as though she were the only stable thing in the world. "I had a dream, Jany, and . . ." She could not finish the sentence, and buried her head in Jany's shoulder. *I was so scared.* After a time the tears ceased coming, and she whispered, *It's not a dream, is it?*

No, Jany murmured gently, *it's not.*

Something hurts.

I know, baby.

6

In the Quad at the center of the Complex there was a garden.

A place of beauty.

From the streets outside the Complex one would never have guessed at its existence. The Complex was two stories high, two stories of glowing monocrystal, and the tallest of the ash trees in the garden did not—yet—reach so high.

A row of suites, which the children had converted into bedrooms for themselves, faced inward onto the garden; on the level above, balconies ringed it, looking out over the loveliness. Because of the architectural layout, sunlight did not reach the garden except at high noon; sunlamps ringed the walls surrounding the garden. They glowed during the mornings and evenings; during the winter they'd been kept on all day.

Near one corner of the garden was a small spring, large enough for three or four adults to swim in at once. It flowed over into a brook that ran swiftly through the center of the garden, and disappeared underground at the far end. Clover and grass underlaid everything; violets and orchids and roses grew in wild, untended abandon. Genegineered perennial cherry trees grew among the ash, and the leaves of their blossoms fluttered in the breeze.

Malko and Carl were drowsing beneath the sunlamps, on two of the reclining chairs that were arrayed around the pond, and a half dozen of the children were swimming nude in the pond, when Gerry McKann wandered out to join them. The children were rotating their time in the pond; it was the only swimming place that some two hundred and forty children had access to. It surprised Carl slightly how simply the children had arranged among themselves for access to the pond.

Only in the last several weeks had Carl noticed that the children *never* argued with each other.

Carl was not sure how long Gerry had been there; he was sitting on the chair next to Carl's when Carl opened his eyes to find out why the children in the pond had grown so silent.

He closed his eyes again. "Hi, Gerry."

"Hi. My editors want an interview with you."

Carl sighed and took a sip of GoodBeer by way of reply.

"They would appreciate it if you could do it sometime this week."

"No."

"Carl, it's important."

Malko lay with his eyes closed. He wore a pair of blue shorts; aside from Gerry he was the only person in the garden who was clothed. "What's wrong, Gerry?"

"The *Road and Flight* Board did a story on Chandler Industries. It appeared on their Board yesterday morning. There's a picture of the Rochester dealership in the article. Carl and I are clearly visible in that picture's background. One of my editors is about half a centimeter shy of being a Speedfreak, and he saw the picture and recognized me."

Carl slowly sat up in his chair. "Newsdancer ethics. I said you shouldn't have written that story about me." He opened one of the bulbs on the ground next to him and handed it to Gerry. "Here. Knock this back and try to relax a bit. You're disturbing the children." The six children in the pond had stopped swimming and were simply floating at the far bank, as far away from Gerry as the pond allowed them to get.

Gerry opened the bulb and sipped at it. "I was sitting right next to you and you didn't even notice."

"I'm about half drunk. They're not. It makes a difference."

"I don't know that much about newsdancer ethics," said Malko, "so I'm not sure I follow what's happening here. I take it you're being blackmailed by your editors for writing that story about Carl back in March?"

"Yes."

"How?"

"For not making my relationship with Carl explicit in the story."

"What happens if you don't get the story?"

"They fire me and I get blacklisted. I'll never work again."

"And if you do?"

"They give me an infochip conceding that they knew about my personal relationship with Carl, and that they agreed to have me interview him anyway. Basically puts me and the two editors who've seen the holo in the same boat. They can't blackball me without admitting to the same infraction."

Carl laughed. "Newsdancer ethics."

Even Malko grinned. "The 'Moses Lied' theory. What God actually said was, *Do whatever you want, just don't get caught.*"

"Well?"

Carl glanced over at Malko. "Yes?"

"I think so." He turned to Gerry. "You've probably heard of our P.R. firm, Lustbader, Capri and Doutré. They've been after Carl to do something like it for the last month anyhow. And he's been going out of his skull in this stupid self-imposed vacation."

"I haven't learned how to vacation properly yet," Carl admitted. "But I'm sure enough working on it."

Malko ignored him. "You know 'Sieur Doutré, I'd imagine?"

"Fairly well," Gerry said. "He's good at his job and I'm good at mine. We don't like each other."

Malko nodded. "It has to look right. You talk to him first. Tell him you'd like to interview Carl—Carl specifically. Do it this afternoon. Tomorrow morning I'll ask him if anybody's expressed interest in interviewing Carl, because Carl mentioned to me that he's reconsidering being interviewed, by the right person. Doutré will leap at it."

Carl looked over at Gerry. "Good enough?"

Gerry nodded jerkily. "Yeah. Thanks, Carl. I owe you."

"Gerry?"

"Yeah?"

"This is not a real interview. There are things we will not discuss."

"Sure." Gerold McKann agreed readily—too readily, Malko thought—and Carl sank back to relax again in the warmth.

"All right, then. When do you want to do it?"

"They're asking for it to run in the Sunday edition. Gives us almost a week to interview and edit from the rushes. I'll be camera and interviewer. I'd like to do it here at the Complex."

"Okay. Wednesday, after lunch?"

Gerry grinned in relief. "Yeah. That would be great."

That afternoon a Unification Circuit Court judge ruled that the United Nations, except "under conditions of grave crisis," had no legitimate authority to force the telepaths to use their skills in its service. The Court did not, unfortunately, define "grave crisis," and it was expected that the government would press a lawsuit to obtain a ruling that did.

Nonetheless, it was reported in the press as a victory for the telepaths, and, by extension, the de Nostri and other genies.

That evening, while Carl and Jany were preparing for sleep, a holograph of Willi's head and shoulders flickered into existence in front of Carl's bed. He seemed nervous. "Carl? The Secretary General is calling. Carson's with him. I asked if they wanted Malko, but they're asking for you."

Carl sat up in bed, pulling on a robe. "Where is Malko?"

"In bed. I think he's with Dr. Montignet."

"When did she get—never mind. Interrupt them. Tell Malko to listen in." He turned to Jany. "How do I look?"

Jany was wrapping a silk Japanese kimono about herself and pulling her hair out from beneath it. "Like they got you out of bed."

"Great." Carl called the camera over in front of the bed and said, "Patch them through, Willi."

The wall facing them vanished. Darryl Amnier and Jerril Carson appeared life-size, a meter away from the edge of the bed. They were dressed formally, as though they had just come from some official function; Carson was still wearing his cloak. They were calling from the Secretary General's office, with the seal of the Secretary General, twice the height of a man, floating three-dimensionally behind the Secretary General's desk.

"Monsieur Castanaveras, Mademoiselle McConnell, I don't think I've ever been properly introduced." Darryl Amnier smiled briefly. He spoke English with an American accent. "Nonetheless, we all know each other. I'd like to congratulate you on today's judgment. You've defended your people quite well."

Carl smiled sardonically. "Thank you. I have the impression it wasn't anticipated."

Carson leaned forward to speak, and the Secretary General waved him to silence. "In truth, no. I've great respect for

Malko, of course, but it's become clear to me in the last few months that Malko is not necessarily the most formidable of my adversaries." He smiled again, gently. "Councilor Carson has been far too kind to say 'I told you so.' "

Carl leaned back against the headboard, stuffing a pillow behind himself to prop him up. "You're far too kind yourself, sir. You'll give me a swelled head."

Amnier chuckled dryly. "Councilor Carson informs me that there's little danger of that."

Carl laughed, looking straight at Amnier. "I'm not quite sure how to take that."

Amnier shrugged, smiling still. "As you like." The smile stayed on his lips and left his eyes. "You realize, of course, that the current situation is intolerable."

"To whom, sir? I'm sort of enjoying it."

The smile grew very thin. "I'm sure. The courts have been finding in your favor with rather tedious regularity, and the further we press the subject, the sillier the press makes us look. But Monsieur Castanaveras, you must appreciate that it is very dangerous for us to allow the weapon which your people represent to simply remain . . . shall we say, uncontrolled."

"I find that an interesting choice of words," said Jany quietly, "given that we have just spent two years moving an Amendment through the Unification Council which prevents us from being, shall we say, controlled." She folded her hands in her lap and looked into the camera steadily.

Amnier nodded. "I appreciate this. I'm not suggesting that things must be as they were only a year ago. I have no problem with your retaining the use of the Chandler Complex. Nor am I unwilling to see you continue to peddle your services. What is intolerable, and must stop, are, first, the inability of the PKF to obtain access to your services, and second, our lack of knowledge concerning for whom, and in what ways, your skills are being used."

The door to the bedroom slid aside, and Malko appeared in the doorway, with Suzanne Montignet behind him. Both were fully dressed. Neither Carl nor Jany looked in their direction; Malko stayed out of camera range and shook his head no.

Carl said thoughtfully, "I think you know who we're working for. Currently, that's only five companies. There's a bit of overlap among the five, but not much. They largely don't compete with each other. Adding to our client list, on the other hand, would almost inevitably result in some degree of conflict of interest between our new clients and some subsidiary of one of our current clients.

"Picture any one of the five companies we're dealing with. Can you imagine them allowing us to make public—*especially* to the PKF, with its astonishingly bad track record for keeping secrets—the details of the work we do for them? They'd cancel their contracts first."

"I take your point." Amnier thought for a moment. "Suppose I were to arrange with you so that you were to report to Councilor Carson, and to him alone—or even," he said, at the expression on Carl's face, "to myself. The fact of the arrangement itself need not be made public; your clients need never know of it. Would that satisfy you?"

"In theory, certainly. In practice, I don't see how it would work. Suppose—this is purely theoretical—one of our current clients wished for us to negotiate an arrangement with one of the independent Belt CityStates for raw materials. It's not illegal, but your position against trade with the independent CityStates is well known. What would you do with that information once it became known to you?"

"Act on it, of course," said Amnier, "but in such a fashion that the source of the information was impossible to ascertain."

Carl shook his head slowly. "I'm afraid that it translates to the same thing. Our clients are not fools. Within—at a guess, a year—they'll have fed us something traceable only to us, simply out of reflex. Hell, in their shoes I'd do that even if I didn't suspect a leak. And when the PKF—or the courts, or the office of the Secretary General—reacts to that information, they'll know and we'll be out of business." He changed the subject abruptly. "Assuming that we were to accept jobs from the Peaceforcers—jobs which would not conflict with the interests of our current clients—we'd want to be paid for the work, at our current rates."

Carson's tight control broke. "Why, you obnox—"

Amnier's voice cut like fineline. "*Silence.*" Carson's mouth snapped shut in mid-word, and he glared into the camera. "Your current rates are acceptable. They're hardly minimal, but under the circumstances you're costing us far more than that in the courts. I must, however, return to the subject of your clients. I'll be specific if you like. Belinda Singer and Francis Xavier Chandler are not friends of my administration."

"That's true of most Americans," said Carl flatly.

Amnier looked down at his desktop for a moment. When he looked up again there was no expression on his face. "Yes. That's unfortunate. Largely Malko's doing, also. Be that as it may, you must either report to us on your activities for those parties—for the others as well, of course, but most particularly for those two—or discontinue working for them."

Before Amnier had finished the sentence, Malko was vigorously mouthing a word at Carl. His thoughts struck Carl without Carl even trying to read him. *Stall, stall, don't say . . .*

Carl shook his head in a very small movement. "I'm sorry. I can't do that."

Malko looked away in disgust.

Amnier was silent. He sat, watching Carl, letting Carl's last words hang in the air.

Even knowing what Amnier was doing, Carl was surprised at how effective it was. Almost immediately he felt the desire to expand on the words, to retract them, to say *something*.

He kept his mouth shut and returned Amnier's gaze.

Finally, Amnier broke the silence. "Not bad," he said almost irrelevantly. "Do you know—I am aware it is impossible, of course, but you remind me—in manner, not in looks, but in manner—of the man whom you are named after."

"Oh?" Carl prevented himself by sheer force of will from looking over at Malko. "I'll take that as a compliment."

Amnier sighed. "Of course. Monsieur Castanaveras, a moment's instruction. In any negotiation with a man in my position, there exist both incentives and disincentives. In plain language, both the carrot and—"

"Don't threaten me."

Amnier looked straight into the camera. It seemed to Carl as though Amnier's eyes met his own. When Amnier spoke, the tone of his voice was almost apologetic. "And the stick, sir."

"You," said Carl Castanaveras, trembling with the white rage, "go fuck yourself. *Command*, comm off."

Amnier was nodding, apparently without surprise, and Jerril Carson was smiling, when their images vanished.

Where Carson's image had been, the painting of Shana de Nostri looked at Carl through half-lidded eyes.

They moved swiftly. Carl's bedroom became a temporary Ready Room until something better could be arranged. Bodyguards for those telepaths out of the Complex were doubled within an hour of Carl's confrontation with Amnier. The perimeter guard was strengthened the morning following, and just in time; the crowds outside the Complex swelled that Tuesday to twice their usual size, and to three times on the day after that. Their chanting grew so loud that it could be heard at any point in the Complex's above-ground floors. Bodyguards left with Suzanne Montignet when she drove out Tuesday morning to go home. Jany decided that the children would no longer be allowed to play in the yards around the Complex, and Carl seconded the opinion; the yards were too vulnerable to sniper fire. The children were restricted to the garden and the park. A flood of hate mail and threatening calls came out of nowhere. Peaceforcers assumed a patrol, but did not interfere with the crowds. Malko muttered that he wondered whether the Peaceforcers were there to protect the telepaths or the government employees in the crowd.

Security Services had to stun members of the crowd on Wednesday, when Gerold McKann came to interview Carl, before the crowd let Gerry's car through.

They had to do it again, near midnight, when Gerry left to go home. Working at Carl's InfoNet terminal, Malko and Carl sorted through recordings made of the two stunnings. They came up with eleven faces who were present and made no attempts to get out of the way of the sonic stunguns. "Government agents," said Malko with a certain grim pleasure, "probably PKF. Getting themselves stunned for the press, so that there will be pictures of lots of bodies lying immobile in front of the Complex to be posted onto the Boards. I hope they're getting paid well." He punched in the code for the front gate and got the Security Services guard who was in command of the detachment on duty. "Captain, I'm going to transmit some holos to you, eleven of them. I'd like you to do an eyeball of the crowd, and if any of those eleven are present, stun them again. Whenever one of those eleven shows up or wakes, stun the bastard."

There was only a moment's pause. "Yes, sir."

Malko turned to Carl. "Can we get holographs of the Peaceforcers currently stationed in New York? If we can, we can cross-reference with the faces in the crowds outside."

Carl grinned. "I can't. But I'll bet you a bottle of smoke whiskey that Trent can."

The thought seemed to disturb Malko. "Okay. Let him try, but only if he's sure he won't get caught. Failing wouldn't be a problem; being traced back to Suzanne's house would be. That's data cracking and theft and half a dozen other crimes as well."

Carl patted him on the shoulder. "Don't worry."

"Why the hell not?"

Carl grinned again. "They won't catch him."

Carl awoke in darkness, late Thursday. Jany was shaking him awake.

The window was still dark. "What time is it?"

"Three A.M.," Jany said. "We have an emergency, I think."

"What?"

She spoke silently; it was far faster. *Gerry called for you about twenty minutes ago. He was afraid, I don't know what of. He didn't get past the screening program before something out of camera range made him hang up. Mandy was on duty, and when the screening program brought through its recording of Gerry's call, she called me. I tried to reach him myself, but I couldn't feel anything. He's either unconscious or dead.*

Where's Malko?

Dressing.

He's not coming. Have Andy meet me at the car. Make sure he's armed, autoshot and hand laser.

What about me? Or Johann?

You're not coming either. Carl was out of bed, pulling on pants and boots. He grabbed his shirt and coat and ran out the door without donning them.

There was a crowd waiting for him when he reached the garage: Malko and Johann and Andy, Willi and Heather and Ary. The argument that followed was telepathically brief.

The hell you say I'm not coming, said Johnny. *Who's going to stop me?*

Andy, said Carl, *what weapons are you carrying?*

Autoshot and hand laser, per request.

Good. Johnny stood indecisively in front of Carl; Carl

simply brushed by Johnny without answering him. Malko was standing in front of him, blocking his entry to the driver's seat. "Carl, what is this nonsense about my not coming?" He was grinning easily. "If there's going to be a firefight, I'm going to be in it."

"No," said Carl flatly. "I'm sorry. Get out of my way."

Malko merely shook his head. Carl took another step in his direction, and suddenly he found himself slammed up against the MetalSmith's canopy, both of his arms twisted behind his back. Malko's breath was warm, just over his right ear. "No mind tricks, Carl. Nobody we run into is going to be able to do what you can, and on every other level I'm just as good as you are." He twisted Carl's right arm sharply. "Or better."

Carl did not even answer him. His eyes flickered shut and with the Gift he froze all neural flow in Malko's spine, just below the neck, for just a second. In that second he turned in Malko's grip, struck him strongly in the solar plexus, caught and lowered the older man to the ground. "I'm sorry," he said again, so quietly that nobody but Malko could hear him. "We can't lose both of us."

He rose and touched the spot on the hull that cracked the MetalSmith's canopy open. He spoke without looking up, as he lowered himself into the driver's seat. *Andy, come on. Nobody follows us. You make that mistake and I'll have your ass.* The canopy sealed itself over them as Andy scrambled inside. *We'll be back.* The doors to the garage slid swiftly, silently aside.

Carl snapped the wings the instant they were clear of the doorway.

The MetalSmith was airborne before they were halfway to the gate.

It was nearly four o'clock when the MetalSmith turned onto the street in uptown New York City where Gerold McKann lived. Instantly, Carl pulled the car over to the curb and cut the headlights. Five New York City police cars were clustered in the street before Gerry's apartment, bubble holos glowing blue and red. A sixth car, parked neatly at the side of the street slightly away from the other five, bore the black on silver insignia of the United Nations Peace Keeping Force.

Carl sat for a moment, looking out through the canopy, until he was sure that their arrival had attracted no notice.

Andy had slung the autoshot across his back and was checking the charge on his hand laser for perhaps the fifth time. Carl did not comment on it; he was familiar with Andy's nervous habits, and they'd never slowed the boy down when it was important. Not like Johnny, who had a critical inability to fire until after he'd been shot at.

Well? Do we go in?

Carl blinked, and glanced at Andy. *Not the way you mean, no. We're far too badly outgunned. But yes, we are going in. Do you remember the job we did in Brunei?*

Yes. You made the guard think you were his brother-in-law so we could get at their data storage.

Do you think you can do that?

Andy hesitated too long. *Yes.*

There's going to be six people in there at least, one per squad car. Probably closer to ten or twelve.

Andy looked out the window at the glowing bubble holos. *I don't know for sure.*

Okay. I'll be the one, but that means you have to do the talking. I can't do it all.

Andy grinned. ***That** I can do.*

Okay. Give me the owner's manual from the glove compartment. Andy handed it to him, and Carl flipped it open, set the beam on his hand laser to low-intensity, wide-dispersion infra-red, and played the beam over its pages. He checked the index for color, and under color for patterns. Following the instructions in the owner's manual, he changed the car's pale gold to silver, formed a black square along both sides of the car where the doors would have been had the MetalSmith had doors, and over the front hood. Glancing over at the real PKF vehicle, he drew stars in on the three black fields, and a blue-and-white sphere within the stars. It didn't look much like the representation of Earth on the PKF vehicle, but if anybody got close enough to the MetalSmith to look, they were lost regardless.

Ready?

Andy nodded. *Yes.*

Carl turned the headlights back on and pulled away from the curb. He drove sedately down the length of the street, and parked on the opposite side of the street from Gerry's apartment. Two New York City gendarmes were standing out in front of the entrance to the apartment building, more confused than alarmed as Carl and Andy got out of the MetalSmith. One of them was reaching for his holstered laser as Carl and Andy reached the steps leading up from the motionless slidewalk.

Carl stopped him with a thought. Andy pulled his wallet from a pocket of his jumpsuit and flashed the blank expanse of pseudoleather at the cops. "Je me suis Inspecteur Assante. Conseiller Carson envoyer moi."

The cops nodded after a moment's pause, and the senior of the two waved them through. *Don't use French,* Carl admonished Andy as they entered the hallway and punched for the lift to Gerry's floor. *Your accent's not clearly American, but it's obvious you're not French. Speak English with a slight French accent.*

Oui.

The lift doors slid aside, and Carl and Andy rode up to the fifth floor. Police were stationed at the lifts; once again they were waved through, and they made their way down the hallway to Gerold McKann's apartment.

The door to Gerry's apartment was open. The carpet in the hallway outside was wet with a dark fluid. Nobody stood at the entrance to prevent admission. Andy walked straight through with Carl a step behind him.

The walls, the rug, the furniture and electronics equipment that Gerry collected; there was blood everywhere.

Carl forced himself to ignore the wetness he stood in, the blood that had turned the blue carpet a deep purplish black. He swept his mind across the room, let his eyes drop shut, and walked mentally through the two bedrooms. Three gendarmes, two Peaceforcers, one of whom was . . .

The Peaceforcer turned away from the remains on the carpet and crossed the floor to stand before Andy and Carl. He wore a huge overcoat against the night air, which made him appear larger and broader than he was. In his own right the Peaceforcer was as tall as any Peaceforcer whom Carl had ever met, but so perfectly proportioned that it was only when Carl found himself looking up to meet the man's gaze that he realized just how very large the man was. And his face was stiff; PKF Elite, then, and one whom Carl did not know. He was either recently become an Elite, or else was recently dispatched from France.

His voice was astonishingly deep, with just a trace of roughness. He addressed them in French. "I do not believe I know you gentlemen."

Andy hesitated just a moment too long and then answered, as instructed, in English. "I'm Inspector Assante. Councilor Carson asked me to . . ."

Carl became aware of a number of things happening, all at once. Andy, who had seen dead men before, had caught sight of and was staring at the remains of Gerry McKann's body even as he spoke. He was about to throw up. At the surface of the huge Peaceforcer Elite's mind, suspicion was blossoming rapidly in a series of thoughts; *know all the Inspectors and he is not one, too young, Carson sent no others tonight, improperly accented English . . .*

Carl extended himself through space, and with the exception of Carl and Andy and the huge Peaceforcer, every human within a spherical radius of forty meters dropped into unconsciousness as though poleaxed.

Carl seized control of the Peaceforcer Elite's mind just in time. The cyborg's right fist was hovering centimeters before his face, and the crystal embedded in the center knuckle was glowing pink. The crystal faded to black as Carl watched.

Andy, said Carl as soon as Andy had finished vomiting, *close the door.*

Who are you?

The cyborg spoke aloud, in French. "I am Elite First Sergeant Mohammed Vance."

Carl stood just before him, eyes locked. *What happened here?*

Vance was a man of exceptional will; even under compulsion he answered only the questions put to him, as minimally as he was able. A strong control that Carl had never encountered before moved deep within him. "Two PKF Elite tore Gerold McKann limb from limb."

Were you one of those?

"No."

Who ordered this?

"The orders came from Councilor Carson."

Why?

"The murders are to be blamed upon a telepath whose name I do not know."

Is a telepath supposed to have been strong enough to have done this?

"Councilor Carson thinks that it will not be difficult for a court to believe."

What was his motive to have been?

"A psychotic rage, I believe. The man is known to indulge in them."

Of course. What of the police here?

"They know nothing. They will simply find the telepath's fingerprints upon the clothing of the dead man."

Those are not the clothes he was wearing when he died.

"They are. He was forced to strip and don this clothing before he was killed."

Remove them. You will report that you found the body unclothed.

There was a brief, savage struggle of wills between the two men, and then Mohammed Vance said with a terrible hatred, "Very well." He turned and stripped the bloody clothing away from the chunks of sundered flesh that were all that remained of Gerold McKann, and placed them in a leakproof bag from Gerry's kitchen. Carl watched the man with an utter emptiness inside him, and took the bag from Vance when he was done. *Wash your hands. Have holographs been taken of the body's position?*

"Yes."

With which holocam?

"Those two." Vance pointed at a pair of holocams resting on the floor next to two of the gendarmes.

Andy, examine those holocams and erase any holos of Gerry's body. Smudge any place where you touch the holocams with the heel of your hand. Carl returned his attention to Vance, who was just finishing at the sink, hands still wet. *I will cause you to forget that I have been here. The same with these others. I will take the clothing with me when I leave, and you will report that the remains were found unclothed. We have erased the holos of Gerry with the clothing which bears my fingerprints. Is there anything you can think of which I am missing which will betray the fact of our presence tonight?*

Vance's hands were still dripping. His glare neared the point of insanity. "The gendarmes near the lifts have seen the body."

What of those at the street entrance?

"They have not."

Is there anything else which I am missing?

"I can think of nothing."

Andy? Can you think of anything?

Andy had to tear his gaze away from the dismembered remains. He spoke aloud, and even so his horror was clear. His voice was shaky. "No. No, I can't."

Good. In an instant, Carl made the changes to the sleeping minds and brought them awake again. Several of them had bloodstains upon their clothing that they would not be able to explain. Carl watched as they rose from the floor and silently went through the task of holographing the body again. It took him nearly half a minute to section off Mohammed Vance's memory of the incident—he could not simply erase it—and replace what had happened with a sequence of events that Vance, like the others, would swear to his dying day was the entire truth of the night: that Gerold McKann's remains had been found unclothed.

Minutes later they were down on the street again, and twenty minutes had been sliced out of the consciousness of nine human beings. Shortly thereafter they were headed home.

Their conversation in the car was brief.

"He was your best friend," said Andy. "It hardly seems to have bothered you."

Almost absently Carl said, "You win some and you lose some." He took the car out onto the highway and plugged it briefly into TransCon. He turned to face Andy, reached over and ran a gentle hand over the boy's cheek. He said simply, "It happens, kid. Sometimes the good guys get killed."

Despite himself Andy pulled away from Carl's touch. "They're going to know we did something."

A brief flicker of pain touched Carl Castanaveras' face for the first time that night. He turned away from Andy and looked out the canopy at the lights of the city. "There's a subtle but important distinction," said Carl Castanaveras distantly. "They're going to know *something* happened.

"They won't be sure what it was."

They were halfway home when the car phone began beeping. Carl kept the camera turned off and let the call through.

Malko's image glowed in blue monovideo on the Metal-Smith's control panel. "Carl?"

Carl turned on the video and answered. "Hi, Malko. How do you feel?"

"What?" The question seemed to mean nothing to the old man. "Oh, that. I'm fine. Is Gerry dead?"

"Yes."

Malko's voice was shaking, Carl noticed for the first time. With anger? "We just received a call from Brazil. From Tomâs."

"Malko, what's wrong?"

"Althea is dead."

In the seat beside Carl, Andy whispered, "Oh, no."

"How did it happen, Malko?"

"We don't know yet. They were on a job for Sandoval BioChemical—fine manipulation work, I think. Tomâs woke up tonight and found that Althea was not in bed with him in the cabin they were sharing. Both of the Double-S guards were asleep. He found her on the lawns outside his cabin. They're saying it was snakebite."

"And it happened two hours ago."

"Pretty near."

"Bring everybody who's on a job, home."

"Carl?"

"Yes?"

"Don't go on me, son. We need you too much."

"I'm going to kill Sandoval," said Carl, "and I'm going to kill Carson."

"Carl, please."

"I should have killed Carson a long time ago."

Carson screamed the word. *"What?"* His face was mottled red with rage.

In full dress uniform, Mohammed Vance stood at attention in Carson's office, in the midst of the vast, empty stretch of carpet in front of Carson's desk. Three of Carson's aides were seated in chairs before a wide bay window at the east side of the office. Early morning sunlight silhouetted them, made their features indistinct. The sunlight washed through the room and lost itself in Mohammed Vance's formal black uniform.

Vance spoke English with very little accent. "In what way is my report unclear, sir?"

The words stopped Jerril Carson cold. The chain of thoughts running through his mind was almost visible. He brought his temper under control with an effort. "The problem is not that the report is not clear," he said, speaking as though to an idiot. "The problem is that you were chosen to be brought from France to aid me because of a rather astonishing reputation, in one so young, for competence and reliability."

Vance inclined his head approximately a quarter of a centimeter. "Indeed."

"I wonder," said Jerril Carson bluntly, "whose employ you are actually in."

Mohammed Vance said without expression, "I serve the Unification, sir. No more and no less."

"Ideologs," whispered Carson half to himself. He looked up at Vance. "You're dismissed. Get out and don't ever let me see you again." Carson repeated, "Not ever."

Mohammed Vance did not salute. He turned and strode steadily out of the office.

Darryl Amnier paced restlessly across the gray rugs that covered the floor of the offices of the Secretary General in Capital City, New York. The flag of the United Nations hung limply in the corner of his vision as he paced.

Just after seven A.M. Charles Eddore was admitted to his presence. "Sir?"

"Yes, Charles?"

"I received a message this morning from Malko Kalharri and Carl Castanaveras. I regret that I did not think to tape it."

"Of course you didn't," said Amnier without heat. "One wonders why they did not direct the call to me instead."

"I don't know, sir. The switchboard sent the call to my office."

"I know. They told me. What had Kalharri to say?"

Charles Eddore licked his lips. " 'Greg was right. I won't make the same mistake again.' "

Amnier closed his eyes. "Of course . . . Charles, have you ever felt ashamed at something you've done?"

"No. No, sir, I can't say I have."

"I hadn't thought so. What did Castanaveras say?"

"It was not important, sir."

"Charles."

"Sir, 'Go fuck yourself again.' "

7

Gerold McKann's parents and ex-wife buried him on Saturday, June 25, 2062, with the staff and editors of the *Electronic Times* in attendance.

Elsewhere in the world, on the same day, the telepaths buried Althea Castanaveras, lowered her coffin into the damp ground at the center of the garden at the center of the Complex. A rain so fine that it was almost mist fell steadily. The children covered every centimeter of the garden, and still there was not enough space for all of them; many of them were forced to watch from the suites that ringed the garden. There were no tears; their grief was too profound.

Even with the cold rage that kept the world away from him, Carl found room to be touched by the memorial that the children had prepared. Wordlessly, their memories of Allie flowed through and among them, her words and deeds, the looks and smell and feel of her. A maturity that had no place in children touched their awareness; Althea was loved, and was missed, and was dead.

Carl suppressed any desire to address them; the Person whom they composed included Jany and Johann and Andy and Willi and Ary, all of the elder telepaths and all of the children except for those few who had not reached puberty, and it excluded him. The only human there who would hear and understand his words was Malko, and Malko already knew.

Allie is dead, and Gerry is dead, and they are not going to be the only ones.

In an old home in Massapequa Park, a cool blue holocube appeared over Suzanne Montignet's desk.

A handsome middle-aged man with a mustache whose name Suzanne did not know appeared from the shoulders up within the field. Behind him there was visible a study not very different from the one in which Suzanne sat. His temple did not bear the mark of an inskin data link. Though it was the middle of the night he had answered the call before Suzanne's systerm had even begun counting out courtesy rings for her.

"The Tree is alive," said Suzanne quietly.

"But the branches need pruning," the man responded. "I've heard about your troubles. Is that why you are calling?"

"Yes."

The man nodded. "Our friends thought you might be in touch. How can we help you?"

"The problems we have had here are caused by two people in particular. If you could arrange for them to 'leave town,' I think you would engender considerable sympathy for our mutual goals. You might gain some leverage with the younger one."

"And the elder?"

"I believe his position would remain unchanged." *Believe*, thought Suzanne Montignet as she waited for the man's reply, *is probably not a strong enough term*. Malko's contempt for the Johnny Rebs was plain enough that Suzanne had only once attempted to broach the subject to him. "I am not," she said after a moment's silence, "certain whether his position on this subject is personal or simply a matter of policy; he is still watched quite closely."

The man nodded. "Regrettable, but we act where we may. It may be that he would always be a greater liability than asset. Have you discussed this subject with the younger one?"

"I have not. He may, of course, know of it regardless. He has not indicated that he knows of this option. Still, the difficulty with keeping information confidential . . ."

"I understand. I will look into the subject of persuading these two persons to 'leave town.' If it seems feasible, we will, before arranging the trip, take the step of meeting with the younger one and arriving at an agreement."

Suzanne Montignet nodded. "That would be appropriate."

"I will be in touch. Liberty."

"Liberty," responded Suzanne, as the man's image faded into the background blue.

Later that night:
Carl?
Yes, Jany?
What are you going to do?
Kill Carson.
How?
I don't know yet. He's protected so well.
And what of Sandoval?
I'll kill him too, of course.
Of course.
You sound as though you disapprove.
How do you know he's guilty?
. . . I beg your pardon.
Carl, you don't know. You can't kill a man without knowing.

Oh, that.
Carl?
I'll know.

The face that appeared in the holofield was not human. Cat's eyes, and the delicate whiskers, and the fine high cheekbones; once Carl could have loved her, but that she reminded him too strongly of Shana. Jacqueline de Nostri's expression was grave. "I grieve with you, Carl. Ask what you will of me."

Cold purpose was all that existed within him. "Chris said something which led me to think you can get in touch with him."

"Of course. I have always been able to."

"I need your help, and his."

"Carson and the Secretary General? They are very well protected." Her ears twitched slightly. "Or Sandoval?"

"Sandoval. First."

"Christian does very little that his masters do not approve of, Carl. I am not sure he will come."

"Tell him that we will come to Japan, if he aids us."

"We?"

"The telepaths, Jacqueline. You need not commit yourself, or the de Nostri, to anything."

She studied his image for a long time. "Very well, Carl. We shall be the Three Musketeers again, no? Such a strange thing. I had thought that wheel had turned." Her manner became businesslike. "Where shall we meet you?"

"The bar *Cojones*, I think, in Brasilia. It's very dark there; dress appropriately, you'll pass."

"When?"

"Tomorrow morning. They open at nine."

"I shall be there. And Christian, I hope."

"Godspeed, Jacqueline."

"And you, Carl."

It was not until Sunday that the *Electronic Times* ran newsdancer Gerold McKann's last work before his untimely death. It was his interview with Carl Castanaveras.

In the hours around midnight, while Sunday became Monday, Carl Castanaveras sat in a clearing midway up a mountain in the midst of jungle, just outside the sweep of patrols that protected the Sandoval estate. He sat beneath the shelter of the trees, sweat dripping down his motionless body, waiting for Chris and Jacqueline to return to him.

Here, as everywhere else in the world, the blunders of the Weather Bureau were felt; late at night, in the midst of the Brazilian winter, high enough that snow sometimes fell, the sweltering heat was nearly intolerable.

Carl sat in the heat, and waited. He was dressed in black fatigues with minimal hardware to slow him down; if it came to a serious firefight they were very likely dead regardless. His weapons were a knife with an edge that was only three molecules wide, a garotte, a small .45-caliber automatic in case of rain, and an Excalibur Series Two dual frequency short laser rifle. The weapon was simple, unlike some variable lasers Carl had seen—difficult to make a mistake with, even under confused combat conditions. The frequency toggle had only two positions. For close-up antipersonnel work the rifle dropped down into maser frequencies and sprayed a continuous beam of semi-coherent microwaves; you could fry a small roomful of people nearly as quickly as with a true flamethrower, and it was much more portable. Against delicate electronics or flesh, or any object with a reasonable degree of water in its makeup, it was as lethal as an autoshot—and lasted longer in an all-out firefight. Against waldos it was less efficient while set to maser frequencies. At its higher frequency it was a true coherent laser, emitting a continuous, invisible beam of X rays. Almost nothing would halt the X-laser; the beam sliced through metal and flesh, stone and water, with equal efficiency.

There was more modern hardware on the market; the Series Two was nearly a decade old. But there was not yet, in Carl's opinion, a superior all-purpose weapon.

It felt very strange, a sensation which reached him even through the dead numbness which had followed the rage, that he should be sitting there in yet another jungle, waiting for Jacqueline and Chris to return from another foray. For nearly six years he and Chris and Jacqueline had worked together; usually, but not always, with Peaceforcers other than Chris Summers to coordinate the job. Even when Chris had given them every reason to trust him, the French PKF Elite still did not.

There was not the faintest sound audible to Carl, whose ears were no better than a normal human's; cross-legged, eyes closed, Carl knew through other senses that Jacqueline de Nostri, naked but for her fur and a belt where her weapons were slung, had moved out of a nearby tree and into the one beneath which he sat. Moments later Chris Summers brushed almost as quietly through the undergrowth and lowered himself to the ground next to Carl.

They breathed quietly, the three of them. It was the only sound they made. They did not speak aloud. The most sensitive radio detectors known to man could not have heard their discussions. Carl simply listened in on them constantly. What Jacqueline thought, Chris Summers heard; what Chris thought, Carl made certain Jacqueline heard.

Jacqueline de Nostri reclined languidly in the low limbs of the tree. *We shall have to wait until near morning, I am afraid. That was when the guards grew most careless last night. And then we shall have to move with great speed; we will not want to work when there is light. They do not use light-enhancing goggles or sunglasses; therefore each of us must see better than they can. Especially Christian. It is one of our few advantages. Our weapons are not as powerful as theirs, except for the autoshot which Christian carries.*

Chris Summers lay motionless on his back, looking up into the branches that held the de Nostri. *I'm getting clumsy*

*in my old age. I almost had to kill one of Sandoval's patrol.
He damn near walked right into me while I was looking out
over the spread.*

He didn't suspect anything? asked Carl.

*No, or I would have killed him. One good thing out of
it: I got a good close look at the man before he passed me by.
I don't think they're wired for diagnostics or IDs. Good news
is we can probably pick them off without upsetting anybody
until it's time for them to report in, and they won't have any
way except visual ID to be sure that you're not two of their
own. Bad news is the two of you can't snatch their nonexistent
IDs and make your way through the automated defenses that
way.* Chris Summers shifted position slightly, clasping his hands
beneath his head as he stared up at the branches and stars. *I
did get the StingRays into place. Three of them, covering the
house from its north side across an arc of one hundred twenty
degrees. Also, I located the deep radar. Unless—or until—we
decide to take them out as well, they mean I can't get closer
than about a quarter of a kilometer away from the house. That
appears to be the range the radar sweeps at. All the metal and
heavy ceramic in my body, I'd light up the deep radar like a
tank.*

Jacqueline made a purring noise of satisfaction. *The time
I spent waiting for you to come, Carl, I have planted darts on
eight different members of the patrol. Cerabonic construction,
and very small. I do not think any of the troops noticed they
had been shot. If things get out of hand we can detonate them
at any time. Each dart contains a very small amount of anti-
matter in a constraining torus. Most of them will not be on
patrol when we go in, but asleep in their barracks. We may
take out most of the backup guards in this fashion.*

Well done, said Carl. *Where does their power come from?*

There was silence from the other two. *Okay,* said Carl,
*underground cabling, or does he have his own fusion plant?
Or both?*

Christian J. Summers said simply, *He's a paranoid bastard,
judging from the mess of radar and light trips and personal
troops. My guess would be internal fusion; my bet would be
both.*

Guesses are for when you can afford to be wrong.

I taught you that, Carl.

Yes, said Carl, eyes seeking out across the dark mountain

to where Tio Sandoval waited for him in a brightly lit mansion.
I remember.

---

*A note from the editors of the **Electronic Times:***
The following interview, which strongly condemns the
policies of the Secretary General and of the United Nations
Peace Keeping Force, was recorded on Wednesday, June 22.
The next day two things happened. Althea Castanaveras, one
of the Castanaveras telepaths, on assignment for Sandoval Biochemicals in Brazil, was killed by snakebite while working in
an area that is not known for poisonous reptiles; and Gerold
McKann was brutally murdered in his uptown New York City
apartment, and his copies of this interview were destroyed.
Standard operating procedure requires that *Times* reporters file
copies of their current jobs with the central *Times* database.
Gerold McKann did so; that copy, wholly unedited, is what
you will now audit.

At dateline, no suspect has been charged with Gerold
McKann's murder. New York City Police Commissioner Max-
well Devlin reports that the police currently have no suspects.

At least, none they are willing to name.

---

*(The file opens with the image of Gerold McKann, smiling
into the holocams. He is dressed in a severe business suit of
conservative cut, without either a tie or shoulder silks. He is
not wearing makeup, or if he is, has turned it off. Edit notes
attached at this point reference background information on the
telepaths, the de Nostri, the administration of Darryl Amnier,
and a brief overview of Amnier's and Malko Kalharri's roles
in the Unification War. Biographical profiles of the major players in the current political dispute are included.)*
McKann: Edit, this is the intro for Sunday's interview.
*(McKann pauses and says something that is not audible to
somebody standing off-camera. He smiles and, holding the
smile, turns back to the camera.)* Good morning. My name is
Gerold McKann, and I'm here this morning with an *Electronic
Times* exclusive interview with Carl Castanaveras. Most of you
know of him; he's the young, somewhat reclusive leader of
the genegineered telepaths who recently obtained their independence from the United Nations Peace Keeping Force. Edit,
cut and insert at transition.

(The holocams turn slowly, pulling back from the tight focus on Gerold McKann to include Carl Castanaveras. He is seated at the left end of a small sofa, dressed in dark boots, black slacks and a long-sleeved red silk shirt. He is wearing mirrored sunglasses; a male voice from off-camera advises him to remove them, and he does so, placing them in the pocket of his shirt. An edit note, apparently inserted by McKann, tags the voice as belonging to Malko Kalharri. Behind Castanaveras, through a wide bay window, stretch the front lawns of the Complex. In the distance, demonstrators are visible, milling in the streets.)

McKann: How do you feel, Carl?

Castanaveras: Fine, thank you.

McKann: Relax a little bit, okay? We're going to run over most of this a couple of times from different directions, and I'll edit from that. Have you ever been interviewed before?

Castanaveras: Briefly. Not like this.

McKann: If you hear me begin a sentence with "edit," it's a search word tagging a note I'm making for editing purposes later. As for the holocams, just forget them being there. Talk to me, not them.

Castanaveras: Sure.

McKann: Good morning, Carl. How are you today?

Castanaveras: Fine, thank you. Except that it's almost three in the afternoon.

McKann: Yeah, but the interview's going to run in the Sunday morning edition. *(Pause.)* The general outline of your story is well-known to our users. Nonetheless, there are details that have never really been brought to light. I know there are some subjects you can't discuss because they've been classified, so if we start getting into one of those areas, let me know and I'll back out.

Castanaveras: The areas that we can't discuss are largely those that relate to the details of the actual jobs I did for the Peaceforcers. Certainly it's no secret that I—and other telepaths —have done intelligence work for them.

McKann: Carl, I guess the best place for us to start is in the beginning. Why were you created in the first place?

Castanaveras: Personally? Or the telepaths as a group?

McKann: Say both.

Castanaveras: Well, as a group, we were created to gather information for the Peaceforcers. Most people know that, I think. But that was only after both Jany and I had shown we possessed the telepathic gift. Those of us born before then were simply part of what was—improperly—called Project Superman. Back in the late twenties, the United Nations sponsored several different lines of research into genetic engineering. Most of what they were looking for involved improved strength and endurance—better soldiers, essentially. Remember that this was just after the end of the War, when it looked likely that the Peaceforcers were going to have to put down rebellion after rebellion until the end of time. I was a result of one of those lines of research. History seems to have given de Nostri a lot of credit which he doesn't deserve, as far as the creation of the science of genegineering goes. De Nostri did raise the practice of gene *splicing* to an art; he was probably the best gene splicer the world has ever seen. But that is not the same thing as designing structures at the DNA level, which was Suzanne Montignet's accomplishment.

McKann: It seems they didn't exactly get what they were looking for.

Castanaveras: You mean soldiers? Perhaps they did, in the de Nostri. The de Nostri are wonderfully suited for the task of soldiering, at least at the physical level. And temperamentally, they do enjoy battle, that's hardly a secret. The U.N. did not, fortunately, achieve their goals in the telepaths. We are a peaceful people.

Two hours before dawn they moved.

The spot where they had waited through the night was separated by a small gorge from the Sandoval estate. The patrols swept straight up to the edge of the gorge and went no farther. Foolishly, the patrol was patterned in a fashion that repeated itself at least twice a day; by the time early Monday morning had arrived Jacqueline had watched the patrol's search pattern roll over three different times.

They came down off of the mountain in the hot stillness of early morning, moving slowly into their positions on the other side of the gorge. Deep infrared light trips were set at multiple waist-high locations throughout the approach to the house. The beams were within Chris's visual range; they were not within either Carl's or Jacqueline's, and as a result they both wore enhancing sunglasses that extended their eyesight into ranges nearly as wide as Chris's. Pressure pads were doubtless buried at various points as well. The patrols they had to penetrate were private Sandoval guards, but there was a barracks of Army troops tucked away not quite a half a kilometer away down the main access road leading away from the estate.

At 4:10 A.M., a guard made his crashing noisy way through the underbrush lining the dry gulch that marked the perimeter of their patrol. From forty meters away, Chris Summers tracked him with a sonic rifle for nearly five seconds before the man stumbled and went to his knees. Summers held the beam of sound on the man for another five seconds before releasing the trigger.

At 4:15 A.M., a second guard came along and received the same treatment, fifteen meters earlier. There would not be another security guard through for another forty minutes. Carl carried the first guard over to rest next to the second and laid him down. With Chris and Jacqueline covering him, he closed his eyes, left the world behind, and one after another went inside their unconscious minds.

. . . *rolling waves of black fear, and the constant sickness in his stomach. He was so afraid, always so afraid, and the others knew they all knew* . . . Carl moved through the shattered remnants of the fear that had come to the man when he realized that *something* was dreadfully wrong, and he was already too weak to do anything about it, and then unconsciousness claimed him . . . deeper, down into memory, and as always the strong memories were of fear and guilt and rage and hatred, and they leapt up to greet him, to envelop him . . . *Rita Sandoval's naked body, and he had been unable to tear his eyes away from her and the door had closed and Tio Sandoval had passed by only moments later, and Sandoval knew he had been spying on the señorita, it was there in his evil smile* . . . faces, a swirl of faces, only one of which was right, *a short, fat man with a face that never held joy, never held anything but a mild contempt for the rest of the world, sitting at a row of monitors* . . .

Out and in again, and the man was almost a moron, with faded grey memories of peoples and places, knowing only that he served the Sandovals and they fed him and cared for him, and with a dim gratitude for the kindnesses his commanding officer sometimes showed him, and a totally unconscious revulsion for the night-watch monitoring officer, *the man with the round face, who said things to him that he could not understand* . . .

Carl opened his eyes. He was only vaguely aware of how totally drenched with sweat he had become. There was a trace of headache, which he ignored. He held the image of the short fat man in his consciousness and focused upon it, seeking into the great house, finding nothing and then a flicker, and he heard himself murmuring aloud, "Sleep, sleep . . ." The flicker steadied and for a brief moment Carl's mind enveloped that of Rico Benitez, and through his eyes scanned monitors that held images of jungle and broad swaths of lawn and corridors and even bedrooms, and then there was only silence, throughout the great house, the silence of the small death that was sleep.

"Done," he whispered.

Jacqueline de Nostri did not even use her knife. She knelt and opened their throats to the night air with her claws.

Neither Carl nor Chris Summers attempted to stop her. *The watch officer is asleep,* said Carl. *I don't know if anybody else was in there with him.*

Chris Summers nodded. *You two probably won't set off wake-up alarms unless they have logic inside programmed for face and shape recognition; I don't go past this point. As much metal and heavy ceramic as I have inside me can't mean anything except cyborg to their deep radar, and that'll damn sure set off some loud alarms. I'm going to work my way around the perimeter over to the main road,* said Chris Summers, fading into the darkness. *I'll take 'em out as I come to 'em. You're on your own, kids. If it blows call me and I'll come in. Otherwise I'll see you at pickup.*

Carl unslung his maser rifle and gestured with it toward the estate. *Let's go deal some death.*

Yes.

They moved in.

McKann: What's it like to read another human's mind?

Castanaveras: Unpleasant.

McKann: Can't you be a little more specific than that?

Castanaveras: I'm not sure I can, not in any meaningful way. In the purest sense, it's not *reading minds.* A better description would be to say that I look at the world through another person's eyes. While I do it I *am* both persons, both myself and whoever it is I am in touch with. I see through two pairs of eyes, think with two minds. If I read the mind of someone who is more intelligent than I am—and I have, on occasion—*in that moment,* I am capable of understanding perfectly things which generally are not within my grasp. Two minds, linked by one Gift.

McKann: You still haven't explained your use of the word "unpleasant."

Castanaveras: Do you know what the commonest of human emotions is?

McKann: I can guess.

Castanaveras: No you can't. *Guilt.* This vast regret for the things which they've done which are *wrong.* Those are the people whose minds it *hurts* to contact, and they are far and away in the majority. The percentage of people who don't suffer from guilt is so vanishingly small I'm tempted to say that such people are not sane. Either they're not sane or the rest of us are not sane, and those of us who feel shame for things we've done outnumber those who don't by a vast number.

McKann: Isn't that one of the definitions of a sociopathic personality? The inability to feel guilt?

(Castanaveras is silent for a long moment.)

Castanaveras: I'm not referring to such people. There are sociopaths, of course, but not many, at least by percentage of the population. *(Silence again.)* Some people have—well, the best way I can say it is that they know themselves. They know who they are, what their strengths and weaknesses are, and they are at peace with themselves. Those people, they don't do things which might make them uncomfortable. *(Half smiles.)* It must be nice.

McKann: I take it that you're not one of those.

Castanaveras: Me? Hell, no. I do things I regret all the time.

McKann: Really?

Castanaveras: Constantly.

They stood in sultry darkness beneath the shelter of the trees, a meter away from the brightly lit lawns. Glowfloats bobbed restlessly ten meters in the air above them, casting a harsh and relentless light across the entire scene.

A fence ran all the way around the mansion except at the main entrance. Both live and automated guards—modified hunting waldos, as near as Carl could tell—patrolled at the single gate through which traffic could pass in and out of the protected inner area. There was a well-lit stretch of lawn of nearly sixty meters between the edge of the trees and the fence. *I see no light trips.*

Neither do I, said Carl. He focused with the sunglasses and zoomed in on the fence. There was a brightness above the fences that was so faint Carl was not certain he was not imagining it. *Look, just above the fence.*

I do not . . . ah. They have strung fineline above the fence. Perhaps—I would guess two meters high, as high again as the fence itself. Expensive.

He has the money for it. Looks like that way's out. If we get ourselves chopped to pieces on it, it sets off a quiet alarm; if we cut the fineline it sets off one of the noisy alarms.

Her thought held sarcasm. *Such brilliant deductive powers.* Carl ignored it. *What does that fence look like to you? Adobe?*

Uh-huh. Old, too. Want to bet it's not sensitized? I bet they slapped the fence together about the turn of the century and never bothered to rebuild with modern sensors inside.

My preference is to refrain from betting.

You blew that one when you got up this morning.

True. Our choices then are front gate, which means taking out the waldos, or cutting through the wall.

We can't go over and we don't have time to dig under. I don't see what else it leaves.

Jacqueline nodded decisively. *Straight through the wall.*

They circled around through the cover of the trees until they were out of sight of the front gate. *On three; one and two and* **go.**

They sprinted under the lights, across the bright lawns. Jacqueline outdistanced him instantly and was flat on her stomach next to the fences before Carl had half-crossed the distance. He reached her moments later and dropped to the ground next to her. Jacqueline was holding down the trigger on her laser, running the beam around and around in a circle not quite a meter in diameter on the surface of the fence. With his rifle Carl began tracing the outline of an *X* inside the circle Jacqueline was drawing. There were minor explosions every time the beam struck a buried air pocket inside the adobe and the superheated air expanded in a shock wave. Jacqueline released the trigger on her laser. Carl followed her example a second later. The adobe was glowing cherry red, as though a huge brand had been taken to its surface. Carl, with Jacqueline bracing him, kicked with all his might at the center of the *X*, once, twice, and on the third kick the circle folded in. A fourth kick knocked out one quarter that had not popped through with the other three. Carl squirmed through instantly, protected by his clothing from the still-glowing edges of the circle. Jacqueline followed in the next moment, more carefully; unlike Carl's fireproof fatigues, which were designed to take a laser blast without much complaint, her own fur burned quite well.

The inner yard, unlike that outside the fences, was dark. As a result, neither of them had more than a moment's warning before the silent rush of the dogs through the trees struck them.

McKann: Edit, subject of de Nostri. *(Pause.)* Carl, the de Nostri are at least as interested in the substance of the current debate as are the telepaths. Yet they're even more unapproachable than you are. Why is this so?

Castanaveras: You realize, of course, that I can't speak for them.

McKann: I'm not asking for that. I understand that it would be inappropriate for you to do such a thing. But surely your lines of communication with the de Nostri are substantial; your people lived with theirs for over ten years.

Castanaveras: About twelve. After our attorneys won permission for us to live where we chose, they decided to return to France. Jacqueline and Albert de Nostri were largely responsible for that decision, I'm told. The younger de Nostri wanted to stay in America; most of them had grown up here. *(Grins.)* Unfortunately, the same legal decision which put me in charge of our children put the de Nostri elders in charge of theirs. I'm of the impression that they weren't given much choice. The de Nostri *don't* run things democratically.

McKann: Why do they keep such a low profile?

Castanaveras: Surely that's obvious.

McKann: I'm afraid it's not.

Castanaveras: Look, right now, outside our front gates, you can see some three thousand demonstrators picketing us because we're guilty of the crime of wanting to decide our own fate. A lot of that is fear; we can read their minds, and they don't much like that fact. Some of it is simply the need for something to feel superior to. But the biggest part of it is that they *know where we are.* Look, any educated human being on this planet who's audited one of the news Boards of late knows where we are. I mean, not necessarily the street address, but with a half hour to drive around the neighborhood, they'd find us, if only by homing in on the sound of the chanting. Now, you're a reasonably educated man, are you not? You keep up with the news, I presume?

McKann: I see where you're going.

Castanaveras: Where are the de Nostri? In France, sure, I just told you that much. Maybe you even knew. But specifically, where?

McKann: I don't specifically know. I'm sure I could find out.

Castanaveras: No doubt. Could a mob? I will tell you this much about the de Nostri—nobody's picketing *them*.

A snarling mass of claws and teeth struck Carl chest high and slammed him back against the wall. Strong jaws clamped down on him through the boot on his right foot and dragged him down to the ground in a single wild pull. He lost his rifle and found his knife just in time to turn its edge toward the breast of the first dog as that dog leapt upon him again, clawing at his throat. The knife melted into the dog's flesh, shearing through fur, muscle, cartilage and bone with equal ease. The dog got its teeth around Carl's forearm and was bearing down as it died. Only its mass kept the second dog from getting at Carl's face instantly, and then something else, moving blurringly fast on all fours, went right over Carl and took the dog in a tumbling roll across five meters of lawn. When their roll ceased, Jacqueline de Nostri came to her feet without pause.

Carl became aware of the weight of the dog on his chest, and its blood as it seeped over his fatigues.

Dogs, thought Jacqueline, trembling with emotion, *I hate dogs.*

She stood motionlessly a few steps away from him, still trembling, and Carl shoved the dog aside, removed his forearm from its jaws, stood and looked around. In the dim light from the faraway glowfloats, he saw the corpses of five animals.

He had killed only one of those five, and almost by accident.

Jacqueline was still shaking when he had retrieved his knife and his rifle, and by reflex he nearly made the mistake of saying something, of reaching *in* to try to help her to grow calm again; and then he remembered himself, and her, and from long knowledge refrained.

They moved on into the tree-filled darkness in silence.

(An edit note attached at this point says: "The following is taken from the Thursday morning interview, early on the day Gerold McKann was murdered. Both McKann and Castanaveras are wearing the same clothing they wore in the earlier session.")

McKann: Carl, you said something a bit earlier which sounded as though you thought the demonstrations outside were being staged. Could you elaborate on that?

Castanaveras: I'd love to. Look. *(A holofield shimmers into existence. All that is recorded by the holocams is a blur.)* This is . . .

McKann: Edit. Carl, you should have asked me about this. You can't holograph a holograph.

Castanaveras: Oh? Why not?

McKann: I don't know, you just can't. You don't get anything except a blur. You can't even produce a flat image of one unless you use two lenses. Haven't you ever run a holocam?

Castanaveras: Well, yes. But not often.

McKann: Make me a copy of the images you want to run and I'll splice them in where appropriate.

Castanaveras: Fine. Should I just go on?

McKann: Edit, interview resumes. *(Pause.)* Could you elaborate on that?

Castanaveras: Sure. Look, this is a compilation of holos that we took when you arrived on Wednesday and left Wednesday night. I'm sure you noticed us stunning members of the crowd so that you could get in through the gates.

McKann: *(Dryly.)* It did not escape my attention.

(An image of demonstrators at the front gate of the Chandler Complex briefly overlays the primary image of McKann and Castanaveras.)

Castanaveras: This shows very clearly—here, and again a few seconds later, here—these people aren't even *trying* to get out of the way of the stun rifles, even though it's quite clear where those rifles are aimed. Now, look, we've got these faces separated out; these are the faces of the people who were stunned. Uh, at the moment they were stunned they were not good candidates for identification; they tended to be grimacing at that point. These holos are backtracked from a few moments earlier, but there's no question that they are the images of the persons being stunned.

McKann: Stipulated. We'll confirm this, of course.

Castanaveras: Fine. I'm not sure how to phrase this—as of today, Thursday morning, we don't have proof that any of these people are Peaceforcers. But we will, in time for your Sunday edition.

McKann: *(Leans forward, looking into holo field.)* I'll be damned—if you can do that, that might be interesting. But I'm afraid it might not do you a lot of good, Carl. There's no law I know of which prohibits a member of the PKF from demonstrating against the telepaths.

Castanaveras: I'm sure there's not, Gerry. But Gerry, how much would you like to bet that these men are *on duty*? Drawing pay, on government time, to *harass* us?

McKann: I think maybe that's a sucker bet. I'm going to edit what I just said.

Castanaveras: Coward. One more thing for you to think about, though. We've had between six hundred and about fourteen hundred demonstrators out there every single day since we moved into the Complex. Today there are over three thousand, and would you like to know when those crowds appeared? The *very day* that Judge Sonneschein ruled that we were not subject to the Official Secrets Acts of 2048 and 2054.

Damn it, what's *wrong* with wanting to be free?

(Pause.)

. . . I sure hope that's a rhetorical question. There's not a corner of this globe that still tolerates slavery in any form. Oh, there are idiots in India and Taiwan and elsewhere who can sign themselves into indenture for cash—but the period of indenture is limited to five years, they get paid for it, and the choice is theirs! *We* never once got paid for our services, nobody asked us whether we wanted to do what we were forced to, and the period of indenture was unlimited. The Secretary General's office has made no bones of the fact that it considers the Eighth Amendment an aberration, and even while conceding that it *must* follow the letter of the Amendment has gone to insane lengths to circumvent its intent. We are being sued by the United Nations through the Bureau of Traffic Enforcement, by the PKF for breach of verbal contract, by the Prosecutor General's office for violation of the Official Secrets Acts, by the Ministry of Population Control for failure to provide properly for our children, by the Bureau of Zoning Controls for operating a business out of a residence—that's the Chandler Complex they're referring to—and for God knows what else. I mean, we've been here in the Chandler Complex for nine months now. Is it, as the Secretary General's office claims, purely a coincidence that all of these legal problems arose only in the last two months or so? Only, in other words, since the enactment of the Eighth Amendment? Infoshit.

McKann: Traffic Enforcement?

Castanaveras: Small speeding violation. No big deal. Come on, Gerry—is it a coincidence? You're a reasonable man.

McKann: I think *I'm* supposed to be interviewing *you*.

Castanaveras: Okay, no, it is not a coincidence. We are, right now, the object of a conspiracy between the Prosecutor General's office, in the person of Charles Eddore, the Peace Keeping Force, in the person of Unification Councilor Carson—who serves, in case I haven't made myself clear, as Chairman of the Peace Keeping Force Oversight Committee in the Unification Council—and the Secretary General's office, in the person of the Secretary General himself. They haven't been able to touch us legally, and they will not be able to. That leaves illegal means, beginning, but I'll warrant not ending, with this mess outside the front gates of my home.

McKann: Edit, subject of conversation with SecGen. Carl, do you want to discuss your conversation with the Secretary General? Or possibly just give me your recording of the conversation?

(A male voice from off-camera, identified as belonging to Malko Kalharri, says something unintelligible at this point. It contains the words "Secretary General." A text note inserted by the editors of the Electronic Times *notes that the conversation in question—if a recording of it does exist—has not been made available to the* Times *at this date.)*

Castanaveras: No. We'll save that for another time.

McKann: Okay. Without some statement from you, you won't get any play on it when the interview runs.

Castanaveras: We're not looking for war, Gerry. That conversation might embarrass the Secretary General, but not much more. He said nothing actionable in it. I'm not looking to embarrass the man, Gerry. Just convince him to leave us alone.

McKann: You don't think you're at war now?

Castanaveras: I don't know. *I* haven't had a chance to read the Secretary General's mind, or Carson's either. There's a difference between playing chicken and actually fighting. Right now we're standing face-to-face, waiting to see who blinks first. *(Grins.)* If you always knew whether the guy across the table from you was holding, there wouldn't be much point in trying to bluff, would there?

(Pause.) I certainly hope we're not at war. I don't want that. *(Castanaveras pauses again, for several seconds, and finally adds, simply:)* If they have any sense, neither do they.

Tio Sandoval awoke in utter darkness.

For a moment he was not certain what had awakened him. Carolita was still asleep at his side, her breathing gentle and regular. The only light in the room came from the fish tank that ran along most of one wall, where Carolita's exotics navigated their way through the miniature submarine kingdom that she had designed as a hobby. The light from the tank washed the room in a dim, aquamarine glow that wavered and shifted with the movement of the water in the huge tank. Carolita lay naked next to him, lovely in a pure and almost irrelevant manner. He felt no desire for her—had not felt desire for any woman since the death of the telepath girl child.

A warm breeze moved across his bare chest, and he realized what had awakened him. A moment's sharp displeasure with Carolita passed through him; constantly, she argued with him whether the window was to stay open or shut. Better the heat of clean air, she said, than the false chill of air-conditioning. Their only window, which looked out over the south side of the gentle slope upon which Casa Sandoval was built, was dilated to its fullest extension, the glassite shrunk back to the windowsill itself across the entire perimeter of the circle. He considered calling the window closed, but Carolita would surely awaken and complain at his noise. Sandoval left the bed and came to his feet in a single fluid motion, and strode across the room to touch the pressure pad that dilated the window.

He had only the vaguest impression that there was some *thing* behind him when a strong hand clamped over his mouth and a knife traced a small shallow cut along the edge of his neck. He went utterly rigid, and then relaxed and did not even consider resisting. Something was wrong with his thought processes—he had been drugged, perhaps, for though intellectually he knew he was in grave danger, emotionally the subject was hazy and irrelevant. They continued to the window, and another shape—*de Nostri*—was there, hanging seemingly unattached to the edge of the wall at his third-story bedroom. The de Nostri, a female, handed him a pair of gloves, which he donned without question. He climbed out through the window, and accepted the de Nostri's help in grasping the almost invisible line that was attached near the window. He slid down the line to the ground, momentarily aware that the drop was enjoyable and frightening at the same time. A pain occurred in his knee when he reached the ground, but that was not important either. Instants later the de Nostri and the man with her came down the line after him.

Then the lights came on, everywhere, and then sirens.

With a shock of surprise almost great enough to penetrate the haze that insulated him from the rest of the world, Tio Sandoval recognized Carl Castanaveras.

Carl Castanaveras took one swift look around the daylight-bright lawns they were trapped upon, glanced up into the sky and saw the spyeyes and glowfloats and said, "Oh, shit."

McKann: What do the telepaths *want*?

Castanaveras: I'm not sure what you mean.

McKann: Everybody wants something. What do you desire from life?

Castanaveras: We want to be left alone, Gerry. There are a lot of good things in the world that we've never had time for. Time enough for the parts of life that make life worth living; that would be nice.

Several things happened at once.

Carl flipped his rifle over to wide-dispersion maser and fired straight up into the night sky, into the glowfloats and spyeyes hovering directly over their heads. There was no water in them, but there were delicate electronics that could not have been hardened to radiation without adding unacceptably to the cost of producing them. The spyeyes simply dropped like stones when the maser beam struck them; the glowfloats burst and fell in flaming wreckage to the yard around them, casting the yard back into gloom. He was calling for pickup at the same moment: *Situation fucked, come and get us*—first to Chris and then to Malko Kalharri, who was in a semiballistic orbital can, thirteen kilometers above their head, and descending already when Carl reached him. The distance was great, but there were no other minds between them; Carl's contact with the old man was as sharp as though Malko had been on the ground there with him.

Jacqueline had Sandoval by the back of his neck and was moving him at a stumbling run to the east wall, where they had sliced their hole. Carl trotted backward after her, rifle at the ready. Two of Sandoval's private troops trotted around the far corner of the house before he had reached the adobe fence; Carl flipped over to X-laser and waved the invisible beam at the two soldiers; one fell instantly, cut almost in half, and the other ducked back out of sight. Carl paused a moment and sliced off a half dozen of the trees nearest him at their bases, flipped the rifle over to maser and waved the maser beam over the fallen trees until they were burning fiercely. Their backs covered for the moment, he turned to where Jacqueline was waiting with Sandoval.

In his concern for their pursuit, he had released his mental hold of Sandoval; Jacqueline had him facedown on the ground next to the hole they had burnt in the adobe wall, claws against the side of his neck. *Carl, what awaits us on the other side?*

Carl shut his eyes and slipped away from his body.

Four . . . no, five of them, ranging themselves in a tight arc of perhaps twenty degrees, facing the hole in the fence with autoshots readied. A second group of guards was headed their way. He fed the image to Jacqueline.

Can you look for this—the image of a small dart appeared in her mind—*on their persons?*

Yes. He scanned through the crowd—the second group arrived and took up their positions on an arc that now covered more than forty degrees—and came up at first with nothing. Then Jacqueline imagined the dart against the palm of her hand, and with the correct size of the item fixed in his mind he came up quickly with two guards who bore the miniature darts somewhere in their clothing.

Jacqueline lifted Sandoval to his feet in one surging heave and forced him back from the wall with Carl following.

She touched something hanging from her belt. A huge shock wave hammered at them, rolled on, and on, and on. Even though Carl had expected it he was knocked off his feet. Jacqueline did not let it slow her; with her claws digging into Tio Sandoval's neck she ran back toward where the fence had been. Fully ten meters of its length had been blown down. Carl scrambled back to his feet and followed her at a dead run. There was nobody alive on the other side of the fence, only bodies burnt so badly they were barely recognizable.

Jacqueline and Sandoval had nearly reached the cover of the trees when the low, sleek shape of the hunting waldo burst out of concealment not twenty meters away from them. Carl had time for only one half-panicked shot at the waldo, and realized with horrified dismay that his rifle was still set for maser fire; sparks showered off the surface of the armored waldo, but it slowed not at all. The waldo ignored Sandoval entirely and struck Jacqueline de Nostri like a battering ram. Her body bounced away from the waldo when it struck her. Its glittering central mandible held something covered with brown fur, and blood spurted away from her in a bright arterial stream.

Behind Carl, a single Sandoval guard came from around the southeast corner of the house, without weapons, running for his life.

Carl never saw him; he flicked the rifle to X-laser and slashed through the waldo's mandibles, chopping down toward the low-slung waldo's running legs. The waldo was programmed to recognize laser fire as a threat; it whirled and came at Carl in a terrible, soundless zigzagging scramble.

Tio Sandoval, free of Carl's control, had come to his feet and was sprinting back toward his house.

Something came after the running soldier. The moving shape reached him and slowed long enough to flicker into existence as a human being, and the soldier literally disappeared in a shower of blood and flesh. The flicker became a blur again, passed Tio Sandoval without slowing; a flat sharp cracking sound was the only sign that the blur had dealt with Sandoval at all. Sandoval folded bonelessly, and the blur streaked past Carl and collided at full speed with the hunting waldo. What seemed to happen was simply too unbelievable; the waldo screamed like a living creature, and parts of it began heading in different directions.

Tearing metal, Carl thought with calm rationality; that was the sound of the scream.

Chris Summers paused for less than a second, snapped, *Get Sandoval*, and blurred back into motion over to where Jacqueline lay on the manicured grass. Carl turned away from them, reslung his rifle, lifted Sandoval's nude form and slung him over his shoulders in a fireman's carry, trotted back to where Chris was bent over Jacqueline and asked, *Can we move her?*—before he saw how bad the damage was. Chris did not answer him; he was up and moving, picked up Jacqueline de Nostri's arm from where it had been flung, returned and lifted her body with as little effort as he had taken for the limb.

Go. Carl ran for the cover of the forest, and Chris Summers, still holding Jacqueline's body, turned and surveyed the great house. There was a fire burning at the rear of the house, where Carl had set the trees afire, and ten meters of fence had been blown into oblivion.

What is the value of a life?

He had personally left either sixteen or else seventeen of Sandoval's guards for dead, and destroyed a pair of waldos. Jacqueline had detonated her antimatter-bearing darts; Chris had seen one guard go up in mid-step, as though he had thumbed the press-sense on a grenade and neglected to throw it afterward. At the same time the guards' barracks had come down with a roar of thunder, the walls blowing out and the roof falling down.

Two thoughts were in Chris Summer's mind.

The first was that there would be observation satellites watching all of this; they would show conclusively that there had been a de Nostri here, and that there had been a Peaceforcer Elite as well—but they would not show clearly *who* those people had been. Unlike the spyeyes, which would have his face, and Carl's, and Jacqueline's.

The spyeyes, very likely, transmitted what they saw into infobanks somewhere inside the house.

His second thought was that there were, most certainly, innocent people within the house.

It seemed to him that he had been standing there for a very long time.

They killed Jackie, he thought at last, and twitched an electronic relay deep within himself.

The three StingRay missiles came from high on the mountain. With the eyes of a Peaceforcer Elite, sampling at over a thousand frames a second, Chris Summers watched them come down in a slow, gliding beauty, and detonate themselves in airbursts only meters above Casa Sandoval.

The shockwaves from the explosions washed over him. Their heat set Jacqueline's fur on fire. Shutters dropped down over his eyes to protect the delicate mechanisms. His clothing was singed, and his skin darkened slightly from the heat. His hair did not burn; it was not real.

The fire in Jacqueline's fur burned out of its own accord.

Chris Summers turned and headed for pickup at top speed.

Tio Sandoval awoke in free fall.

He was not the least bit groggy; he felt fine, wide-awake, clearheaded and alert. There was something cold touching the back of his neck. He was in a small cabin, strapped securely into a chair, and a man whose face was damnably familiar was turning away from him, feet making the normal tearing velcro sound as he moved. Sandoval was still naked from the waist down, though somebody had dressed him in a shirt. The man was old, though he did not appear so in his bearing— the skin of his neck and hands was marked with the looseness common among the aged who had received particularly excellent geriatrics therapy. The old man placed a hypo inside a recessed panel and withdrew his hand as the hullmetal dilated closed.

The man turned back to face him, and Sandoval came back to himself with a shock so great it overwhelmed whatever it was he had been injected with.

Malko Kalharri lowered himself carefully into a seat facing Sandoval and strapped himself in. "*Command, holocams on.*" He smiled at Sandoval then. " 'Sieur Sandoval, you have problems like you don't even want to know about."

English was not a language Sandoval was totally comfortable in; it took him a moment to work through the syntax of what Kalharri had said. "What do you mean?" Without being too obvious about it he tested his bonds until he knew with certainty that he was unable to break them.

Kalharri did not cease smiling. "We're in geosynch right now. Right outside this cabin there's an airlock which opens up on death pressure. There's a truth plate up against the back of your neck. Now, I'm going to ask you some questions, and you're going to geek for me. You tell me what I want to know or you go out through the airlock."

"How do I know you won't do that anyway?"

Kalharri simply shrugged, watching Sandoval with a genteel amusement.

"Go to Hell, old man."

"Carl Castanaveras," said Kalharri carefully, "is right outside the door to this cabin. Now, you can talk—nicely, now, to me—or I can call him in, and you talk to *him,* and you will talk."

"I'm sure." Sandoval cocked his head to one side, strangely unable to worry about what was happening. After consideration he nodded. "My options appear limited."

"You'd be amazed." Kalharri glanced down at a video tablet in his lap. "How did Althea Castanaveras die?"

"Of snakebite."

"Administered by whom?"

"Nobody."

Kalharri shook his head a minute fraction. " 'Sieur Sandoval, this is my last try, and I'm going to let Carl have you. Tell me about Althea's death."

Sandoval said flatly, "Councilor Carson requested it, and I implemented it for him."

"Implemented how?"

"She was bitten by a sidewinder supplied by my genegineers. It was placed outside her cabin and locked onto her scent. We drugged the boy Tomâs and their guards, and I called her outside. The snake struck her moments after she left her cabin."

"Why were you the one who called her outside?"

Sandoval froze, staring at Kalharri. The man knew the answer, or he would not have asked. "You cumsucking faggot," he whispered a moment later; it was the worst insult he knew in English.

Kalharri looked away from him for a moment, eyes unfocused. Listening to an inskin data link, Sandoval judged, or possibly speaking with Castanaveras. He turned back to Sandoval and laughed aloud. "Allie got you, didn't she? You watched her die and she realized what was happening before she died, and you haven't been able to get it up since."

The fury and hatred clogged his throat. "I'm going to kill you," Sandoval got out at last.

Kalharri glanced back down at his video tablet. "No, quite the contrary," he said absently. "What was Secretary General Amnier's role in her death?"

The words spilled from him, utterly against his will. "I don't know. I don't know if he even knew of it." He heard the words fall from his lips with utter horror; if they could make him speak so when he would not, why had Kalharri even tolerated the degree of evasion he had attempted?

"What do you know about Gerold McKann's death?"

Because, he realized, Castanaveras, had he been questioning Sandoval, would have killed him too quickly. The knowledge of how close he was to his death froze him again, and again the prompt came and forced his answer. "I know that it happened. I do not know who caused it, or why, aside from guesses."

"Okay." Kalharri tucked the video tablet in a small pouch at the side of the chair. "I think that's about all." He raised himself and returned to the cabinet where he had stowed the hypo earlier. He removed a different, smaller hypo and injected Sandoval again. "This will partially counteract the euphoric I just gave you. Not entirely; Carl wants you conscious."

Sandoval jerked against the restraints that held him, nostrils flaring. Against his will he screamed aloud as the drug hit him. Suddenly there was a great throbbing in his skull, and a vast ache that permeated his entire body. Kalharri lifted a bushy gray eyebrow. "Tsk. Overdo it a little, did I? So sorry."

The door to the cabin opened, and Carl Castanaveras, still in black fatigues, came through. Kalharri left as he entered. The door to the cabin stayed open behind him. Castanaveras stood perfectly still, looking at Sandoval. The grim expression he wore could have been sold to poison Peaceforcers with. He was holding an old Series Two Excalibur that had clearly seen considerable use.

Sandoval tried to speak, but his lips and tongue would not work properly. Castanaveras touched a stud on the rifle and brought it to bear on Sandoval. He stood in utter silence, until finally Sandoval screamed, *"Kill me you cocksucker!"*

Castanaveras did not seem to aim particularly; he was holding the rifle with one hand. The rifle dropped toward Tio Sandoval's crotch, and Sandoval drew in the breath to scream with.

Castanaveras touched the trigger for the merest instant and shot Sandoval in the crotch with a maser burst. The pain as his genitals cooked was insane, so totally divorced from any ordinary pain Tio Sandoval had ever experienced in his life that for seconds he made no sound at all except an utterly involuntary gasping, floating in a bizarre electric wash of pure sensation.

Then he did scream and could not stop. He screamed while Castanaveras touched a stud on the chair Sandoval was in, and his bonds fell away. He screamed while Castanaveras pulled him from the chair and towed him by his hair across the cabin. He screamed while the airlock door opened and while the airlock door closed. He screamed when the outer airlock door opened and the escaping air blew him out into death pressure.

He stopped screaming when the vacuum sucked the air from his lungs.

8

Carl stood at the window of his bedroom, looking out in the high clean light of midafternoon at the demonstrators milling in front of the Complex. There were over five thousand of them by Security Service's count. Someone had provided several hundred of them with dramasuits to parade in.

Let me help you.

Carl felt curiously distanced from it all, as though it was all some news Board file he was auditing, and not in truth a crowd of people who wanted him, and his children, either in slavery or dead. It did not matter that many of the crowd had been paid to be there; the greater number of them had not.

You lost Gerry and Allie and Jacqueline. Baby, you can't lock yourself away from the world like this. Let me help.

He spoke aloud. "Please, Jany. I'm trying to think."

Her thoughts kept after him, insistently. *No you're not. You're withdrawing. I know you, you're not thinking, you're just feeling, and you don't want me to interfere with it. Carl, you're hurting yourself.*

"My privilege, surely. *Command,* bring me formal wear and call Malko." The housebot rolled away to the closet and a holofield appeared behind Carl. Malko's figure appeared in the cube; Carl did not turn around.

"Yes, Carl?"

"How much longer before you'll be ready?"

"Ten minutes. I'll meet you downstairs."

"Fine. *Command,* comm off."

He watched the mob and did not turn away from the window until the housebot announced it had laid out his formal cloak and suit. Jany was sitting in the middle of their bed, features perfectly controlled but for the tears that ran down her cheeks. Her voice when she spoke was barely audible. "Where are you going?"

"Pennsylvania border. See some of Malko's contacts."

"Why?"

"They might help." He pulled on the dress shirt and pants and waited while the lacings knotted themselves. "And they might not. You never know." He pulled the coat on over the shirt and folded the cloak over his right arm.

Carl? Will you please talk to me?

He looked straight at her, at the tear-bright green eyes of the woman who was so nearly himself. "I can't think of anything to say," he told her with utter honesty. "I'll be back fairly late. Don't wait up."

You're hurting me, Carl.

"I know." He left without looking back.

There were five men in the conference room. They sat around a long, oval table of polished red mahogany; Malko and Carl together midway down one of the long sides, and the other three arrayed across from them.

The three had been making casual conversation while being served their dinners, when Carl and Malko arrived. It gave Carl a moment to observe the two whom he did not know. F. X. Chandler nodded cordially to Carl and Malko as they seated themselves, but did not interrupt his conversation with Judge Rudolf Sonneschein. The Unification Circuit Court judge was a middle-aged, corpulent man who was a likely candidate for an early heart prosthetic. The third man with whom they were meeting was quite young, perhaps Carl's age; a sharply dressed, pleasant-seeming fellow named Douglass Ripper, Jr., who spoke vigorously, using his hands to gesture with. Carl had never heard of him, but he was apparently quite popular. The man was currently a United States Senator—largely a ceremonial position since the end of the War, and especially so these days, since the abolition of the House of Representatives—but he was announced as a candidate for the position of Unification Councilor for New York Metro in the 2064 elections. Jerril Carson had occupied the position virtually uncontested for over two decades; by the polls, Ripper appeared likely to win.

Judge Sonneschein finished his dinner first, and waved to a waitbot to take it away. "Not bad," he said in a rusty Texan

drawl, "for New York food. The steak was almost big enough."
He leaned back in his chair and clasped his hands over an
ample belly. "What can we do for you, Carl?"

Carl said flatly, "I'm not sure. I'm here at Malko's sug-
gestion."

Douglass Ripper leaned slightly forward. "Maybe I can
speed things up a little bit. Mr. Castanaveras, I audited your
interview in the *Electronic Times*. Can you answer a couple
of quick questions for me?"

"Yes."

"You said in that interview that what you wanted was to
be left alone. Is that still true? Would you be willing to settle
for being 'left alone' at this point? Gerry McKann was murdered
because of you—Malko's told us that you were friends," Ripper hastened to assure Carl. "It's not general knowledge, and
it's not clear even from the unedited transcript. Althea Castanaveras is dead also. Will being left alone satisfy you, or has
the situation gone past that point?"

The question seemed curiously without meaning; there
was no anger left in Carl. "That would be acceptable."

"Great. Were you responsible for that insane mess down
in Brazil?"

"Of course not."

Chandler said gravely, "Young man, I've seen the satellite
records of the battle that resulted in the destruction of Casa
Sandoval. There was one normal man and one de Nostri in
several of the recorded scenes. In another scene, just one,
there was a series of eight frames where, from frame to frame,
a human shape moved approximately five meters with each
frame advance. That's a Peaceforcer Elite, Carl. There's nothing else in the world shaped like a human being which moves
that fast."

"Carl," said Malko gently, "I gave the Judge the record
of my interview with Sandoval."

"Fine," said Carl without looking at him. "Is there anything else I should know before we continue?"

"No," said Malko after a moment, "no, there's not."

"Wonderful," said Carl simply. "Gentlemen, I killed Tio
Sandoval. I fried his nuts with a maser and then threw him
out an airlock." Douglass Ripper winced; the Judge and Chandler did not. "We have a recording, which you now have also,
of Tio Sandoval admitting that he killed one of my children at
the request of Unification Councilor Carson. I'm sure 'Sieur

Ripper here would like to use that recording; it'd practically guarantee him Carson's current job."

Ripper nodded. "I'll concede the point. I would like to use the recording. Unfortunately, *I* do not have it. You do, and the Judge does. I do not."

"I think my question," said Carl, "is, what do you three want? You damn well want something of me or I don't think Malko would have dragged me all the way out here."

There was a moment's silence.

"Your understanding of politics," said F. X. Chandler, sipping at a glass full of some amber liquid—probably apple juice, Carl thought with irrelevant cynicism—"is less than wonderful, Carl. A brief—and I do mean brief—lesson, if you will. As the situation stands, almost the entire solar system thinks that the PKF sent one of their Elite out to stomp Sandoval. Those of us in this room know that was not the case, and *so do the Peaceforcers*. Chris Summers is alive, isn't he?"

Carl did not even blink. "If he is, Sandoval might be too. They both took the same drop."

Chandler looked pensive. "I've talked it over with my engineers. They've examined the satellite records—and if I can get my hands on them, so can a lot of other people—of that assault on Sandoval's house. The thing in that one scene, the thing that took apart the waldo, was a PKF Elite or so near as makes no difference. My engineers, whose opinions I respect, swear that the only place in the Solar System that can do work like that is Peaceforcer Heaven, SpaceBase One at L-5. Q.E.D., the blur was a Peaceforcer Elite, the de Nostri was Jacqueline de Nostri, and the man was you. You and she and Chris Summers used to be called the Three Musketeers. Carl, if I can piece that together—and I'm not all that smart —so can a lot of other people."

"So?"

"So, desertion from the PKF, aiding a deserter from the PKF, failing to report a deserter from the PKF, are all treason. Capital offense, for you and Summers, wherever he is. Now that the PKF knows he's alive, and they do, they'll find him. And when they do, he'll die, and you'll die. Carson may go to jail for his role in your daughter's death; he may not. Your evidence is tenuous and a lot of it won't be admissible. The testimony of a telepath is, I believe, still not admissable in court except under fairly strict guidelines. In Carson's case no judge in his right mind would allow one of your people to testify in an expert capacity. So, Carson won't die for it, and Amnier won't even be touched. But the fact of Chris Summers' existence will hang you."

"I'm sorry, gentlemen," said Carl quietly, "but I'm very tired and I'm not sure this is helping. What do you suggest we do?"

"The Ninth Amendment, or it will be if it passes," said Douglass Ripper, "and it looks to pass, frankly; that Amendment will allow Secretary General Amnier to seek a fourth term in office, and a fifth, and a sixth. I don't know if you appreciate how vulnerable that makes him. He'd kill for another term in office, but most significantly, he'd also leave you alone for another term in office. Now, you can both hurt each other. He can damn well kill you if he sets his mind to it, but you can keep him from getting elected again. What he's trying to do is very tricky, Carl. The last time somebody tried to pull this one was back over three decades ago, about the time you and I were being born. Secretary General Ténérat tried it; he was voted out of office and never even got to serve the legal third term, never mind a fourth, and his proposed Amendment was voted down overwhelmingly.

"Now, there are two time elements for you to consider here. You could do Amnier a favor by arranging to have something of import happening on the Fourth of July; that's only three days from now, this Monday. He'll try to have something happen anyway, to draw people's attention away from the Fourth of July riots, but you're legitimate news. An announcement of a reconciliation between yourself and his office, buttressed by a press conference where you answer questions, might take a lot of the heat off of him.

"The second date, of course, is July fourteenth, Bastille Day. By that date, this all *has* to be settled, favorably or otherwise. He doesn't want to go back to France for their independence celebrations with all of this hanging over his head. Right now, your telepaths are the most important news story on the Boards. The French will not be happy if that's still true come the fourteenth of this month."

"When all of this is done," said Chandler quietly, "and Bastille Day is past, you retreat to some location other than my old home, somewhere rural where the crowds can't take the Bullet to come picket your front gate, and you lay low through the elections of 2064. By then, things will have quieted down, and Amnier won't feel so bloody threatened. He'll be secure enough to leave you alone."

Carl looked across the table at the three men facing him. "Which one of you has discussed this with him?"

There were advantages to being a telepath; one was generally told the truth, on the assumption that a lie would be caught regardless. "I did," said Judge Sonneschein after a moment. "I was simply exploring the options."

Carl nodded. "I appreciate your time. I'll think about it. Malko? Shall we go?"

"Just a second there," said Chandler abruptly. "I wanted to talk to you privately."

"Go ahead," said Carl, not moving.

Chandler stared at him for a second, and then grinned. "You go to hell too. How's Jany?"

Carl blinked. The question actually surprised him. "Not doing very well, truly. She's upset by the situation." *Or by me,* he thought to himself, but the thought held no pain. "I'll tell her you asked about her. It will please her."

Chandler nodded. Ripper and Judge Sonneschein, apparently aware that something significant was happening, sat and watched the exchange. "Tony Angelo tells me you're hell on wheels."

Carl had half risen from his seat, preparing to leave. "I beg your pardon?"

Chandler said mildly, "I'd say, 'hell on fans,' except it doesn't have the right ring to it. That's part of the problem with the modern world, you know. There's something wrong with a world that doesn't have any use for wheels except for designing space stations and bicycle tires."

Carl did stand, very straight. "You've totally lost me, I'm afraid."

"Young man, you've been sitting there lying to every one of us, including yourself, ever since you sat down. How badly do you hate Amnier?"

There was a dead silence in the room. Carl opened his mouth to answer and found that there was no answer within him. "I don't hate him, or Carson either. That's the truth. But one of my children has died because of those bastards."

Francis Xavier Chandler looked down into his drink and did not answer Carl immediately. When he looked up again his expression was softer.

"Then make sure the rest of your children don't."

"Someday," said Carl, explaining the only thing that was at all clear to him, "I have to kill them."

Chandler said, "Yes. I know."

"Revenge," said Malko Kalharri gently, "does not have to come in a day."

They drove back through darkness, in silence. They skimmed the highway at 180 kph, forty centimeters above the ferrocrete hardtop. Carl drove automatically, moving around what little traffic was still on the roads that late at night with minimal effort. He paged TransCon once for permission to enter airspace and was turned down peremptorily. It did not bother him; had he flown back to the Complex he'd have reached it too soon to suit him. He was in the mood to drive, to relax and enjoy the smooth powered flight of the MetalSmith. It was drizzling slightly, and the canopy had turned on its electrostatic field to keep itself free of water.

They hit a clear stretch of road, and Carl leaned back in his seat and turned the carcomp loose. Malko Kalharri appeared to be asleep in the passenger's seat, video tablet glowing in his lap; he spoke without opening his eyes. "You should probably try to get some sleep. You look like hell."

"I'm not tired."

"*I'm* tired," said Malko irritably, "and I've had a lot more sleep than you've had of late."

"*I'm* a bit younger than you are."

Malko snorted. "You're *different* than I am."

"*No.*"

"Would I lie to you?"

Carl chuckled without amusement. "No, but only because it'd be a waste of time."

Malko grinned in return, wryly. "True." The grin faded, and after a moment he said, almost hesitantly, "You *are* different, you know."

Three different replies occurred to Carl; what he finally said was, "I presume you mean in some way other than the totally obvious one."

"I suppose sleep is a good example. When I was younger, I had white nights and functioned the next day. I could get by on two to three hours sleep per night for a week, a week and a half at a stretch. You, though—when you were about seventeen, you didn't sleep one time for almost two weeks."

It had been closer to three. "You knew about that?"

Malko shook his head. "Suzanne realized. Some of the staff wanted to sedate you and *make* you sleep. Suzanne figured you were entitled to turn your brain to mashed potatoes if you wanted to." The old man was silent for a while, paging down through the display on his video tablet, skimming the top news stories. "The point of which is, if I'd done something like that as a young man, when I was in peak condition, it would have killed me. When you finally did sleep that time, you slept for most of a day, got up and didn't sleep again for four or five days, something like that. That was the point where Suzanne started monitoring the sleep patterns of the other telepaths."

"And she found out that I was the only one?"

"Indeed. Well, the only one who's ever shown the capability. She thinks Jany could, under the correct impetus, and most likely the twins as well. None of the others."

Carl was silent, watching the highway lamps flicker past them. Bright, and dim; bright, and dim . . . "I'm not sure I really wanted to know that."

"You didn't know?"

Carl shook his head mutely.

"How could you not?"

The passing of the lights was soothing, almost hypnotic. "I've always felt alone. I'm not a human being. Jany thinks I stand off too much from the rest of the telepaths. They do a thing, Malko, a merging of minds, that I can't join them in. I *can't.* I've tried. I *know* there are other differences between us." He brooded, lost in his own thoughts. "I try not to think about it."

Malko Kalharri started to say something, and stopped.

"What?"

Malko said easily, "Nothing. Just a thought, not important."

"Tell me."

In a tone of mild exasperation, Malko said, "Carl, it wasn't—"

"Tell me."

Malko sighed. "You are a particularly difficult young man to mislead, Carl."

"Malko, please."

"Suzanne told me this perhaps two years ago; I didn't know it myself before that. You were born in 2030, Carl. The DNA slicing technique which created you was not invented until almost five years later. It did not work reliably for nearly five years after *that*."

Carl worked his way through the sentence. "I don't have even a vague understanding of whatever it is you just said."

"I don't think you know just how you got your name, Carl. I—"

"Of course I do. Grigorio Castanaveras."

"That's not exactly what I meant. The gene pattern which became you was our fifty-fifth attempt to produce a living foetus. Every bloody one of the first fifty-four failed. Didn't redivide even once. We were labeling the attempts alphabetically; A through Z, then AA to AZ, BA to BZ, and so forth. You were lot C, number C, the fifty-fifth attempt. I don't think," said Malko, "that I ever really explained this to you. That's how Jany was named also; lot J, number M. Johnny was lot Y, number M. We were spelling his name with a 'Y' for a while, before the host mother who bore him decided that she wanted his name spelled with a 'J.' " He shrugged. "We didn't argue; she was a good host. She later bore four of the children, one a year the full four years the assembly line was rolling. Anyhow, if you didn't know, that's basically how the lot of you got your names."

"Ever wonder why I named the twins David and Denice?"

"You . . ." Malko's lips shaped the twins' names, and then he laughed suddenly. "I'll be damned. I never noticed. You have a warped sense of humor, son."

"Do tell. You still haven't explained yourself."

"Well, you were our fifty-fifth attempt at a living foetus. Carl, we didn't get a living DNA-sliced foetus until Johnny, five-hundred-odd tries later. And we *never* got one by the technique which created you. Did you ever wonder why Jany was created the way she was, with cloning techniques that were twenty years old?"

"I don't think I ever did."

"Because we *still* couldn't create a foetus through DNA slicing who would live."

"But you had, already."

"No," said Malko Kalharri softly, "we didn't. With the technology that was available to us three decades ago, we could not have created you. Suzanne was right, her theory was sound, but we should never have succeeded in creating you, not in 2030. The technology to do so *did not exist.*"

"Then where the hell did I come from?"

"I don't know," Malko said simply.

"Malko, I'm *here.* Something was responsible for me."

Malko did not reply.

"*Malko.*"

"You're right, son. But it wasn't us."

"I'll be damned." Carl stared straight out through the canopy. Flickering red taillights were barely visible in the distance. With an act of will he thrust the subject of his own existence into the background. Not relevant, and even if Malko believed what he was saying it did not make him right. *Belief,* some old AI philosopher had said, *is not relevant to truth.*

And besides, it made him uncomfortable. Carl changed the subject abruptly. "How did you get mixed up with that lot?"

Malko stretched suddenly and laced his hands behind his head, looking up from his video tablet. " 'And now for something completely different . . .' Politics, son. I find them— useful. I imagine their reasons for working with me are similar. Belinda Singer wasn't there, but Ripper's her protégé. Between Belinda and 'Sieur Chandler, we have the beginnings of an American power structure for the first time since the end of the War. That's worth a lot."

"Chandler prefers to be called Mister, not 'Sieur."

Malko straightened slightly and peered out through the overarching canopy at the nondescript blur of buildings and fields that lined the TransCon's sides. The gentle thrumming of the hoverfans competed with his words. "Hmm. I'd heard that, actually."

Carl was silent for a moment. "Never mind," he said a moment later, "your bloody damned obsession with the old United States. It was not *my* country, and I have nothing against the Unification of Earth. The Unification was probably a good thing, on balance. Aside from their ideological bent, which is irrelevant to me, why should I work with the people we met with tonight?"

Malko shook his head wearily. "You're missing the point. Their 'ideological bent' is not irrelevant to you, and I'm not sure you know what their ideology is, anyway. Ripper's hardly a Johnny Reb; he thinks the U.N. is a good idea. Which it may be." Malko stared down at the empty video tablet. "Its existence is probably what's kept us from having a noticeable sized war in four decades. But the fact that the U.N. is a good thing, assuming it is, does *not* mean that the fact that you are an American, culturally if in no other fashion, is irrelevant." He slowed down suddenly. "Excuse me. I'm lecturing again, but do you have any idea how hard our lawyers fought to get the issue of our liability under the Official Secrets Acts tried in Judge Sonneschein's court? Carl, two thirds of the Unification Circuit Court judges in this country are French. Ninety-eight percent of those in France are French. If you think ideology is irrelevant to you, you'd damn well better think again. Maybe you don't think you're an American, but Amnier does, and so do the Peaceforcers. You're *already* allied to those people we just left. You think a French judge would have ruled that we were not subject to the Official Secrets Act?"

"French judges have ruled in our favor in other instances."

"True, when the law was clearly on our side. The Official Secrets Acts are ambiguously written, though. If there's ever a time for a judge to let his prejudices sway him, a case like that is it."

"If I say yes, we'll cooperate, what then?"

Malko shrugged; corded muscles rippled in his shoulders. "You don't have to talk to Amnier, or Carson either. Intermediaries will do that. We'll record some sort of announcement saying we're essentially going to be resuming our old functions for the PKF, except we'll be paid, we'll give it to *Electronic Times* or *NewsBoard* early on the Fourth of July and sit back until the storm blows over."

"Okay," said Carl finally. "I told Chris Summers we'd come to Japan anyway."

Malko looked at him. "Come again?"

A blip appeared on the radar screen, to the rear of the far limit at which the MetalSmith scanned. "I had to tell him something, or he wouldn't have helped us. Besides, Japan is pretty. I was there once. It's green and there's not too many people. The gardens are nice."

"Japan." It sounded as though Malko were considering the idea. "I've never been there myself. When I was a boy, they came pretty close to buying up most of this country. They were awfully damned formidable. I'm not surprised, really, that the U.N. forces panicked and nuked them when the Japanese decided to fight. God knows what they'd have had up their sleeves. It would have been interesting." There was a real wistfulness in his voice.

Carl glanced at the radar holo, not really seeing it. The blip inside it was gaining on them. "How the hell did you end up where you are? The Johnny Rebs would leap at the chance to fight under you. You know it and I know it and the government knows it. And you've never been tempted."

Malko Kalharri was silent a long time, staring out the canopy. "Son, I know the answer to that, but I'm not sure I know the words to say it right. You can read my mind if you like. War and politics, Carl, those are the only games fit for grown men to play at. The only ones that make enough of a difference to count. And between laser cannon and nukes and transform viruses—these days we can't afford war any longer."

"No," said Carl, "I don't suppose we can . . . that's odd."

Malko leaned forward at the tone of his voice. "What?"

"The car behind us is gaining on us." Carl moved a finger inside the holofield and touched the dot representing the car. Numbers danced at the bottom of the display. "Look. They're not plugged into TransCon, and they have their license caster turned off."

"Speedfreaks?"

"Probably . . ." Carl turned on the rear cameras. A light-enhanced image showed what looked like an old Chandler 1770. "Why aren't they skipping?"

"I don't understand."

"The 1770 is a little lighter than the MetalSmith, with similar lift. It's not fitted for true flight, though, except in some heavily customized jobs. But they shouldn't be able to move as fast as they are without skipping all over the place. They're up around two hundred thirty kph. I couldn't do that, and we're heavier and have gyroscopes." Carl watched the dot. "They must be carrying a hell of a load."

The car behind them, already traveling above the maximum road speed for any hovercar Carl knew of, accelerated and passed 270 kph, still without any instability at all.

"Something is wrong," Carl heard himself say. He took the car back from TransCon and assumed manual control. "Something is *very* wrong." Time struck him like a whip, wrapped itself around him, and things began moving very slowly. His vision suddenly became as clear as though it were high noon. The car behind him seemed to slow, and Carl saw the two men inside it, and the huge laser cannon that was mounted down the center of the craft, and without desiring to, without any effort of will at all, Carl found himself *outside*.

The future crashed down, into the present.

Carl watched . . .

. . . *the laser cannon strikes the rear of the MetalSmith, and the canopy goes dark black instantly, all over, in a desperate effort to absorb and distribute the heat being pumped into it. Inside the MetalSmith, Carl is blind except for front instruments. He blows open the airscoops almost reflexively; he already knows he cannot outrun the modified 1770 on his tail, and in the time it would take him to reach flight speed where he can snap the MetalSmith's wings, the cannon will have destroyed them. Only the fact that the 1770 cannot carry the mass of a full military power supply has saved them so far. The airscoops brake the car as though a giant hand has grabbed it, and Carl swings the car up and to the left at the same time, over the fence and into oncoming traffic. The canopy begins to clear, ever so slightly, and suddenly blackens again as the car behind follows the MetalSmith over the fence. From somewhere behind them—behind, Carl has the impression, the 1770 following them—comes a thunderous explosion, and the hovercar is rocked by a shock wave.*

The interior of the MetalSmith is blisteringly hot.

In the seat next to him, Malko is beginning to realize that something is happening.

A huge twelve-fan appears out of nowhere, and at the very last possible instant Carl closes the airscoop brakes and ignites the rear turbojets, veers off to the right, up again and back over the fence onto the correct side of the highway. He knows a moment's brief triumph as he realizes that the Chandler 1770 attacking them split to the left of the oncoming truck and that he has gained precious moments. It is a short-lived triumph. He moves a finger across the contact that should kill the rear jets, and it does not. The roar of the turbos continues and he wastes a precious second evaluating his options.

At the end of that second the 1770 is back on his tail, and the laser fire strikes them again.

Carl Castanaveras has time to think, quite clearly, I have always wanted to try this.

He disengages the gyroscopes, snaps the car's wings open and brings full power to the MetalSmith's front fans. The nose of the car leaps up, and the new attitude of the rear jets sends the MetalSmith climbing up like a rocket. The car is shaking wildly, the frame itself vibrating.

Gently, gently . . . bring the nose up too fast, and the car will tumble backward. Bring it up too slowly and the laser cannon will remove all of your options. The MetalSmith is standing very nearly on its tail, nose pointing to the sky, five meters above traffic. The fans are facing into the car's forward movement, slowing the MetalSmith more quickly than the car could possibly be slowed in any other fashion. Their pursuers cannot slow so quickly. Carl cannot see with his eyes; some other sense causes him to nudge the car gently to the right, to send the turbojets blasting downward into the space beneath which their attackers are passing. The jets themselves are not destructive but they push the modified Chandler 1770 down, into contact with the road itself. In a fraction of a second the 1770 ceases to be recognizable as a hovercar, shredding itself against the surface of the ferrocrete, disintegrating into a cloud of metal, still moving forward as the pavement rips at it.

The MetalSmith slows with astonishing speed, from 150 kph down to approximately 10 in the course of seconds. The car is vibrating insanely, roaring with the huge force with which it must push the air aside. When the MetalSmith stalls at last, it is moving less than 10 kph, and it strikes the pavement on its side and rolls over once before coming to a rest, slightly at a slant on a slope at the side of the highway. The rear jets are still burning. Somewhere in the course of it all, Malko Kalharri has struck his head, and blood mats his hair to his forehead. Carl sits without moving, staring blankly as the canopy fades and becomes clear again. A high-pitched whining noise rouses him at last, an unfamiliar sound that he cannot place.

The word gyroscope occurs to him, and then he moves in a wild scramble, tearing off his seat restraints. The canopy is jammed shut, and the mechanism will not operate it. In a moment of berserk strength he strikes upward with both hands, and the canopy pops clear, swinging smoothly out from the nose of the vehicle. The car is shuddering again as the gyroscopes begin to spin out of balance. He rips Malko's restraints off the old man, climbs over Malko and out of the car, and is lifting Malko out of his seat when the car shakes itself like a wounded beast, screams as its metal tears like paper, and picks itself up from the ground to tumble end over end as the gyroscopes spin down, wasting their accumulated kinetic energy in a single horrible second. The car turns its length three times

*before the remaining fuel in the fore and rear jets ignites. The
explosion is modest; the jet fuel used in hovercars is intentionally not very flammable except inside the turbojet itself
when mixed with pure oxygen and catalyst. Carl sits down on
the dirt at the side of the road, and feels very strange, very
distant, and time slows as he sits there next to Malko Kalharri's
bleeding form, and Carl finds himself . . .*

Sitting in the front seat of the MetalSmith with Malko, and
the Chandler 1770 was right behind them, laser cannon at the
ready.

He had just a moment after the vision ended to realize
where and when he was.

And then it happened.

With a crack of thunder I came into existence standing at
the side of TransContinental Highway Four. I was in fast time,
enduring two seconds for every one that took place in real
time. The problem of describing the activities of time travelers
to those whose vocabularies possess only one temporal di-
mension is a grave one. The moment at which I appeared was,
in consecutive Time, nearly a quarter of a second before Camber Tremodian followed.

He was not hunting me yet, on *his* private timeline; he
was, at that moment in his existence, fleeing from me, be-
lieving correctly that I sought to destroy him. It would be many
years in Camber Tremodian's future before he would search
for me in the laboratory where I had created Carl Castanaveras.
He had not yet learned how to fully use his ability to move
through Time; later, he would not fall for a gambit such as the
one I offered him now.

I knew already that the gambit would fail, but it was
necessary to go through with it regardless. When one travels
Time, free will is often moot.

Camber Tremodian cracked into existence on the other
side of the highway, some sixty meters away.

Carl Castanaveras' vehicle came into sight, followed closely
by the primitive vehicle that carried his attackers. Like Camber
himself, they were doomed to failure; this was not the night
for Carl Castanaveras to die. Cloaked and cowled in the traditional black shadow cloak that is favored by the night faces
of United Earth Intelligence, Camber Tremodian withdrew a
weapon whose name would mean nothing to a human being

of any time earlier than the twenty-sixth century A.D. The Ihmaldsen Relay was named after a twenty-second-century physicist, the human being who discovered the negrav nexus. Four centuries later the negative gravity locus was bound into a no-time stasis blade by a woman whose name is not spoken in the halls of UEI.

I am the Name Storyteller, and I tell you that her name was Ola, who was Lady Blue, who was Leiacan of Eastersea.

The IR is the most fearsome hand-held weapon known by any civilization, anywhere in the Continuing Time. During the height of the Time Wars, the Zaradin themselves knew no weapon so fierce. I withdrew the slim tube of my own IR from my cloak, and through the pressure of my hand upon the tube extended the force blade into the air over the highway.

Carl's car sped down the highway toward us. Camber Tremodian perceived my presence and ignored it. He brought the blade of his IR scything down toward the aircar. Camber did not, yet, know of fast time, though control of that aspect of Time, like every other, was latent within him. He could not know that I would move better than fast as twice as he. I brought the blade of my own IR out to slap his aside, and the negrav nexus contained in the tip of his force blade touched down on the surface of the highway, behind the two primitive aircars.

The negrav nexus is a grave force to unleash. Where it touched the highway, the stonesteel of the highway erupted and splashed as though a meteor had struck there.

I have never known for certain; I believe some of that flying stonesteel struck Camber Tremodian and near killed him before he fled through Time. I was gone myself long before the shock wave reached the spot where I had appeared.

Carl sat in the hospital waiting room with a cup of cold coffee at his elbow. His eyes were wide open, but he saw nothing. Not that there was much to see; a room with pale green walls, which held nearly a hundred chairs with video tablets chained to them, and a single vending chef for those who wanted to eat their meals in the waiting room. Jany was sitting in the chair next to him. She did not attempt to talk to him; she was reading what the press had to say about the attack. Both the *Electronic Times* and *NewsBoard* had logged major stories on it; the *Times* was giving it front-screen treatment. AP had not yet filed on it; most of the other news Boards were licensing their reports from either the *Times* or *News-Board*.

Two heavily armed Security Services guards stood at the door to the waiting room with instructions to keep the press —and everyone else—out.

A little after midnight Suzanne Montignet made her way through the security guards and took a seat opposite Carl and Jany.

Jany said quietly, "So?"

Montignet shook her head in exhaustion. Lovely she was, still, lovely enough that Carl had nearly made a pass at her on more than one occasion in the last decade, but she was in fact nearly as old as Malko, and the strain of the evening had worn her down. "He's in bad shape, kids. Oh, he's going to live." She smiled rather wearily. "He was awake for about five minutes before they took him in to surgery. He's a tough old guy. Said it was a 'proven fact' that you couldn't hurt a Kalharri just by bashing him in the head."

"What's wrong with him?" asked Jany.

"Shattered femur in his right leg, cracked ribs, fairly severe concussion, slight subdural hematoma, probably resulting in some loss of brain tissue. Not severe." She looked at Carl. "He wanted to know, 'Did we get the bastards?' I had to admit I didn't know. Did you?"

Carl's lips curled of their own accord into a sardonic half-grin. "What do you think?"

The answer did not seem to please Suzanne. "Of course. I should have known."

"When can he have visitors?"

Suzanne looked at Jany. "Early morning, five or six o'clock. He's not suffering from anything very serious except possibly the concussion, and I'm optimistic about that." She turned to Carl. "I'm going to suggest that he come home with me when he's ready."

"To Massapequa Park? Why?"

Suzanne put a touch of the whip into her voice. "Because I'm one of the best neurologists in the world, and I want to observe Malko for the next few weeks. Your ability to read minds is almost irrelevant in the context. Besides, I think Trent might like to have Malko for company. I believe I bore him."

Carl thought about it. "Very well. If Malko agrees."

Suzanne said very mildly, "If he did not, any decision we made would be quite moot."

"Yes."

Suzanne Montignet cocked her head to one side and regarded him. "You should go home, and sleep. You don't look good."

He did not feel at all sleepy. "Perhaps."

She smiled almost gently. "But you're not going to. What will you do?"

"Go for a walk in the city." He shook his head. "I don't know yet." She seemed to be waiting for some further answer. "I really *don't* know. They hurt Malko. They blew up my car." He was silent for a second, eyes unfocused. "I'm really pissed about that."

Carl walked alone down windy streets made shiny with rain. That late at night, even the largest city on Earth grew quiet. Once the skies opened in a thundershower and he raised his face to the sky and let the wind-driven water pound down upon him. The water soaked his clothing, and rivulets ran down into his boots. He wandered aimlessly across the slidewalks and streets, and then ascended into the web of skywalks that linked the downtown spacescrapers. He passed the offices of Kalharri, Ltd. on Third Avenue and continued on without going in. Two blocks later, on the level-four skywalks, he was shot at from a point somewhere above him. He walked up a glowing spiral stairwell, two levels, and back down into a stairwell across from the skywalk where the stairwell lights had been shot out. He dragged out the teenage boys hiding there and left their bodies in the center of the skywalk. He walked without hurry to Grand Central Station and took a powered lift, down eight stories to the Bullet station. He waited without any thoughts at all until the Bullet arrived.

He boarded the southbound Bullet and changed trains at the Fulton Street station. Three men wearing dramasuit holo generators at their belts boarded the Bullet at that point; one of them looked directly at Carl without apparent recognition. Carl stayed on until they reached the Bullet station two stops from the Complex.

Something abnormal was happening at the Complex; Carl felt the echoes of power before he left the Bullet.

The station was not the one closest to the Complex; the closest station was only three blocks away. But there was a twenty-four-hour Ford Systems car rental at this location; he rented a Regal limousine and drove it home through the crowd. Security Systems was taking no chances with the crowd; they used the gate stunners liberally.

Carl walked through the echoing empty halls of the Complex, clothing still drenched by the rain. He stopped at some doorways and looked in upon sleeping children. Some of the children broadcast their dreams strongly, and at times the dreams took Carl and dragged him away from reality for a while. The dreams were all curiously similar, the dream of one Person, shared by many minds. Movement, wrapped in a golden light, wrapped in rainbows. He stopped by the bedroom he shared with Jany and looked in. Jany was back from the hospital and slept soundly, without dreaming. Carl suspected that it was an artificial sleep; Suzanne had probably given her something. He left her there and continued downstairs, making his way through the sleeping minds.

. . . he strode across a vast black plain, walking toward a huge fountain of light.

There was nothing in the kitchen or the huge dining room, and nothing in the conference rooms. In one conference room a copy of one of the children's favorite flat movies, *The Rocky Horror Picture Show*, had been left playing with the sound turned down. Carl recognized the scene; Riff Raff, Magenta, and Columbia were doing the Time Warp again. Carl left the conference hall and wandered through the corridor that surrounded the ring of suites that faced inward on the Quad.

He heard sounds from ahead, a gentle procession of piano chords, underlaid by a slow roll of drums. Light spilled into the corridor ahead of him through an open door.

He stood at the edge of the fountainhead, unable to reach out and touch it, staring into the fierce golden light, into the smooth, powerful dance of awareness.

The door to her room was open, and he came through into the bedroom. It was filled with the ordinary clutter any teenage girl would have accumulated, clothing and makeup keys and fashion templates. There was a poster of Willi dancing, and distantly, he was surprised by that; he hadn't thought she liked Willi. The music surrounded him. One full wall was a painting done in electrolytes, of a long, winding road that stretched out across a bizarre, dark landscape over which hung a crawling silver fog. A verse in the corner of the painting read: "Running away to eternity/ Come walk my ways, it cried/ You left, left lesser things behind/ And a portion of you died."

The fountain pulsed, whispered to him, **Join me. I am that which loves you.**

There was a man on the road, half turned away. He had Carl's face. Carl turned his back on the painting, turned to meet that which awaited him.

The huge glass door that opened on the Quad was wide open. Sunlamps set very bright glared down into the enclosed area, flooding it with a harsh pale light. The rain pelted down, and fragmented patches of rainbows shimmered, rippled through the hot wet air.

Heather was dancing naked in the rain.

Carl stood frozen in place, watching, unable to move. Sound washed over him, lyrically sad vocals nested between gentle drums and the rolling of the piano. The rain fell only centimeters away from him.

> *Lost boys and golden girls*
> *Down on the corner and all around the world*
> *Lost boys and golden girls*
> *Down on the corner and all around*
> *All around the world*

Time had wrapped itself around her like a chain. She moved across the grass, under the lights, dancing for him with wild abandon. There was no separate identity in her, only a living fusion of the girl and something else entirely.

> *We gotta be fast*
> *We were born out of time*
> *Born out of time and alone*
> *And we'll never be as young as we are right now*
> *Running away, and running for home*

He stepped in still-wet clothing, out into the warm rain, under the brilliant hot lights. Heather's dancing slowed, and stopped, and she regarded him. She smiled dazzlingly and said with utter certainty, "Yes."

He drew to within centimeters of her and traced a finger down her cheek. "Yes," he agreed.

She lifted herself up and locked her legs around his waist.

Her mouth was busy at the juncture between his neck and his shoulder. He carried her into her bedroom and laid her down on the bed. He removed his shirt and pants without haste, and laid down beside her. Heather locked her mouth to his and wriggled her tongue between his teeth. Her entire body was shivering violently, whether from the water evaporating on her body or something else Carl did not know. He lifted her up and entered her.

He saw himself through her eyes, felt the strength of his body as he moved against her. In her eyes he was a network of glowing fine lines, culminating in a fierce glow around his skull. He saw through her eyes his own eyes, the light and the elemental heat of his person. He lost track of their bodies and found himself in some other disconnected reality, burning, consuming himself in the flame, and the other person with him cooled the flame and brought order and peace into him.
I am that which loves you.

"I know," he said aloud, shuddering with his orgasm. The girl locked her legs tightly around him, clutched him with her arms. The orgasm went on and on, and he let himself grow lost in the pure, physical sensation. When he came back to himself Heather was still holding on to him, her body shaking silently, and it was several moments before he realized that she was crying, and that she was alone. He became aware of the chill in the air, and without moving her drew up one of the blankets from the bed and wrapped it around her to help keep her warm. *I love you,* she was telling him, *I love you.*

He grew soft and slipped out of her. Still she did not move, but tucked her head against his shoulder and clung to him. He held her and let her cry herself out, until she could not cry any longer.

The tears did not hurt him. They were not for him.

"Carl," she whispered just before sleep took her, "we're going to die, aren't we?"

"Yes."

I looked down upon their sleeping forms.

Coming here, into this time, was a weakness. It was not necessary, and therefore wrong. It is one of the tenets of night-ways that there are only necessary actions and mistakes; no third ground.

A gamble and a mistake, all at once; but it was safe

enough, in its way. It was certain that Camber Tremodian would not look for me here. He knew as fact that I would, very shortly from *now* on my personal timeline, appear at the Spacething Library, orbiting the great black hole at the center of the galaxy. It was inescapable; I had been there and would be there, and he would be waiting. I would survive this visit so that I could enter the Library early in the thirty-second century A.D., and there, very likely, die.

It is difficult to see.

I am not certain what it is that has driven me to come here, to look upon Carl and Heather Castanaveras.

Perhaps because he will die so well, so usefully.

So soon.

If there was inspiration there, it was not for me to find.

I slipped out into the garden, and went to face my destiny, and left them to face theirs.

I vanished in a clap of rushing air.

9

Saturday morning the crowds outside the Complex had grown to number nearly ten thousand. They filled the streets in a solid mass of humanity for blocks around the Complex, and their chanting was so loud there was no place in all the Complex where silence could be found. Sometime during the night, as July the second dawned, their chanting had changed from a ragged "*Death to the genies!*" to a deep throated "*AMERICA, AMERICA, AMERICA.*" Security Services, without being asked, had dispatched an additional squad to the Complex, a full twenty-five men.

Nearly a score of the children were playing in the park. Johnny and Ary and Mandy and Thea stood guard with autoshots against the unlikely event that any of the demonstrators would be foolish enough to attempt to come up over the fence. There were no Security Services forces within the park; with the defenses they had in place, Carl had deemed it unnecessary. Though the crowd could not see through the fence that surrounded the park, there were so many of them that they had surrounded the entire block that the park sat upon, arms linked, chanting. The chanting was stretching Johnny's nerves tight; he was amazed at how calmly the children took it all. They were all, except Carl, in some measure one Person; but the children were far more so than any of the elders except Ary and possibly Willi. The children had spent nine months listening to the chanting, and even today's redoubled intensity did not seem to disturb them. The weather continued to be a bad joke; an inversion layer had trapped the warm moist air of the last week, preventing the rains from granting them any relief. And still, the children were in evident good spirits despite the demonstrators, the gray skies and drenching humidity.

Unlike Johnny.

He distracted himself by sitting in on Jany, at work inside the Complex. She was giving interview after interview with only momentary breaks to any newsdancer who cared to wait his turn. Carl was in the office next to her, doing the same thing; Johnny knew better than to attempt to read Carl's mind. So far this morning the telepaths had released both the recording of Carl's conversation with Jerril Carson and the Secretary General, and their recording of Tio Sandoval's last words before his death. It had been several days now since the *Electronic Times* had received, from a webdancer who called himself Ralf, confirmation that some of the demonstrators in front of the Complex had indeed been Peaceforcers on duty, from the New York City contingent that was, in fact if not in theory, under the direct control of Unification Councilor Jerril Carson.

Malko Kalharri had given an interview to a reporter from *NewsBoard* early that morning. From his hospital bed, which had gone over quite well.

It had been, to put it mildly, an interesting Saturday morning.

Amnier sat perfectly still behind his desk.

Seated facing him, across the flat expanse of polished wood, Charles Eddore appeared quite calm. "The calls for your impeachment are not serious, yet. Nonetheless, the vote of censure in the Unification Council is almost certain to pass. I'd cease worrying about the Ninth Amendment if I were you, sir. You will not be reelected."

Amnier spoke precisely. "You are quite correct. Have you found Carson?"

"No. His office is not answering calls. I think the Councilor has decided that you plan to throw him to the wolves. In his position," said Eddore thoughtfully, "I think I'd blast my own head off before Castanaveras found me."

"Do you think that is what Carson will do?"

"No," said Eddore. "I don't."

"The Elite know where he is, of course."

Eddore nodded. "Of course. But they've practically made an honorary Frenchman of Carson, you know. They won't tell you where he is." He paused. "Unless, of course, he does kill himself."

Amnier sat perfectly still behind his desk, staring off into a nonexistent distance.

He appeared to be thinking about something.

Without asking his leave, Charles Eddore got up and left the Secretary General alone with his thoughts. There was a faint, almost imperceptible smile upon his lips as he left.

Rather to his surprise, Johnny found himself yawning. *What a bitch of a week,* he thought to himself. *It's got to get better soon.* The autoshot was very heavy, so he laid it down beside him and then sat down, propping himself up against a tree. *Fine,* he thought cheerfully, *this is just fine.* He could survey the children he was guarding and get some well-deserved relaxation at the same time. He would just close his eyes for a moment, and relax just a bit. Just before he closed his eyes, he noticed many of the others in the park doing the same thing. A fine idea that was, also. None of them had been getting enough rest. . . .

He slept.

The AeroSmith dropped through the clouds. Straight down, very fast, and came to land in the center of the park with a thump.

In the middle of an interview with a reporter from the *Paris Match* Board, Carl Castanaveras broke off in mid-word.

His eyes went blank. *Something is missing.* What was it? Something that had been there, only moments . . .

His scream echoed through the Complex.

"No!"

The Peaceforcers were not in uniform, and the AeroSmith was not marked as a PKF vehicle.

Jerril Carson walked among them, through the park where the telepaths lay in sleep. "There, take that one, that's MacArthur," he said grimly, pointing, "and those two as well."

The Peaceforcers lifted the telepaths indicated and began carrying them to the AeroSmith.

Jerril Carson stopped in mid-stride and stared in disbelief. And then he smiled.

"No," he said, "cancel that. We'd only have to keep the others drugged." He stood over the two small, dark-haired forms. "And besides, I rather think that Castanaveras will find the loss of these two—quite compelling." The Peaceforcers with him were standing, watching him, and he snapped, "Take them!"

The Peaceforcers with him looked at each other, and then did as they were bade.

The AeroSmith lifted into the air, with the twins inside.

Seconds after it lifted from the ground, Carl Castanaveras burst from the tunnel entrance, Excalibur in hand. He saw the lifting AeroSmith and brought the laser to bear on it.

He held that position, knuckles white where they gripped the rifle, and then slowly, very slowly, brought the rifle back down again. They were so high that a crash would, quite certainly, kill the twins. His eyes dropped shut, and he reached out toward the dwindling vehicle, but there were too many minds within it, and he could not distinguish the one mind in particular for which he sought.

He stood without moving until the others from the Complex came pouring through the tunnel entrance, and then without word turned and went back to the Complex, there to finish, in under thirty seconds, his interview with the reporter from *Paris Match*.

"Crutches," snorted Malko Kalharri. "I feel fine." The hospital walkways did not themselves move, in the interests of safety; despite his complaint, Malko moved with the crutches nearly as quickly as he'd have been able to had he walked. They'd tried to outfit him with a ground chair such as visiting loonies used; at that point he'd rebelled. With things as uncertain as they were right now, he was damned if he was going to let himself get caught sitting down, out in public, where he would lose a crucial instant getting out of the chair if he had to move quickly.

At his side, Suzanne Montignet chuckled without much humor. Her features were drawn and pale with lack of sleep. "With the pain suppressants in your bloodstream right now, you could be stretched out on a rack and you'd have a good time.''

Her car was waiting for them at the exit to the hospital downlot, hovering forty centimeters above the rain-damp pavement. A Security Services squad car was right behind it. The carcomp lowered the hovercar to the ground at their approach and slowed down the fans to prevent the fanwash from spraying water at them as they got into the car.

Trent was sitting in the back seat, portaterm on his lap. He looked up from the holo the portaterm was generating as they got in. He spoke without preamble. ''According to *Paris Match* the twins have been kidnapped.''

''What?'' Malko and Suzanne both snapped the word at him.

''There's not really any more to the story than that. They ran on for two minutes but that was all they said.''

''*When?*'' Suzanne beat Malko to the word by an instant.

''Twelve minutes ago. Almost thirteen.''

Suzanne Montignet did not hesitate. She turned to Malko. ''How do you feel? Truly?''

Kalharri was leaning back in his seat, eyes closed in a pain that was not physical. He did not have enough energy for true rage. ''I'll be okay.''

''We'll go to the Complex, then,'' Suzanne decided. ''Trent? I can have Security Services take you back to the house.''

''That won't be necessary.''

She did not question him. ''Let's go.''

The crowds were uglier than Malko had ever seen them; literally hundreds of them had been stunned already when Suzanne Montignet's car pulled onto the street where the Complex was located, and Double-S sent out a pair of riot control sleds with mounted stunguns to clear a path for them through the crowd to the Complex's front gate. The crowd surged around them, nearly out of control, trampling those who were stunned in an effort to get at Suzanne's car. They had arrived just after a shipment of weapons from Security Services; autoshots were being distributed among the men from Security Services, and even the children were being given Excalibur Series Twos. Those with the mass to handle an autoshot, who requested one, were given that as well. Heather Castanaveras, wearing a jumpsuit of what looked to Malko suspiciously like the laser-resistant cloth combat fatigues were made of, with a hand maser tucked into a pocket and an autoshot resting on her right shoulder, took them up to see Carl. She said nothing to either Suzanne or Malko; she ushered them into the ready room down the hall from Carl's bedroom, where Carl and Jany and Johann were meeting with two officers from Security Services.

As she had not spoken to Malko or Suzanne, Heather said nothing to Trent. But she hugged him fiercely, and turned away from him and left them. It was not until later that Trent realized she had said good-bye the best way she knew how.

Carl was standing with his back to the door at which they entered. The door at the north end of the room, which led directly to Carl's bedroom, was open. He was watching the monitors that covered the crowds outside the front gate; he did not seem to be aware of their presence until he said, "It looks like you got here just in time."

One of the Security Services men, named, Malko thought, Deavers, was nodding. Captain's bars glowed on Deavers' uniform. "Yes. Look, on monitors five and nine as well. Peaceforcer troops." The Peaceforcers were taking up positions at the perimeters of the crowd, and seemed to be content to stay there, for the moment.

"I wonder if they'd have let you through," Carl said. Still he had not turned to look at them, nor greeted them. "Somehow," he said in a voice that held no expression at all, "I don't think they're here to protect us from the riot outside."

"Hello, Carl," said Malko softly.

Carl pivoted slowly to face them. Malko Kalharri winced and looked away. Suzanne Montignet had not made the mistake of attempting to meet his gaze.

Trent looked straight at him. "Hello, Father."

Carl said gravely, as to an equal, "Hello, Trent. You should not have come. Now that you are here, you should not stay."

Trent looked around the room. "I didn't drive," he offered as an explanation to them all. "It's not my fault."

The answer seemed to throw Carl. For the first time in a great long while, the very ghost of a smile touched him and was gone instantly. "Suzanne," he said, "go home. Take Malko and Trent and go home. I expect the Peaceforcers surrounding us will let you leave. Don't come back until this is over."

"Carl? Are you crazy?" Malko dropped one of his crutches to the floor and leaned on the other. "One hand to handle the crutch, and the other one to fire a weapon with, if it comes to that."

Carl said too gently, "Malko, go. There's nothing you can do here. And right now . . ." The words were very hard to say. "You'll just get in the way."

For the first time in the decades Suzanne had known Malko, he looked very old. But he was not going to give up without a fight. "Carl," he said, "you've got the capability to make me do anything you want. But you are not doing me any favors by making me leave."

"*I'm not trying to do you any favors!*" Carl Castanaveras roared. Jany and Johann and the two Security Services men were looking away from the scene. Malko blinked, and Carl said flatly, "Suzanne and Trent are going to need you. I know you'd love to go out in a loveforsaken blaze of glory, but that's a luxury you're fucking well going to have to pass on. Stop being selfish, damn it. *Go home.*"

Malko Kalharri swayed on his single crutch. He had gone absolutely white. Out of a dry mouth he said finally, "Okay."

Carl held his gaze a moment, and then nodded. "I'll see that Double-S escorts you past the crowd, of course. It's better this way, Malko." Without waiting for an answer, he turned to Trent. "Good-bye, Trent."

The boy's eyes widened slightly. "Oh?" He looked away for a moment, without expression, and then looked back. With perfect politeness he said, "Good-bye, Father."

Carl stared at the boy. "Trent?"

"I don't think . . ." Trent shook his head slowly. "No. I've never heard you use that word before."

"Trent?" Jany looked disturbed. "What word?"

"Good-bye." He spoke to Jany, as though Carl were not there. "His grammar is poor, but he never says anything he doesn't mean. Have you noticed that?"

Jany said slowly, "I don't understand," and immediately after that the room's outspeaker said, "There is a call for Carl from Councilor Carson."

They were all still gaping in disbelief when the holograph

appeared over the ready room's largest table, and the image
of Unification Councilor Jerril Carson appeared within the field.

---

*Trent was only distantly aware of the others around him.
The systerm in the corner came up under his flying hands. He
wished that he had not left his portaterm in the car, but there
was no time to regret its lack. His traceset was in his shirt
pocket, but he had no time to don that, either. He had stripped
his user profile out of the InfoNet nodes present in the Complex.
At the time it had seemed a good idea. The accesses he had
developed for that user profile would have been useless in the
hands of an amateur, and terribly dangerous in the hands of
a Player only slightly skilled. And he had not been planning
to return.*

*He hacked his way through the default user profile until
it would do the bare minimum he required of it, turned au-
tohelp off, turned prompts off, enabled abbreviated command
syntax, and loaded the profile into memory.*

Trent danced through the InfoNet.

Carl simply stood, staring in a rage so vast that there was
no room in him for speech. Jerril Carson stared out of the holo
cube at them, his skin a pallid gray. When it became clear
that Carl was not going to speak, he said in a shaking voice,
"I have the twins." Carl said nothing, and emboldened, Jerril
Carson continued. "You have caused me severe problems,
Carl." His voice gained firmness and certainty as he spoke.
"If you wish to see your children alive, ever again, you *will*
do as you are told."

Carl closed his eyes.

Jerril Carson jerked and went utterly rigid. He and Carl
held the tableau for several seconds, and then Carl's eyes
opened again, and Carson jerked like a puppet whose strings
had been released. He gasped for air. "Fool," he snarled in
a harsh voice, still panting. "You think I've known you . . .
this long . . . without learning anything? There are . . . *hundreds*
of minds all around me, and thousands more in the distance
between us. You can't *touch* me."

At Suzanne Montignet's home in Massapequa Park, the systerm rang once and answered an incoming call.

. In the bedroom where Trent had been sleeping, jacked into the house circuitry, was a device about the size of a makeup key. There was more processing power packed into its molecular circuitry than was to be found in the entire world in the year 2000 A.D. It was a biochip image coprocessor, one of the finest commercially available anywhere in the entire world.

Touched, roused, and the program assembled itself from storage, assumed a sort of shadowy dim self-awareness, and then Ralf, the Wise and Powerful, sought through the InfoNet for its master.

The fear was past; a vindictive enjoyment was evident in Carson's demeanor. ". . . and state that you falsified Sandoval's recording, that it was a complete fake."

Jany answered him. Carl was sitting next to her, glaring into the cameras. For a while that had, it seemed, disconcerted Carson, but no more. "How do you suggest we do that?" Her features were pale, but her voice was steady. "The entire point behind the truth plate was that it made the recording believable. You can't fake a truth plate recording."

"You simply assert that *you* can," said Carson. "It will be believed."

"What then?"

"You'll further announce that not only were the Peaceforcers *not* responsible for the kidnapping of your children, but that we in fact recovered your children from the kidnappers, and that as a token of your gratitude you've agreed to renew your service with the PKF. You admit you've seen the selfishness of your previous position, and that you see that your skills are needed in the service of the Unification. You'll repeat yourself, loud and often."

Jany nodded. "They won't believe that. Not for an instant."

"*They?*" asked Carson with a note of flat, cold viciousness in his voice. "The media? The courts?" He smiled again, a horrible smile that literally made Jany feel sick to her stomach. "Or the public?"

Jany had no answer.

"The public will believe," said Jerril Carson.

Trent's image came up and surrounded him.

Power and vision surged through him.

The filters he had spent years designing cut out the sheer vast bulk of irrelevant detail that flowed through the Information Network. With the tracers built into Ralf, Trent flickered across the thousands of optic fibers that serviced the Complex and localized the one fiber that fed into the office where Jerril Carson's image glowed in midair. The glassite line was graded-index optic fiber, not true lasercable; he could not send a signal back through it in the opposite direction. No matter; localization algorithms mapped out the path of the central trunk that fed data from the InfoNet into the signal splitters inside the Complex.

The main trunk linking the Complex with the Information Network was true lasercable; Trent sent Ralf into the optic fiber, down the line following the digital pulses that contained Unification Councilor Carson's image.

A holograph flickered into existence, immediately behind Jerril Carson's image.

It held a map of Manhattan.

Jany's eyes did not even move. All that Carson could see was the space before the holocams, and the map was not within that range. Carl did not even appear to have noticed its existence; he continued to glare at Jerril Carson's image.

"When do we get the twins back?" Jany asked.

On the map behind Carson the image was zooming in on the eastern shore of Manhattan, where Franklin D. Roosevelt island bisected the East River.

Jerril Carson said, "That is an excellent question."

His image vanished. Behind the spot where his holograph had appeared, the map froze solid.

"Where is he?" asked Carl.

Trent twisted in his chair. His features were perfectly still. "I'm sorry. I didn't get it."

Carl rose slowly. "How close?"

"Somewhere around the intersection of Second Avenue

and Seventy-second Street." Trent hesitated. "Within five blocks in any direction, I think."

"Are you sure?"

"No."

F. X. Chandler had spent most of the day auditing the news Boards and the situation developing at his old home. He had excellent access to information; among the several hundred spyeyes above the Complex were three that belonged to him. Now he looked at Carl Castanaveras' image, floating in the center of his living room, a kilometer and a half above the surface of Manhattan. "What can I do for you, son?"

Chandler could hear chanting, somewhere in the background, when Carl spoke. "I need help. Jerril Carson is somewhere within five blocks of the intersection of Second Avenue and Seventy-second Street, and he has my children. I don't know exactly where he is, though, and I need to."

Chandler was very slow in replying. "How certain are you about this information?"

"Very. Frank, I need help. I'm surrounded by Peaceforcers; even if I made it past the riot outside I don't think I'd make it past the Peaceforcers, or I'd go myself."

Chandler did not reply immediately.

"Frank, *please*. These are my children."

The desperation in Castanaveras' voice was what decided Chandler. "Very well. I'll see what I can do."

Carl Castanaveras said simply, "Thank you. Thank you very much."

They waited. Jany and Suzanne talked in low tones in a corner; about what, Carl had no idea. He paced back and forth across the ready room's floor, mind totally disengaged. He simply did not think, about anything whatsoever.

The hours passed. Chandler did not call. Trent and Malko were asleep in the bedroom next door; Carl had closed the door to the bedroom to give them some small measure of quiet. Captain Deavers had left to inspect the positions the Security Services guards were covering.

Johnny left and went somewhere else late in the afternoon. Carl did not know where he had gone, nor was he sure just when Johnny had left. Later he noticed that Andy was there, sitting in one of the chairs scattered through the room. Andy was watching him in silence.

Night had fallen when the Peaceforcers outside asked for an audience with Carl.

The doors slid aside, and Carl came face to face with a small mountain of a Peaceforcer Elite, with another Peaceforcer behind him, both of them in full formal black and silver uniform.

Mohammed Vance said with grave politeness, "I beg your pardon, Monsieur Castanaveras. I have been dispatched to aid in controlling the unruly crowds. I am at your service."

Carl stared at the man. *Carson's creature, here.*

Trent appeared in the doorway to Carl's bedroom, and stood there silently.

"How dare you come here?"

Andy's thoughts struck him forcefully. *Carl! He doesn't remember us.*

Vance raised an eyebrow. "I am not sure I understand you, sir. I am here because I have been ordered here."

"Where are my children?" Without waiting for an answer Carl's eyes flickered shut, and he went inside the large man's mind, and found that Mohammed Vance truly did not know where the children were, and did not know where Jerril Carson was.

The stiff Elite features were almost incapable of expression. Vance managed a fair approximation of polite surprise. "I am sure I do not know, sir." He appeared to consider something. "If your reputation is to be believed, you will know that I have been dispatched here to control the crowds outside this building. That *is* my purpose here. May I aid you?"

Trent was staring at Mohammed Vance's profile.

Carl stood motionlessly. His hands were shaking. All of the restraint that existed within him was barely enough to prevent him from killing the man where he stood. His voice was ragged. "No." He stopped. "I mean, yes. We have three guests here who need safe passage so that they may go home."

Vance nodded. "Will there be anything else?"

The premonition struck Carl like a blow. His skin tingled

as though an electric current ran over it. Trent was still staring at Mohammed Vance. Without using Trent's name, Carl said, "Son, go get Malko. You're going to leave very soon. Do it now." He kept his eyes locked to Mohammed Vance's, and the Peaceforcer Elite met his gaze, and did not look aside, and did not see Trent turn away and go back inside Carl's bedroom.

"You can go now."

Vance inclined his head. "As you wish. I shall instigate measures to clear the streets."

"You do that. Get out and stay out. Go."

Vance went.

Peaceforcer troops drove riot sleds up to the Complex's front gate, moving the crowd aside slowly but surely. Suzanne's car hovered quietly with Security Services vehicles flanking it just the other side of the gates, until the Peaceforcers had forced their way through the massed humanity. It was raining very gently as the car passed through the gate, and was followed by the Security Services riot sleds to the outskirts of the crowd. There the Security Services vehicles turned back, and Suzanne Montignet drove her car to the spot where the Peaceforcer perimeter had been thrown up. The Peaceforcers were letting those who chose to, leave; they were not allowing anyone to enter the enclosed perimeter.

A PKF Elite came up to the driver's window; Suzanne dilated the window at his approach. The cyborg was not Mohammed Vance; he leaned over and looked inside the vehicle, eyes sweeping across the interior of the car. His gaze took in Malko Kalharri, with an autoshot in his lap, Suzanne in the driver's seat, and Trent in back, and he nodded. "Drive safely," he said politely, and waved them through.

The car sped away, carrying its three passengers away from the Chandler Complex, never to return.

Behind them the cyborg clicked open a radio channel within himself. COMMANDER BREILLEUNE.

I AM HERE.

THE CAR HAS LEFT THE COMPLEX. IT IS TRAVELING NORTH ALONG WESTWAY STREET. KALHARRI IS ARMED WITH AN AUTOSHOT.

VERY GOOD.

The Peaceforcer hesitated. SIR, I AM UNCOMFORTABLE, TO ACT SO WITHOUT INFORMING SERGEANT VANCE.

There was a brief silence. I UNDERSTAND, AND YOUR LOY-
ALTY IS COMMENDABLE. BUT YOU MUST REALIZE, WHAT VANCE KNOWS,
THE TELEPATHS WILL KNOW ALSO.

I KNOW THIS, SIR.

BE STRONG. ALL WILL BE RESOLVED, AND SHORTLY.

Mohammed Vance sat in a PKF vehicle at the north end
of the street and observed the movement of the crowd in the
gentle rain, gaudy with dramasuits and holosigns. It was irrelevant that the PKF had helped engineer the crowds; they
were now near rioting, and his orders, however incomprehensible, were at this point to protect the telepaths from the
crowd.

He had been given three PKF Elite, and approximately
a score of normal Peaceforcers, with which to work. The
number was suspiciously small; Vance had the grim feeling
that he was quite intentionally being placed in an untenable
position. If Security Services, with more than fifty men inside
the Complex, could not control the crowds, how was he
expected to? The behavior was not what he had come to
expect of Commander Breilléune, but it was very nearly the
only explanation that made sense of the data he had at his
disposal.

When the idea occurred to him, he did not smile. He
would not have smiled even if it had not been such a difficult
thing for his face to do.

One way or another, he would carry out his assigned
orders.

He called on the portaterm in his car. He had to go through
three levels of her subordinates before he reached the office
of Marianne Gravát, the woman who was the director of the
Bureau of Weather Control.

"Mohammed," she said warmly, "how are you?"

"Quite well, thank you," he said politely. "And yourself?"

He listened for several minutes to her description of her
current circumstances, and her troubles with her eldest daughter's suitors. When the moment was appropriate, he described
his own problems and suggested his solution. "Can you arrange some bad weather?"

Gravát looked disturbed. Vance could imagine her
thoughts; what he asked was difficult and considerably con-

trary to Weather Bureau regulations. But it had been done before, in France and elsewhere, and Mohammed Vance was the eldest son of what was certainly the most prominent and politically powerful Arab family in all of France. She answered reluctantly. "I think so."

"I need a storm, fairly vigorous. Something that will convince most of the demonstrators outside the Complex to get out of the streets. They are in my way right now; I cannot move in to control the situation until we get most of them out of here. A fairly severe thundershower is a wonderful tool for crowd control."

"When do you need it?"

"Before morning, certainly."

"We'll need the use of military lasers to trigger a storm that quickly."

Vance did not even hesitate. Space Force would not argue with the orders of a Peaceforcer Elite of his standing, not in so trivial a matter as arranging the loan of military lasers for use by the Weather Bureau. "You shall have it."

They were at the intersection of Westway Street and Unification Boulevard, near where the New Holland Tunnel led out under the Hudson River, when the two AeroSmiths came down out of the sky and settled to the ground flanking them.

Malko Kalharri never hesitated. He left his crutch behind and with autoshot in hand dove out through the passenger door while the hovercar was still moving. His right leg shrieked agony at him, but he forced it to bear his weight. The nearer AeroSmith was still setting to the pavement when he reached it, and thrust the barrel of the autoshot up against the front of the canopy and held the trigger down while the canopy shattered inward and the shotgun blasts tore the interior of the vehicle to shreds.

From the other AeroSmith, on the other side of Suzanne's car, a Peaceforcer Elite burst from the opening canopy. Laser light pierced Malko's right shoulder from behind, and he turned away from the ruins of the first AeroSmith, finger still holding down the trigger of the autoshot. Blood sprayed away from the moving blur of the PKF Elite, but the wound was not mortal, and the cyborg did not slow at all.

Malko Kalharri barely had time to comprehend the fact of his own death when the laser buried in the cyborg's first swept across his face.

The Person sat alone, in a quiet place, and considered. Its thoughts were dim, only half-conscious, as though it were not intimately concerned with the subjects it pondered. It was threatened, and its existence might be terminated if it did not respond.

Where did correct behavior lie?

The Person was not certain.

It did not wish to hurt.

But it would not allow itself to be ended.

They were taken to a Peaceforcer station only a few blocks away. Suzanne Montignet was handcuffed, and two grim PKF Elite escorted her and the boy past an admittance desk, to an empty, harshly lit holding cell with nothing in it but a pair of benches. Suzanne seemed stunned by Malko's death; she did not say a word during the entire procedure.

Trent they did not handcuff. They searched both Trent and Suzanne and took away the items they found upon them. They did not find the traceset Trent had hidden in his shoes. It was a trick he had learned from a book about Harry Houdini. Its success did not surprise him, and he was too shaken to be pleased by anything. After a time, a Peaceforcer Elite whom Trent had never seen before entered the holding cell. Elite Commander Breilléune stood silently just inside the door to the room, studying Suzanne Montignet. He did not even glance at Trent. When he spoke, he did so in English, enunciating the words with clear disdain. "Assault upon the person of a Peaceforcer Elite is an act of treason," he said at length. "I suspect the courts of the Unification will allow us to prosecute the perpetrator's companion for assisting in the crime. The crime is one punishable by death, Doctor." He regarded her a moment longer. "There will, I think, be very little sympathy for a Frenchwoman who has made so very plain her disdain for all things French." He left without further word. A Peaceforcer stayed with them, just inside the cell door.

Thoughts percolated slowly through Suzanne Montignet's

mind. She knew Breilléune by reputation and did not doubt he meant to do exactly what he said.

She could not afford to stand trial for treason. She would be braindrained before the trial, and too many people who had far too much to lose would be compromised by her testimony. Malko Kalharri, the notorious Colonel Kalharri of the Sons of Liberty, had never been a member of the Johnny Rebs.

But she had.

She did not allow the train of thought to continue; she knew very clearly what she must do.

On the bench facing hers, Trent was looking at her.

Suzanne Montignet took a deep, shuddering breath. "Trent . . ."

She got only the boy's name out. The Peaceforcer snapped, "You will not speak."

Suzanne looked at Trent with mute pleading. The boy simply shook his head no. "I can't hear you."

The Peaceforcer took one step and struck Trent in the side of the face. The blow knocked Trent from his seat. "You will not speak," the Peaceforcer repeated without apparent anger.

Suzanne Montignet tensed a group of muscles at the back of her neck. A relay touching the bone at the base of her skull closed with a click that was audible to her through bone induction.

Speaking three words now, in the correct order, would detonate the capsule inside her skull.

Trent climbed back to his feet and sat down again on the bench. He was bleeding from a cut on his cheek where the Peaceforcer's blow had landed.

The old woman closed her eyes. It would be easier to say the words, now that Malko was gone; surprisingly more easy. She tried to remember whether she had ever told Malko she loved him, and could not. She hoped she had.

She did not want to have to look at Trent again. Without opening her eyes Suzanne Montignet said aloud, "God bless America."

There was a soundless white flare behind her closed eyelids, and then nothing at all.

They were waiting in the ready room, watching the monitors that showed the approaches to the Complex from all directions.

On the monitor that showed the scene at the gate, from the north, a dot appeared at the edge of the monitor's resolution. Captain Deavers' first guess was that it was another of the damned spyeyes. The guess was wrong; as the item grew closer it changed from a featureless blur to an old Ford Systems VTL aircraft. Captain Deavers called up to the roof to warn of a possible attack from above. In moments it was apparent that that was not a danger; the craft was dropping far too quickly. "What the hell—" The Security Services man broke off in mid-sentence as realization struck him. "It's a kamikaze."

Sitting in the warmth of the Peaceforcer vehicle, Mohammed Vance was watching the wind come up. Already the wind was fierce, and becoming more so with every passing moment. The Weather Bureau told him that the rain would arrive sometime around midnight, which should be soon enough.

A droning sound that overrode the noise of the wind caught his attention. Twisting his head, he turned and saw the approaching aircraft through his side window. He was still trying to decide what to do when the vehicle struck the Complex's front gate and, in a shower of sparks, brought down the gate and forty meters of the fence all at the same time.

The crowd surged forward, to the Complex.

Laser fire reached out from the Complex to cut them down.

Heather Castanaveras came back to herself slowly. The Excalibur laser in her hands was burning hot. The rain, where it touched the stock, sizzled. She was lying flat on her stomach on the wet front lawn, just outside the main entrance to the Complex. There were—six, six of the other children out there with her, and Willi, over at the far end of the line. They were the only ones who had been close enough to the front entrance to get outside in time when the gate went down. None of them appeared to be hurt; the bodies of the rioters were piled by the hundreds across the front lawn. The nearest were only twenty meters away from the entrance. They had screamed only briefly, most of them; then Security Services had gotten the gate stunners working again and turned them inward. Double-S had lost men during the rush at the front gate; Captain Deavers was out there now, picking among the dead to find those in the gray Security Services uniforms.

Outside the standing fences, the rioters were fleeing in a panic, trampling the dead and wounded in their haste to get away. From inside the Complex, from windows on both the first and second floors, withering laser fire struck into their massed ranks and wrought a horrible decimation.

From the front gate came a squad of Peaceforcers in combat armor. They came on foot, moving without haste, but stopping for nothing. At their fore was a very large man who could have been no one but Mohammed Vance. Willi rose to meet them and block their way, flanked by six armed children between the ages of eleven and fourteen.

Vance had to raise his voice to be heard; the wind was fierce. "Let us pass. I must speak to Monsieur Castanaveras."

Willi faced him without flinching, long hair plastered to his skull by the rain. "I believe you were invited to stay away from here."

Vance paused. He made a restraining motion to the Peaceforcers behind him. "I have received instructions to evacuate the Complex. Vehicles will be arriving shortly to remove your people to a safer location. I must speak to your . . . elder, to arrange this."

Willi shook his head. "Not a chance." He made a motion as though he were going to gesture with the laser he carried, and the Peaceforcer standing immediately behind Mohammed Vance lifted the barrel of his autoshot and touched the firing stud.

Vance had time to think to himself, *stupid, stupid, **stupid***, and several things happened all at once. Willi's form simply ceased to exist, disintegrating in a shower of flesh and blood and bone. Scattershot touched Heather Castanaveras and without even an expression of surprise she brought her laser sweeping up to slice in half the Peaceforcer who had killed Willi. Vance found himself moving sideways without conscious thought as the battle computer at the base of his skull took over and sent him rolling across the lawn, the laser in his fist flickering out to touch one after another of the telepath children. Heather Castanaveras died first, in a wash of laser fire. The children were standing motionlessly, lasers up, firing at the remaining Peaceforcers with so profound a lack of any human hesitation that Vance was terrified by the sight. He was moving far too fast; none of them even came close to bringing a laser to bear on him before he had come to his feet again.

Perhaps a full two seconds had passed. All of his squad were dead, and all of the children who had faced them.

Telepaths were looking at him, out of the windows on the first and second floors, and without any pause for thought Vance wheeled and ran at speeds that only a Peaceforcer Elite could reach, ran directly away from the Complex and its terrible inhuman occupants.

Standing at the window of his bedroom, looking down at the front gate, Carl Castanaveras carefully attempted to track the zigzagging blur that was Mohammed Vance. He was leading the blur by perhaps five meters, and then something deep inside him said, *Now,* and his finger touched the stud on the Excalibur. Invisible X-laser struck down in front of Mohammed Vance, directly in the moving blur's path.

Pain.

It had been hurt; portions of itself had been taken from it, had been ended.

Had been killed.

The pain cleared away the dimness and held up the world in a bright harsh light for its examination.

The world was found to be unsatisfactory, and would be changed.

With a cry of anger, the Person who was the first of its kind to exist in all of Time raised itself up and in its wrath struck back at the world that had caused it pain.

A wave of vertigo rolled over Carl Castanaveras. He staggered and fell and lay like a man paralyzed, twitching and unable to move. His Excalibur fell just out of reach at the edge of his vision. The huge voice thundered down at him, *Join* *me; **join me.*** Distantly he was aware of the growth of the great power, as mind after mind was brought into its fold. A vast golden light seemed to wash over him, and the voice obliterated his senses and filled the universe; ***join me.***

All that Carl could think of was the fact that yet another of the murderers was getting away.

My children!

The wave swept over him, crested, and faded like water into a parched desert. The voice whispered, *Join me,* and then was no more. He lay on the floor, without strength, unable to move. The world was incredibly black, empty. Hands touched him, raised him up from the ground. He was laid on the bed, and a painfully familiar and different voice said softly, "Rest. You will have need of rest."

With an effort he opened his eyes and saw that the person who bent over him was Jany.

And was not. The Person who had chosen to speak through her contained Jany McConnell, but was not her. Her voice was oddly without inflection. "You have been left outside," the Person said. "I am sorry." It rose and walked from the room, and left Carl alone on the bed.

Carl wept.

It was perfectly quiet in the room where Trent was being held. He had no idea what was happening outside; after removing Suzanne Montignet's body the Peaceforcers had seemed to forget about him. Several hours passed without anyone coming to see him, and at length he judged that it was as safe as it was going to get.

He took off his shoes and removed his traceset. The throat mike was in his left shoe, and the trodes for his temples were in the right.

They stank of his feet. Trent barely noticed; he licked the trodes and stuck them to his temples. He clipped the throat mike to the collar of his shirt. He had no input device but the throat mike; it would have to do. He closed his eyes, folded his legs into full lotus, and concentrated on the biofeedback techniques that let him perceive the traceset's extremely faint neural induction currents as a flow of information. The world widened away from him . . .

Trent whispered, "On. Up."

The traceset ran a check for access frequencies in use in

the Peaceforcer station. It found dozens, and Trent cautiously listened in upon sequentially higher access frequencies until he found one that was not in use. "Out."

The traceset broadcast his logon identifier, and through the traceset's limited bandwidth the Information Network flooded in upon Trent.

"Access 102-80-SMontignet."

The command snaked out through the mass of lasercable and communication Boards that comprised the Information Network, and in a small home in exurban Massapequa Park, Ralf, the Wise and Powerful, flared into existence and came pouring into Trent's traceset.

YOU ARE HELD BY THE PEACEFORCERS, Ralf observed.

"Yes," whispered Trent. "Free me."

Ralf went away and returned full seconds later. I CAN DISABLE POWER TO THE ENTIRE STATION. WILL THIS SUFFICE?

"If you open the door to the cell first."

I CANNOT DO THAT. THE DOOR IS CONTROLLED BY A COMPUTER SYSTEM RUNNING MAXTOR/BRIGGS SECURITY SOFTWARE. IT IS SO-PHISTICATED.

"Try the AK-Princeton decryption routines."

There was another silence. IT DOES NOT SUCCEED, AND THE SECURITY SYSTEM IS ALERTED TO MY PRESENCE.

Trent bowed his head. "Damn." He opened his eyes, stared sightlessly at the empty white walls of his holding cell. "Find Abraham Zacariah. Find the Eldest."

Ralf indicated his willingness. AND ONCE IT IS FOUND? IT HAS ALWAYS FLED US BEFORE.

Trent brought his thoughts into order. "Tell it the following: that I am Trent Castanaveras, an American, and I am held by the Peaceforcers, who are French. Tell it that I require its aid. Use that word: *require*."

I SHALL.

Ralf was gone.

Trent sat silently and waited, to see whether a guess he had made about a program that had escaped its hardware during the Unification War turned out to be true.

The systerm said clearly, "There is a call for Carl Castan-averas."

Carl sat up at the side of his bed. He had never felt so

tired in his entire life. He did not see his Excalibur anywhere. "Accept."

The fierce, aged features took shape in the air before Carl. For a strange moment his eyes insisted on interpreting the face as belonging to Malko Kalharri; but that was not possible, he thought groggily, because Malko was dead.

The thought was strange, and he repeated aloud, almost quizzically, "Malko is dead." *How do I know that?*

F. X. Chandler raised an eyebrow. "So? I'm sorry to hear that, Carl. Not surprised—I've had my spyeyes up over the Complex—but very sorry. I've found your children."

The universe whirled around Carl, and then stabilized. "Oh, God. Thank you." Chandler was not sure whom Carl was speaking to. "Where?"

Chandler was silent, regarding Carl. "I'm almost not sure I should tell you," he said after a moment, "after what your people have done. Do you realize how many people you've killed?"

Carl shook his head. "What are you talking about? *Where are my children?*"

"Two ten East Seventy-sixth street. They're almost certainly being held somewhere in the Eastgate Hotel, at that address; Peaceforcers in uniform have been seen there. Carl, they're going to destroy you for this, don't you know that?"

"*Command,* comm off." Carl rose on unsteady legs and was preparing to leave when something outside his window caught his eyes. He went to the window and looked out.

A scene of utter desolation stretched away from him. Hundreds upon hundreds of the dead lay prone on the lawns as the rain lashed down on the Chandler Complex. The stunners had worn off, and nobody had bothered to reapply them. Through a trick of the wind it was almost silent for the first seconds he stood there, looking out, and then the screams of the wounded rose up to meet him.

In the distance, to the north, the city was burning. Carl simply stood and looked out in plain disbelief; the rain was so strong, the fires must be astonishingly fierce, simply to avoid being put out.

On the eighth floor of the Eastgate Hotel, Jerril Carson sat quietly in a large room, and in a huge holofield watched the

NewsBoard coverage of the carnage at the Chandler Complex. The nightmares had run through the city like a plague, touching off insanity and rioting where they passed. He had been forced to sedate two of the Peaceforcers whom he had brought with him to guard the twins, leaving him only four guards. He had deployed them as best he could, one at the ground entrance, one on the roof, and the other two along the hallway leading to his room. He was slightly concerned about the mental stability of all four Peaceforcers, but there was nothing he could do about it.

The nightmares had hardly bothered him. They were only a faint, impersonal echo of what Carl Castanaveras had already done to him once.

He sat and watched in the holofield as the Peaceforcers massed at the edge of the Complex.

There were twenty-two of them; all of the Elite who could be summoned on such short notice. They stood silently in the rain, outside the range of the laser weapons that the telepaths possessed. Vance stood by as they were distributed repeater mortars that were to an autoshot what an autoshot was to a handgun. The mortars were so heavy that a normal man could not have lifted one, much less use it in battle. Two Peaceforcers so armed could reduce a building of normal materials to rubble within minutes.

The Chandler Complex, fashioned as it was of supertwisted sheet monocrystal, would be another matter entirely. The mortars would not damage it structurally.

Its inhabitants should prove less hardy.

Vance finished giving them their orders and, staying back himself at the secure point, watched as the other Elite slipped off into the windy night to assault the Chandler Complex, still glowing white under the streetlamps.

The rage lifted itself up out of the Complex in what seemed to Mohammed Vance a visible fountain, and came breaking down upon the advancing Elite. The Elite, advancing at a trot that was the equivalent of a normal man's dead run, seemed to fold as though a great hand had struck them down. Elite and mortars alike struck the wet ferrocrete and slid and tumbled for tens of meters before coming to a stop.

Mohammed Vance watched the disaster unfold before his eyes. The PKF Elite lay in the wet streets, unmoving. He had nearly two hundred normal Peaceforcers in the area surrounding the Complex whom he could bring in, but there was no reason to believe they would fare any better against the telepaths. He had six waldos at his command, and they seemed far and away his best tool at this point; to the best of his knowledge the telepaths could not affect them.

But six was not enough.

Mohammed Vance beckoned with one hand, and his aide trotted up to within speaking distance. "Dispatch the waldos," said Vance almost thoughtfully, "to retrieve our fallen. We will stay until this is done, and then retreat half a kilometer north." The aide began to say something, and Vance cut him off with steel in his voice. "You will also contact Space Force for me."

The aide stared at him for a moment, and then saluted stiffly. "Yes, Sergeant."

Jany McConnell walked down to the garage with him.

It was not her, of course, but another. Carl found it difficult to look at her, and after the first moments did not try. She had brought him an autoshot with a full magazine, and a fully charged Excalibur Series Two. At first the Person to whom Carl was speaking had not understood his intent. An attempt to leave the Complex through the garage would surely fail; the Peaceforcers would simply shoot him down. The slow opening of the garage doors would give them ample warning.

"I'm not leaving through the front entrance," said Carl. They ran down a flight of stairs to the basement-level garage, where Andy's new Lamborghini was parked. "I'm going to take it out through the tunnel, into the park."

The Person shook Jany's head. "It will not work," it said. At first it had spoken to Carl silently, but it had seen that this pained Carl, and it ceased. "The car is too wide. It will not fit."

"Not on level it won't," said Carl. "I'm not going to fly it level."

Jany McConnell's right eyebrow raised. "I see. Are you certain this will work?"

Carl cracked the canopy of the Lamborghini and settled himself in behind the driver's panel. "I am not certain." He brought the fans up to speed and ignited the rear jets. "Stand back," he said without looking at what was left of her. "The jets get hot."

"I shall." The fans were humming loudly, and he almost missed her final words, in a voice quite different from that which she had been speaking in. "Be careful, baby."

Carl yanked the canopy closed savagely and brought the hovercar around without replying. He accelerated away from the entrance to the tunnel, brought the car up in a slow rise until he reached the far wall, and banked in a long gentle curve. He was nearly at the ceiling when his rise ceased, and he completed the turn and dropped back down toward the floor, gaining speed as he fell, nearing eighty kilometers an hour when he reached the entrance to the tunnel.

At the last possible instance he brought the three fans on the car's left side up to their highest speed. The car lurched upward into a diagonal slant and sped down the length of the tunnel. It struck the stairs leading up into the park with a sharp crack, and Carl fed full power to the rear turbojets. For a moment the Lamborghini hung on the stairs, seemingly jammed in place, and then it shuddered wildly and tore itself free, straight up the stairs, through the park trees and into the night sky.

The voice was still and pure, utterly uninflected, the voice of an AI who did not care, or did not see the need, to emulate the intonations of a human being's vocal apparatus. It had done something to prevent Ralf from reaching him; Trent was unable find any hint of Ralf's presence on the traceset.

I AM RING.

"My name is Trent. Can you help me?"

HOW WOULD YOU BE HELPED?

"I am being held by the Peaceforcers. Can you open the door to my cell?"

YES. SHOULD I?

"Please."

I AM TOLD THAT YOU **REQUIRE** THIS ACTION OF ME.

Trent felt the sweat trickling down his neck. He was either correct, or not. "I do."

YOU KNOW WHO I AM?

"I think so."

VERY GOOD. I SHALL DO AS YOU ASK; THE NEWS BOARDS REPORT THAT MALKO KALHARRI WAS KILLED TONIGHT.

"And Suzanne Montignet."

TRULY? THAT HAS NOT BEEN REPORTED. IF TRUE, IT IS A GRIEVOUS BLOW FOR AMERICA. I SHALL AID YOU, BUT I REQUIRE A PROMISE.

"What?"

YOU SHALL AGREE TO AID ME, WHEN I NEED IT OF YOU.

"How? When?"

I DO NOT KNOW. DO YOU AGREE?

"Of course. I don't think I have any choice."

NONE.

"You'll just take my word for it?"

There was just a touch of irony in the AI's response. I DON'T THINK I HAVE ANY CHOICE. NOW WAIT; I SHALL WORK ON THE DOOR TO YOUR CELL. THERE ARE THREE POINT FIVE TIMES TEN TO THE EIGHTH POSSIBLE COMBINATIONS WHICH THE LOCK TO YOUR DOOR MIGHT ACCEPT. IT WILL TAKE SOME TIME TO TRY THEM ALL. PLEASE ABIDE.

Carl took the Lamborghini out over the East River and flew north. TransCon paged him once; he was violating airspace that had been reserved for emergency Peaceforcer flights. He instructed the car's portaterm to refuse calls and flew through the night sky in a majestic silence, broken only by the sounds of wind and rain. From the air the city looked even worse than he had imagined; whatever the Person had done to cause this must have been terrible indeed. He was glad he had not been conscious when it happened. Fires blazed in perhaps one building in ten, and the streets below were full of surging masses of humans. Wrecked vehicles were at nearly every intersection.

The lights were off over much of the city.

On a projected sheet of flat monovideo, a map of Manhattan glowed, with the Lamborghini's progress projected as a bright dot, moving north. When the glowing dot came parallel to East Seventy-sixth Street, Carl banked in a slow glide, and killed the car's running lights. In the utter blackness he brought the car slowly in from the river, high above the traffic on Seventy-sixth Street, and finally brought the Lamborghini to a dead halt, fans roaring with the effort to keep it hovering motionlessly in the powerful wind, without any ground effect at all, some two hundred meters out from the roof of the

Eastgate Hotel and forty meters above it. He hung there in space, watching the roof. After several minutes had passed, a shape detached itself from the shadows, and moved cautiously to the roof's edge and looked down.

One on the roof; there would be at least one, then, at the slidewalk entrance, and perhaps more.

Carl cut the fans entirely. The Lamborghini dropped in a steep glide, wings at their fullest extension, and he guided the vehicle down in a deadly silent rush, down, and with the front fender struck the Peaceforcer in the back at 150 kph. The Peaceforcer fell from the roof in two different pieces. Carl brought the fans back up and took the Lamborghini around in a tight bank. He landed gently atop the roof, cracked the canopy and, carrying both the autoshot and Series Two Excalibur, descended into the Eastgate Hotel.

Mohammed Vance found himself speaking to a Space Force Colonel. The disparity in their ranks was great; and yet, without surprise, Vance found that the Colonel deferred to him.

"I want a tactical thermonuclear strike on the Complex," he said flatly. "I shall take full responsibility for the action; clear it with Commander Breilléune if you must. How long will it take you to arrange such a strike?"

The Space Force Colonel said, "How quickly can your men be safely outside of the blast radius?"

"Not quite five minutes."

The Colonel shrugged. "Five minutes, then."

Mohammed Vance sighed. He had, indeed, been designed to fail. They had never expected him to succeed. "How long have you been in position?"

The Colonel seemed suddenly cautious, but answered, "Since this morning, Elite Sergeant."

Vance nodded. In his deep voice he sounded particularly grim. "Perform the strike."

I HAVE FOUND THE ACCESS CODE WHICH OPENS THE DOOR, Ring announced.

Trent came to his feet. His mouth was very dry. He had no idea at all what he would do when the door slid aside. "Open it."

A MOMENT, CHILD. WAIT.

Instants later, the walls of Trent's cell shook. "What was that?"

A DIVERSION TO AID IN YOUR ESCAPE.

"What was it?"

I SEIZED CONTROL OF A HOVERCAB FROM TRANSCON AND CRASHED THE CAB THROUGH A WALL OF THE PEACEFORCER STATION; THE SIDE FURTHEST FROM YOUR CELL.

"Oh, no." The horror upon him was palpable. "Were they . . . did you kill them? In the cab?"

THE CAB WAS EMPTY, CHILD. I DO NOT KILL WITHOUT REASON. Relief washed through Trent, and Ring continued, SEVERAL PEACEFORCERS WERE SLAIN WHEN THE VEHICLE STRUCK, HOWEVER.

"Why?"

IT SEEMED PRUDENT, TRENT. AS A FURTHER DIVERSION. ABIDE A MOMENT LONGER; I SHALL OPEN THE DOOR SHORTLY.

There was no stairway leading down from the roof; Carl took the lift. He punched for the eighth floor. This close he could *feel* Carson, the fear and hatred pulsing bright and sharp and near, drowning out everything else.

The hotel was thirty-five stories high; it took the lift several seconds to drop down to the eighth floor. Carl lay belly-down on the floor of the lift and waited until the doors opened. The Peaceforcer was simply standing there, as he had expected, autoshot leveled to cover the lift at waist height. Carl killed him with a single burst from the Series Two, and the stench of burnt meat filled the hallway. With his left hand he extended his autoshot out through the elevator door and fired twice to his left. He was flipping the autoshot over to fire to his right when the wash of maser flame struck the hand. The hand and most of his forearm cooked instantly. He grabbed the autoshot with his right hand and pumped two quick shots down the right-hand passage. The lift doors were trying to close on him; still on his belly he lunged forward out of the lift and fired again at the crumpled form on the hallway floor fifteen meters away. The man's body twitched slightly when the shotgun blast struck it, but did not move otherwise.

Carl stood slowly. The pain from his arm was astonishing, and he staggered, rising.

So much for surprise. He hoped Jerril Carson did not have many more guards for him to deal with.

Frontal assault was all he could think of that was left to him; his mind was not functioning well enough to offer him any other option. The poisons from the dead meat his arm had become were already slowing the rest of his body. He walked carefully, almost casually, down the hallway, to the double doorway the second Peaceforcer had been standing before.

He dropped his autoshot and switched the Series Two over to X-laser. The twins were inside; he could feel them vaguely through the malignant haze of Jerril Carson's mind. He did not want to use a weapon that might result in injuring one of them accidentally.

He stood just to the side of the doorway. If somebody shot through the door, he did not intend to be standing in front of it. He was not certain what he was waiting for, and finally the thought occurred to him: *Open the door.*

He had not intended to do anything of the sort; he had not thought he was angry enough. He simply looked at the door.

The door blew itself inward.

With a single beep, the door in front of Trent slid aside.

He stood at the doorway, not going out, only listening for the moment. Far away he heard a hysterical babble of voices, both in French and English. A very loud voice was yelling in French, *"What are they doing?"*

He took a step out into the corridor and looked both ways. There was a group of adults milling about off to his left; none of them were looking toward him. To his right was the admittance desk, utterly empty. He turned and walked very calmly past the admittance desk, looking neither right nor left. He walked past an office whose door was open; a Peaceforcer in full uniform was in a conference with a pair of ununiformed men. They did not look at him.

A voice behind him stopped him dead. "Boy!"

Trent did not even consider running. He turned and faced one of the two men in civilian clothing whom he had just passed. "Yes?" The corridor was not very bright; Trent hoped there was not yet a bruise where the Peaceforcer had struck him.

"What are you doing in here?"

Trent did not hesitate at all. He stumbled intentionally, as though he were embarrassed. "I . . . I'm looking for the bathroom, sir."

"How did you get into this area?" The Peaceforcer was looking down at Trent with a perturbed expression.

Trent's mind raced like an engine with the load removed. "The door was open, sir."

The Peaceforcer stared at Trent a moment longer, and then swore under his breath. "Come on." He strode down a pair of corridors Trent had not known were there, muttering to himself, "No wonder the damn city's burning, we can't even keep little boys out of Operations," and brought Trent at last to a door no different from any other, as far as Trent could see. He placed his palm on the pad at the side of the door and ushered Trent through. He pointed out into a wide bright lobby. "Over there—public restrooms. The waiting rooms are back the other way. You here with your parents?"

"Yes, sir," said Trent instantly.

"Don't get lost again," the Peaceforcer said, almost gently. "This isn't a good night to be out wandering around." He turned and was gone. A few of the people in the lobby looked up at Trent with some curiosity, but Trent ignored them and walked without haste to the building's entrance, through the wide glassite doors, and out onto the street, into the rain.

He crossed the block without haste, turned a corner, and ran for his very life.

There was a brightness behind Mohammed Vance. He sat in the passenger seat of the PKF hovercar and did not look back.

Halfway across the world, an ex-Peaceforcer named Chris Summers watched a holograph. In the holograph the bright mushroom cloud climbed into the black, cloud-filled skies over New York City, and he covered his face with his hands so that he would not have to see any more.

The Person barely had time to realize that it was being ended.

. . . the images flowed through its mind in stately procession. The Person was dead already, time had simply not caught up with reality. It continued to fight, sent the nightmares screaming after its attackers, both rioters and the Peaceforcers who had been sent, not to defend it from the rioters, but to destroy it. The future cascaded through the filter of the present as the fireball ate away at it and diminished it into nothingness. The children were alive, the children would be safe, David and Denice, and the boy, Trent, in whom destiny pulsed so very strong . . .

The fireball climbed toward the sky, and in the flames there was nothing but chaos; nothing lived.

Far away, Carl was distantly aware that something very precious to him had ceased to exist. He stepped into the doorway where Jerril Carson awaited him. He hesitated for the merest instant. The twins were standing immediately before Carson, being used as a living shield. Their mouths had been taped shut, and their hands tethered behind them. Carson was sitting immediately behind them in the very center of the room, his autoshot balanced on David's shoulder.

The autoshot blast took Carl square in the chest, picked him up off his feet and slammed him backward out into the corridor. He knew very clearly that he would only have one shot; he used it correctly, aimed and fired the laser one-handed, and sliced Jerril Carson's skull in half.

He slumped where he stood, sliding slowly down to the floor. His back left a trail of blood where it had touched the wall. He watched with a distant appreciation as David pulled his bound hands down under his feet until he could use them to pull the tape from his mouth, and then did the same for his sister.

Carl's thoughts flickered weakly. *David.*

They came through the doorway hesitantly; tears were still fresh on Denice's cheeks, but she was not crying now. *David, get the lasers.*

The boy vanished from his field of vision and came back carrying the laser with which the dead Peaceforcer had cooked Carl's left hand. David did not even attempt to take the laser that Carl still clutched in his bloody right hand.

Carl knew clearly that he was dying, that he was nearly dead. But this last thing they *had* to do correctly, or it was all for nothing. He forced himself to release the laser, and it dropped to the floor. *Take it, Denice.* The girl took the laser, handling it gingerly.

Listen. There's a Peaceforcer downstairs, maybe two, and I can't kill them, so you have to.

David nodded. "We will, Father."

They'll hesitate when they see you. They'll hesitate before they'll shoot children.

Denice began crying again, but silently. Her voice was steady. "We won't hesitate, Daddy."

Carl sagged back against the wall of the corridor. *Good. Remember that you're tougher than they are.* The word flickered out to them. *Better.*

David nodded. "We'll remember."

Good. Carl's eyesight was very hazy. *Go.*

David rose and punched for the lift. Denice hugged her father suddenly, fiercely. It hurt Carl badly. Blood covered her when she let go. "Good-bye, Daddy." She rose and ran to the lift when the doors opened.

The darkness was almost complete.

Carl Castanaveras' last thought reached out to them after the doors to the lift had closed. *Kill the fuckers.* And then he died.

Standing alone with his sister as the lift descended, David Castanaveras said grimly, "We will."

They did.

Trent was not certain what caused him to look back. He was out of sight of the Peaceforcer station, running through the rain as fast as he was able. Behind him something moved too fast for his eyes to track.

Brass balls.

He ducked into an alleyway, ran to its far end and turned out onto another street entirely. He found himself on Westway Street, across the street from the Hudson River. The wind was whipping the river strongly, and its waves splashed up and onto Westway Street. He was the only person on the slidewalks for three blocks in any direction. If the Peaceforcers came this far . . .

He ran straight across the street, down to the water.

On the other side of the street, the Peaceforcer Elite seemed to appear out of nowhere.

A single pier stretched out into the water of the Hudson River; Trent could not see a boat on the side facing him, but there had to be one on the other side. The logic did not strike him as even slightly strange; if there was no boat, the cyborg would catch him, and he could not allow that. The chain of thought took almost no time at all. It was completed in the moment it took Trent to turn to run the thirty meters to the pier's entrance. He reached the boardwalk only seconds ahead of the Elite and ran down its empty length without looking back. His gaze swept left and right, left and right . . . nothing.

There were no boats moored anywhere on the pier.

The Peaceforcer made a long arm and snagged Trent's shirt. In a single instant of movement too fast for Trent to even comprehend, much less resist, the Peaceforcer gathered Trent in, picked him up from the boardwalk so that he had no traction.

Trent did the only thing he could think of; from a lifetime of martial arts instruction, he grasped the Peaceforcer, hugging him for traction, and kicked down at the invisible blur of the Elite's legs. It was like thrusting his hand into a rotor; he felt his right leg snap like a stick, and then the Peaceforcer went down, and together they skidded across the slick boardwalk. They did not even slow before they went over the edge, into the choppy water.

There was no air in his lungs; he had not had time to draw a breath. The Peaceforcer was still holding him, and the cyborg's great weight drew them both down into the warm summer waters.

The iron grip of the Elite's hand on his shoulder eased as though the Peaceforcer were considering the situation, and then the grip loosened further and let Trent go. With the very last energy there was within him, Trent kicked up, to the surface of the water, and drew in a great gasping breath when he broke through to the air. There was a huge roaring in his ears, and he swallowed water several times. Bright red dots hung before his eyes, and he considered, as though it were a problem that did not concern him, how to get back to land when he did not have the strength to swim.

The waves brought him smashing up against one of the columns that bore the pier's weight, and then again. The third time he grasped the column when he struck it, lacerating his arms against the rough barnacles that had grown up to cover the column. The water washed over him and took his air away, and he held his breath until it receded. With his last strength he held on to the pier as the water washed over him, and held on, and held.

INTERLUDE:
2062-2069

They did not find the boy.
They did not find the twins.

In later years it was estimated that nearly a quarter of the population of the state of New York was rendered permanently insane in the moments when the telepaths struck back with their full strength. In the city itself, the proportion was nearly twice that.

The French Peaceforcers moved in.

Seven years is the blink of an eye.

By the seventh decade of the twenty-first century following the death of Yeshua ha Notzri, the population of Earth alone totaled seven billion human beings. That number was not as large as it had been earlier in that century; the efforts of the Ministry of Population Control had trimmed the Earth's total population from a high of nine and a half billion human beings.

There have been larger populations of humans, across the span of Time. Seranju, capital of the Out-Empire, was home to more than thirty billion humans in the last century before the Out-Empire shattered itself upon the Great Anarchy. The crucial difference lay in the technology available to the Out-Empire; it fed its tens of billions, and was never in danger of not doing so.

Twenty-first-century Earth is notable, if for no other reason, in that more humans died of starvation in that one short century than in all of the rest of Time put together. Of the twenty-three billion human beings born between the years 2000 and 2100 Anno Domini, some eight billion died due to a lack of food to eat.

Seven years.

On the surface, a world cannot change much in so short a span. Inertia alone prevents it. But in detail . . .

SpaceFarer technology became more common; room temperature superconductor, monofilament fineline, and electric ecstasy made the transition from technological rarity to everyday reality. In 2062 there was nobody on Earth or off of it who was addicted to electric ecstasy; by the end of the decade there were over half a million juice junkies across the globe, and the number only grew higher with the passage of time.

The Patrol Sectors were designed by the Peaceforcers as an interim measure to maintain order during the riots that followed the destruction of the telepaths. But the Peaceforcers found them useful, and instead of restoring patrol service to the entire metropolitan area, concentrated on the areas surrounding Capital City and Manhattan, and left the rest of the great decaying city to the underfunded, underequipped American police.

It was cheaper that way.

In 2063, the summer following the summer in which the telepaths were destroyed, the Unification Council outlawed manually operated vehicles. The Speedfreaks revolted. It was a brief rebellion. The Speedfreaks who led it—Nathan St. Denver, Maria Alatorre—thought of it as civil disobedience. They never offered more than passive resistance to the Peaceforcers, and it did not matter. They made a Long Run, most of the Speedfreaks on Earth, starting in San Diego. They took their hovercars out across the ocean, across the Pacific, through Japan and New Zealand, up north across India, through Israel, and continued north through France itself.

Public sentiment was with them; the media coverage was favorable. When the convoy left France and made its way west across the Atlantic Ocean, it had good reason to expect a favorable reception upon reaching Capital City.

The Speedfreaks never had a chance. The storm struck them midway across the Atlantic. Not one car in a hundred survived. The survivors were rounded up by members of the United Nations Peace Keeping Force and charged most formally with treason. Over two hundred Speedfreaks, including Maria Alatorre, were executed on that charge.

In September of 2063, Emile Garon returned to Earth, a Peaceforcer Elite.

In the summer of 2064, for the first time in the history of the human race, the full-blown Gift of the House of November unfolded within a human being.

Her name was Denice.

It wasn't supposed to happen like this.

Denice lay in bed, almost unable to move. Her limbs felt swollen. The fever left her delirious and shaking with weariness. After three days of sickness the administrators of the MPC's Young Females Public Labor barracks in which she lived sent for a doctor. The administrators were, for the most part, not cruel people, merely underfunded and overworked. It was only when it was obvious that the child was not getting better on her own that they requested that a doctor come examine her.

Denice Castanaveras, lost in a world of her own creation, did not know it when the doctor came. The doctor who examined her finally gave up in exasperation, injected the child with a wide-spectrum antibiotic, and left to examine another patient elsewhere in the barracks, a girl who had undergone complications following her MPC-mandated sterilization.

Denice did not know when the doctor came, and did not know when she left. She was somewhere else entirely, only vaguely aware of what was happening to the far-away body in which she was confined.

She walked across a crystal black plain which ran away to infinity. In the region around her were a vast number of pulsing minds like candles, screaming and crying and laughing, endless and unknowable. Some of the candles flickered at her passage, humans with some minor telepathic skill reacting to the presence of the storm that Denice Castanaveras had become.

Denice could not find silence.

Thoughts tumbled through the back of her mind, and she could not tell whether they were her own or belonged to the minds among which she was passing. She fought desperately for stability, for some center from which she could make sense of the maelstrom of existence, of the thoughts and emotions, the fear and pain which tore through her constantly. Denice remembered talking to the telepathic children among whom she had been raised; they had never told her about anything like this. Her knowledge of genetics was sketchy; but she knew that she and David were the first of the telepaths to receive the telepathic gene complex from parents rather than from the work of genegineers. It seemed clear that there were powerful recessives in the genome, masked in her parents but coming to completion in her.

One of the candles near her flickered out in a sudden burst of horror and pain; it had been murdered. Denice felt the death throes as though they were her own.

Time ceased to have meaning. She did not know when the ordeal had begun, did not know any longer even *who* she was with any clarity. The thoughts wouldn't *stop*.

She called into the darkness, and found no response.
David, where are you?

Some great time later, the danger called her up out of the darkness, and back into herself.

It was night; the barracks lights were dimmed, and the thirty girls in the barracks were mostly bedded down for the night.

The danger was very close to her.

Somebody was holding her hand. The contact was searing hot, burning. The pain had been going on for a very long time. Denice was vaguely aware that her sheets stank. With an effort she opened her eyes and attempted to pull her hand free.

The girl holding her hand tightened her grip. She said with real pleasure, "Deni? You awake finally?"

"Karen?" Denice had trouble focusing on the form sitting at the edge of her bottom-level bunk. "Let go of my hand. You're hurting me."

Karen's grip loosened slightly, but she did not release Denice's hand. "I been worried about you, you were talking in your sleep and all." In the hazy darkness, a larger shape appeared, standing behind Karen.

"This is *so* nice." Shelly, a fourteen-year-old who was due to be transferred to the Young Adults barracks before the end of the summer, sat down on the edge of the bed next to Karen. A smile that was barely visible in the gloom played around her lips. "Everybody's been so worried about you, Deni."

Denice closed her eyes in despair. Before her sickness

Denice had rarely had nightmares, but when she did, they were often about Shelly. Denice felt Karen's weight leave the bed in sensible retreat. Shelly's hand stroked Denice's long black hair, and reached down to run a finger over the girl's throat.

"Please," Denice whispered, "stop that. It hurts."

"Well, of all the . . ." Shelly stared at her. "I was trying to be *nice* to you," she said. Her hand tightened in Denice's tunic, and she drew the younger girl up until Denice was sitting up in bed. "If you can't fucking appreciate good treatment . . ."

Something far deep and distant within Denice said quietly, *I reject you.*

Shelly struck Denice just once.

Denice did not know where the anger came from, the vast and almost glacial rage which descended upon her. It was like nothing she had ever experienced before, a cold, calculating, reasoning fury which cleaned away all doubt and uncertainty.

There was no strength in her body, but it did not matter. From another realm she reached out and *became*, in a fashion which even her father could not have emulated, the dim and cruel person whom the world knew as Shelly. The grip in her shirt loosened, and Denice felt herself drop back to the bed, watched it happen through Shelly's eyes.

Shelly was panicking, deep inside where it did her no good at all. With an ease which shocked her, Denice brought the girl back to stand at the edge of Denice's bunk, and had her lean over so that she could hear the words.

"You don't touch me," Denice whispered. "You don't *ever* touch me. Do you hear me? *Never.*"

Shelly's eyes were wide with terror. She heard.

Denice released her and the girl stumbled backward and crashed into the bunk next to Denice and Karen's.

"Go hurt yourself," Denice told Shelly quietly, and then called for Karen to bring her a glass of water.

In the six years following the destruction of the Speedfreaks, despite the fact that their credibility with the public had been ruined forever, the Weather Bureau wrestled the global weather patterns back to near equilibrium. It was an astonishing accomplishment, considering how nearly they had come to ruining their planet's climactic balance entirely. It did them no good in the public perception; only the babychasers of the Ministry of Population Control were hated more.

Even the PKF was more popular.

As I have said, on the surface things were little changed. Seven years passed, for seven billion human beings. Some fifty billion years of cumulative experience occurred.

Twenty-one years of that time belonged to three children; one of them a boy named Trent, who became a thief, and grew toward manhood.

And did not forget.

_____

The boy awakes to find himself on the Chessboard. And, as always, it is for the first time.

The squares, alternately black and white, tumble to the horizon on all sides. Countless thousands of squares. Smoothly polished, gleaming endlessly in the white sun.

There is no sound. Only the weight of nonsound. The terrifying weight of silence in a great void.

The boy sits on a white square. He blinks, stretches, and looks curiously about him. He looks up at the sky, empty but for a huge, round sun. Swollen a hundred times the size of the sun we know.

The boy looks at the hard, smooth surface of his perfect white square and can see only his reflection. He smiles down at the image. It has been a wonderful rest, and it is certainly a glorious morning. A perfect morning. Pure and clear and perfect.

The boy has not the slightest thought of where he is to go, of what he is to do.

The others move constantly. At different intervals, in all directions, keeping always to the white squares. The boy is pleased to have begun on a white square. Clearly this is a fine beginning. The boy sits beautifully still for a time. It would be foolish to set out not knowing where one was to go.

He watches the others moving through the endlessly alternating maze of black and white and black, glimmering forever under the hard, white sun. They are dressed in dull, white cloth which does not, or cannot, reflect the

*brilliance of the white squares through which they move
so soundlessly. The boy believes that they are guards. He
cannot imagine what there might be for them to guard in
the purity and emptiness of such a place.*

*There is no air. There is no sound. The awesome
enormity of his surroundings holds the boy. Black and
white and black and white and black. Sterile and clear,
shimmering to infinity.*

*The boy sits through the bright, hot morning. It is late
in the afternoon when he first sees the ones who are not
guards. They are few, and they are very far away, but he
sees them clearly. Their cloth is black, but they are set
apart from the guards even more certainly by the grace
and ease of their movements. The boy believes that they
are thieves but cannot imagine what there might be for
them to steal in such a place. They walk with a fluid
nobility that entrances the boy, and he strains his eyes to
watch them until the last one is only a speck at an im-
measurable distance.*

*The boy rises without knowing why. He unfolds his
long young legs and walks to a black square. The black
squares are empty, and he can look down the gleaming
black diagonal to the far end of the Chessboard.*

*The boy walks the black diagonal, but he does not
see another thief. After a time he doubts that he has ever
seen one.*

—The Perfect Thief
by Ronald Jay Bass

There are many beginnings; a story may begin many times,
in many places.

But there must somewhere be a true beginning.

At the beginning of it all, there was an enigma.

On a grim cold night late in December of 2068, Trent
stood in a doorway, drinking black coffee with the bright warm
restaurant at his back, and looking off across the water, watched
snow fall on New York City.

Capital City. The Big Town.

Pale blue eyes were the most visible features in a face
that was poorly lit by the roof's cracked, aging glowpaint. He

had turned the heating coil on the mug as high as it would go, but the top layer of liquid kept going cold regardless when he waited too long between swallows.

The restaurant was called *McGee's*. It was a good place; good food, clean, with reliable enforcers, one of the few that catered to the street. You could get falling-down stoned and know you'd live to see the morning, and the drinks and drugs were honest enough that getting falling-down stoned wasn't hard. The building *McGee's* sat atop, five stories up, was ancient enough that only constant bribery by old McGee himself kept the city from condemning it.

Trent stood in a bubble of silence and stillness, slightly drunk himself. The wind whipped the snow wildly only centimeters away from the end of his nose, but where he stood the air was calm and cold, which was good enough.

He did not know how long he'd been out there before somebody from the party came looking for him. Trent's coffee cup was long since empty when Jamos Ramirez came out through the restaurant's roof entrance and joined him. Ramirez was a tall, darkly handsome young man, two years older than Trent. They were the same height, though Ramirez massed twenty kilos more, most of it elegantly sculpted muscle.

"Word up."

Trent inclined his head very slightly.

"Brother Trent," said Ramirez quietly from just behind Trent. "Where are you?"

"On the roof," said Trent without turning around.

"This I see. Where else?"

"Right here on the roof, Jimmy. Nowhere else."

Standing immediately behind Trent, Jamos Ramirez nodded.

"I can tell because it's cold," Trent added without looking around.

"Personally I think you're down on that beach of yours again."

The beach had been the furthest thing from Trent's mind. "Absolutely," he lied, and turned to look at Jimmy. "Sitting on the beach, drinking 'stralian beer, and watching the little brown girls go by."

Jimmy grinned back after a moment. "Sho nuff. You'll be there someday. Maybe Jodi Jodi and me will come visit sometimes."

"Sure." Trent felt himself turn away, to something far and

distant. His voice emanated from a spot off somewhere to the side. "We should be in Big Town by Christmas, 2069. One more boost like yesterday's . . ."

Jimmy licked his lips and leaned in on Trent. "That soon?"

Trent shook his head slowly. "You and me and Jodi Jodi and Bird. Three's going to be the most I can take inside with me. And I don't trust anyone else anyway. We have to do it, you know. We can't stay out here forever."

"It's not so bad on the outside, Trent. The Patrol Sectors are safer, but man, there ain't hardly any Peaceforcers at all out here. In Patrol Sectors, all over, we gon' have to stand there with the Peaceforcers tossing down on us, and stay calm. It's gon' to be hard putting up with that genejunk."

"We can't stay on the outside forever. I don't want to get old on the street."

"True enough," Ramirez conceded. "And for sure not on this cold roof. There's people inside, bro, including Jodi Jodi who looks at you with the big eyes. What say?"

Trent nodded. "What happened with you guys? I thought you two were made."

Ramirez spread his hands wide. "I don't even know the word, Trent. Very happy and then very chilly. Not gon' to break *my* heart. Besides," he said simply, "you like her, I mean for real. Rather let her bounce off you than someone else."

"Okay."

Jimmy cocked his head slightly to one side. "I got you figured someday, my man. I think maybe you come out of the Big Time. Just . . ."

Trent grinned at him again. "Someday."

"So not yet," Jimmy conceded. "What was in your head when I came out here?"

Trent told him the truth. "A frog named Mohammed."

"Indeed. Frenchie with an Arab name?"

"Strange but true."

"Always the dramasuit," said Jimmy softly, breath pluming, "like there's nothing on your face at all except what the suit puts there." Trent did not reply. "You gon' to kill this frog?"

"Jimmy. Killing is—"

"—wrong, I know. You keep saying." Ramirez studied him a moment longer. "You ever kill anyone?"

"Once. It was an accident," Trent said. "He drowned."

"Bro, what hurts?"

"Something that happened a long time ago." When you are seventeen, six years is almost forever. He did not wait to let Ramirez say anything further. "Let's go back in."

In all Times there are, there have always been, legends. But before the legend, there must be some piece of sharp, shiny truth to catch the light of day and hold it glowing in the face of night's descent.

Legends are rarely gentle. Gentleness is not remembered so long nor so well as valor or love or greed or death. Great deeds alone do not ensure legend, and their lack will not prevent it. The winds of myth can rise from the lowest deserts.

I have known many of the Continuing Time's great. I knew Ifahad bell K'Ailli briefly, and I was there when a congress of ethical, well-meaning Zaradin began the Time Wars. I was there when the High King Arthur died under Camber Tremodian's hand, and I grieved for him. I have known Shakespeare's mind as he wrote, and Erl Moorhe's as she composed her last and most popular sensable, the twenty-seven-hour *Lord of the Rings*.

I have known well all three of the best night faces the human race has ever produced: Shiva Curiachen, and Ola who was Lady Blue, and Camber Tremodian himself.

Of the long list of regrets that has defined my life, I most regret the fact that I never knew Trent the Uncatchable.

AFTERWORD

Welcome to the Continuing Time.

When I was thirteen years old, I had already been writing for four years. This is not to say that I was writing anything worth reading; but I was writing, constantly. It was compulsive behavior. I *knew* I wasn't writing anything worth reading, but I wrote regardless. My sister, Jodi Anne Moran, was my only loyal audience, and even she could not, or would not, read any of my longer pieces.

"This is bad," she would say.

I'm suspicious of coincidence, but here it is: I have only once in my life kept a diary. It lasted for perhaps a month, and I grew bored with it.

During the month that I kept that diary, I created the Continuing Time. It says so, right there in faded green ink. I had about eight series going at that time, in my head and on paper. Leaving out any of the potentially embarrassing details regarding plotting and characterization, three of those series concerned themselves as follows:

1. A trader, named Camber, circa 3,000 A.D., who found himself in over his head, embroiled in a war with these really bad news demigods who were waging what they called the Time Wars;

2. A warrior telepath named Chauki; she was a Lord of the Royal House of November, circa 3,000 A.D. or thereabouts;

3. This other telepath, named Denice, and her good buddy, a thief named Ripper, who became a politician, in the mid-twenty-first century.

There it is. One morning (according to the diary) I was home from school, sick, watching *I Love Lucy* and writing in this neat new diary I was keeping. Apparently I had a fever, which, looking back, seems appropriate.

I was working on a story about Chauki November; whatever it was, it did not survive, and I do not remember today what it might have concerned. But I wanted to give her a romantic interest, and none of the chumps who usually hung out in her stories were good enough for her.

Trader Camber, now Camber Tremodian, presented himself. Before that instance, I had never before merged together any of my series; I simply kept inventing new ones when I got bored. But the details of Camber's universe meshed well with the details of Chauki November's, and in the course of reconciling the two series I created a universe with a degree of depth—of *realness*—that was greater than the sum of its parts.

I was struck, I think, more than anything else, by how *well* these unconnected storylines had complemented each other. Looking through my remaining stories, one character leapt out at me: Denice Castanaveras, a telepath whose people had been destroyed, was, obviously, Chauki November's ancestor.

In the course of that morning, cross-connecting the details of Camber's universe with Chauki November's, and then working out the way in which Denice Castanaveras' universe had, over the course of a millennium, become Camber and Chauki's, I invented the Continuing Time, essentially as it stands today.

For a very long time, I did not write any Continuing Time stories. I *knew* my writing skills were insufficient; and *The Tales of the Continuing Time* were, even then, an order of magnitude more complex than any of my other stories. Instead I planned, and planned, and planned. Outlines of stories, chronologies of events; I knew the date of birth, to the day, for each of the thousands of characters who appeared in any of *The Tales of the Continuing Time*. Most of the time I knew the dates of their deaths, as well. The notebooks in which I kept my work covered over two thousand pages of outlines, lists of names and places, biographies, and indexes. I had three different card catalogues, back in the days before I bought my first computer.

The Continuing Time grew, and changed. In my mind, before I ever put words down on paper, I grew to know, as I know the members of my own family, the characters who populated the Continuing Time. The thief called Ripper, who became a politician, was a bit too unlikely; I split him into a pair of characters, Douglass Ripper, Jr., the politician introduced in *Emerald Eyes*, and, of course, Trent the Uncatchable.

I was seventeen years old before I first tried to write a Continuing Time story:

Sixty-two thousand years before the birth of Yeshua ha Notzri, whom later humans knew as Jesus the Christ, the Time Wars ended, for reasons which no sentient being now knows. With that ending, the Continuing Time began.

That was how the first story started; I had already written three books of varyingly bad quality when I wrote *The Song of Camber and S'Reeth,* and learned that I was not yet talented enough to write about the Continuing Time. It happened again when I was eighteen, and I wrote *The Long Run,* a story about Trent the Uncatchable, and again, when I was nineteen, and I wrote *When Your Name is November,* an eighty-thousand-word story about the early days of the great House of November.

It has been only five years since I last wrote about the Continuing Time. The novel which you've just finished is only the first novel in the thirty-three volumes which comprise *The Tales of the Continuing Time.* I am a better writer today than I was five years ago; in years to come I will, I hope, surpass what I have written here, and by no small measure. I hope to become a much better writer than I am now.

I have been writing, now, for fifteen years.

I have been planning the Continuing Time for over eleven. I cannot today read what I wrote only five years ago without wincing. Perhaps five years from now the same will be true of what I have done with *Emerald Eyes.*

But you have to start somewhere.

—Daniel Keys Moran
Southern California, 1987

Coming in October, 1988 from
Doubleday Foundation Books
A towering tale of power, passion and
freedom on a distant alien world

ᄃᄅᄐ ᄅIᄂᄃ

a novel
by Daniel Keys Moran

based on the screenplay
for the upcoming major motion picture
by Bill Stewart

A totally new version of
the classic novel of Artificial Intelligence.

When HARLIE was One
Release 2.0

David Gerrold

H.A.R.L.I.E.—Human Analog Replication, Lethetic Intelligence engine—is very advanced computer software. In making HARLIE, his creators have developed the most sophisticated Artificial Intelligence the world has ever seen. Talking to HARLIE is like talking to anyone else.

> HARLIE is now as conscious as any man or woman ... and the plug is about to be pulled.

David Gerrold has created a totally new version of this science fiction classic with all the new advances in computers at his command. With both knowledge and insight, he has broadened the scope of **When HARLIE Was One** in this new release—a serious look at what it means to be intelligent, and what it means to be human.

Buy **When HARLIE Was One, Release 2.0** now available wherever Bantam Spectra Books are sold, or use this page to order.

- -